Tension Running High

Lee was edging slowly in from the doorway. The reckless redhead was too confident, he realized uneasily. The barroom was full of Smoke Tree men—handpicked by Hawken for their readiness to pull trigger on any and all occasions—cold-eyed gunmen who would seize the first opening to make an end quickly of the matter, including Sandy and his two loyal friends. An instant's inattention would find a half score guns emptying lead at the trio.

Smoke Tree Range

ARTHUR
HENRY
GOODEN

LEISURE BOOKS 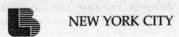 NEW YORK CITY

To Louise

A LEISURE BOOK®

October 2009

Published by special arrangement with Golden West Literary Agency.

Dorchester Publishing Co., Inc.
200 Madison Avenue
New York, NY 10016

ISBN 10: 0-8439-6308-5
ISBN 13: 978-0-8439-6308-3
E-ISBN: 978-1-4285-0752-4

The name "Leisure Books" and the stylized "L" with design are trademarks of Dorchester Publishing Co., Inc.

Printed in the United States of America.

10 9 8 7 6 5 4 3 2 1

Visit us online at www.dorchesterpub.com.

Smoke Tree Range

I
Crawling Sands

Nan eyed the venerable mesquite tree with wonder and respect. It was quite the hugest mesquite she had ever seen, at least a hundred yards in circumference and lifting its prickly thatch a full twenty feet above the desert floor. The red mare, too, showed a lively interest in the vast mass of thickly clustered branches; she pricked up attentive ears, nickered and pawed the ground, a performance that perplexed and disturbed the girl. She had the uncomfortable feeling that unseen eyes were watching her; a thought, she told herself, which was absurd.

She was a slim boyish figure in the big cowboy saddle. An old black sombrero was pulled over tawny chestnut hair and she wore overalls under leather chaps, and high-heeled boots and spurs, all much the worse for wear. A yellow bandanna knotted loosely under the collar of her dark blue flannel shirt added a touch of color; and thrust in the holster of the belt buckled to slender waist was a light but serviceable thirty-two six-shooter. At a distance any chance observer would easily have mistaken her for some youthful cow-puncher.

Approaching sunset was drawing a softening veil over the fierce, hot beauty of the landscape; long shadows crawled across the sun-baked desert floor—weird distortions of gaunt cacti and grotesque Joshua trees, of mesquite and greasewood, of graceful flowing palo verde and stark and lean ocotillos; a scene that enchanted—and chilled—bred an awe close on terror.

Nan sensed vaguely a brooding savagery—dimly divined cruel sheathed claws.

She sat lightly erect in the saddle, attentively absorbing further details—the titanic sweep of rugged brown hills that reached down from a lofty mountain ridge where snow clung to sheltered cranny and crevice. They were fantastic, violent hills. The girl thought vaguely of mighty cataclysmic forces.

Rust-red cliffs, the mouth of a narrow canyon, framed a solitary palm-tree, bearded with hoary, pendent withered fronds and lifting a royal crown of living green to the hot blue sky. Other splashes of green marked the twisting ascent of the canyon. Nan surmised that the lofty peak was the source of a stream that dropped down between the painted cliffs to subterranean gravel beds deep beneath the blistering sands.

She shifted her gaze to the bleak dunes lying to the east. They rose hundreds of feet in places above the surrounding levels—huge flattened domes of sand, now suffused with changing lights and shadows, soft rose and delicate lavender—a curious transition to an orange yellow that quickly deepened to an ominous murky brown. Nan stirred uneasily in the saddle, riveted suddenly apprehensive eyes on a dun haze pushing over the blue horizon. The dark outline of the distant saw-toothed ridges toward which the sun stooped was dissolving in a rising saffron sea; and the sun was now a molten red disk, swimming in the saffron sea and drawn oddly close to her. Wind came in fretful gusts, lifted dust devils that whirled in frenzied dance across the dunes; the desert that all the day had brooded in sullen apathy, was awakening—was coming to life with shuddering sighs. The girl shivered a little. She was beginning to fear this harsh, fierce desert; instinctively she sensed violence.

Swiftly the brown murk billowed into the heavens, blotted out the blue sky; wind whispered and moaned through the chaparral and flurries of sand rattled like hail against a nearby giant Joshua tree from which the life-sap had been long gone, a gaunt gray skeleton of the desert, its dry old bones swaying and creaking with each savage thrust of the rising gale. A frightened rabbit scurried for the shelter of the venerable mesquite; a coyote slunk across the trail, melted like a wraith into the swirling yellow mist.

The red mare snorted, laid back her ears; Nan felt the sleek, powerful body tremble under the saddle. She glanced about, conscious of a terrifying helplessness; and with incredible suddenness the wind was a hurricane, blasting across the desert dunes—a shrieking, ravening demoniac fury that tore at prickly shrub and sturdy cactus—that ruthlessly scourged the slender sinuous ocotillos until they leaned and writhed like tortured shapes from an inferno. The sky dropped down to the harassed and moaning desert floor, an angry brown pall that shrouded the world.

Wind and sand stung the girl's face, brought water to her eyes; an uprooted thorny shrub clawed like a wildcat at the mare's heels, drove her into a frenzy. Appalled by the thought of the surrounding savage tangle of bristling cacti Nan slipped foot from stirrup and threw herself from the saddle. She landed on her feet, shaken, trembling—gamely clinging with both hands to the snorting mare's bridle. The struggle flung her against the needle-sharp spines of a *cholla*, drew a startled cry of pain that to her amazement was answered by a man's voice; a shout of encouragement that was lost in a crackling volley of sound as the ancient Joshua tree parted at last from its weary old roots and crashed to the sobbing earth.

Nan lay very still in the wreckage of shattered branches, dimly aware of the mysterious voice again challenging the wild cacophony of the storm. Her answering cry was a pitiful moan that the wind sneeringly smothered with howls of derision. She tried to get to her feet, was indescribably shocked to realize that the stubby arms of the prostrate massive bole held her in a vise-like clutch. She was hopelessly trapped, doomed to a lingering death—a grave under the hissing, crawling sand.

Her brain whirled. She fought off the faintness and again sent out a little cry. This time she was answered by a shrill neigh from the red mare, floundering in the chaparral. Hope revived in her. Surely the man would hear Linda Rosa—be guided in the right direction!

She lay very still, ears straining for the sound of approaching feet. She could hear him, now, stumbling through the brown murk; and suddenly he was bending over her, was gently extricating her from the death clutch of the stricken Joshua tree. The feel of those powerful arms lifting her back to life was too much for Nan; with a little inarticulate moan she sank into unconsciousness.

There was a curiously startled look in the man's eyes as he turned away with his limp burden and ploughed through the storm, head lowered against the blinding flurries of sand, his wide-brimmed hat held as a shield over the white triangle of face pressed to his shoulder.

He reached the lee side of the big mesquite tree, its vast bulk a welcome barrier against the desert's savage onslaught. Above the sinister hiss of slithering sand sounded the red mare's neigh. She galloped up, nostrils blowing. The man's taut expression softened. The mare was a mustang, of the same Arab strain brought over from old Spain by Cortez and his fellow adventuring conquistadores. Her lineage ran back to the tents of Kedar. It was her heritage to put her trust in man.

They moved on to a small opening in the side of the mesquite, a sort of tunnel into which the man turned with his burden. The red mare followed confidently. The darkness was complete, but the man proceeded with the sureness of one who was in his own home.

Nan's eyes fluttered open, stared up blankly at the anxious face bending over her. The owner of the face drew back, relief in the slow smile he gave her. He was holding a dripping wet cloth, the girl saw. She put both hands to her cheeks, realized that her face was sopping wet.

The man smiled again. "Seemed the thing to do," he explained. He held out the makeshift sponge. "You might as well wipe some of that grit out of your eyes—"

Nan took the thing and mutely dabbed at her eyes and cheeks. The cool wetness was refreshing, cleared her brain. She sat up.

"It's the first time in my life I've fainted," she confided.

"It was one time nobody could blame you for fainting," declared the man. "It's all over now," he added, "you're quite safe, here—"

A feeling of peace, security, came to Nan. There was strength in this tall stranger's calm, unhurried voice, an unshakable serenity in the eyes attentively regarding her.

"You—you saved my life—" her voice was unsteady, "I would have died—"

"It's all over," he repeated gently. "No need to worry, now—"

"I—I was frightened to death," Nan confessed. "I—I'll always hate the desert—"

"The desert can be beautiful—as well as cruel," he told her. "In the Spring, when the desert smiles, you learn to forget its harshness."

She was absorbing her surroundings as well as she could by the lone candle stuck into an empty tomato can. There was not much she could see beyond the faint glow thrown out by the candle. She was sitting on some blankets thrown over a pile of straw, she realized, and the man was leaning against what appeared to be the massive, gnarled trunk of a tree. From somewhere beyond the surrounding wall of darkness she could hear the stamp of horses' hoofs, could hear the wild cries of the storm-wracked desert—the sinister sound of crawling sand.

He saw her bewilderment. "Can't you guess where you are?" Amusement lurked in his voice.

Nan shook her head.

"You're inside the old mesquite tree."

She stared at him with growing amazement.

"The Indians have used this old mesquite as a sort of wayside inn for generations," he went on. "It spreads over a lot of ground—hundreds of square feet."

"But it looks like a mass of brambly branches," protested the girl.

"The lower limbs and branches and brush have been lopped off and cleared out from time to time," he explained. "The clearing around the trunk has grown bigger and bigger. Many a desert rat prospector has found shelter for himself and his burros in the heart of this old mesquite. You'll find them here and there in the Colorado Desert, but not as big as this old fellow."

"I wouldn't have dreamed there was such a place here," marveled Nan.

"There's only one small opening," he informed her.

"I keep it closed with a sort of brush door made of mesquite branches."

Nan pondered for a moment. "You mean it's a—a sort of hiding place?" she asked in a puzzled voice.

The man shrugged dusty shoulders. "Let's call it a *sanctuary*—from the storm," he evaded. He rolled and lit a cigarette. "That cowboy rig you wear had me fooled," he drawled. "Thought you were some kid puncher, until I dragged you from under that old Joshua tree."

Nan colored, but met his amused look squarely. "It's a miracle you were able to find me," she told him soberly. Distress clouded her face. "I'm worried to death about my poor Linda Rosa—out there in that dreadful sandstorm."

"If you mean your red mare—you needn't worry," he reassured. "She's snug as a bug in a rug—keeping company with my Palomino horse." He gestured into the darkness.

Nan's relieved smile thanked him. "What a—a Good Samaritan you are, Mister—*Mister Stranger*—"

"Cary," he told her, "Lee Cary."

"I'm Nan Page," acknowledged the girl. She glanced around dubiously. "How long will this last, this awful sandstorm?"

Lee's reply was not reassuring. "No telling how long," he informed her tersely.

"You mean I may have to stay here—all night!" Nan's voice was troubled.

"You'll be safe enough here," Lee assured her a bit coldly.

"It's not that," she hastened to explain. "It's my people I'm thinking about. They'll be worried—"

"Nothing we can do about it," Lee said grimly. "Listen . . . blowing worse than ever—"

Nan nodded dismally. She could hear the sinister hiss of the sand driving before the gale and the moaning of the wind as it shook the giant mesquite. Lee watched her for a moment, sympathy—and a hint of curiosity—in his eyes.

"At least we can eat," he suddenly said with a boyish grin. He turned away, vanished into the blackness beyond the candlelight.

Nan stared thoughtfully at the flickering candle. She wished that she could have a better look at her mysterious young host. One little candle in that dark place was so inefficient. She wouldn't know him again if she met him face-to-face in broad daylight—not unless he spoke. Nan felt that she would never forget his quiet unhurried voice. Only her own dire extremity, she reflected, had forced him to disclose his weird sanctuary in the mesquite. Was he a fugitive from the law, she wondered, or a rustler, seeking to evade the fatal wrath of angry cattlemen? Instinctively she felt drawn to his defense.

He was back in a few brief moments, bearing an armful of mesquite twigs and roots which he piled in a heap near a fireplace built of stones. From his pocket he extracted two fresh candles. He lit and placed them in holders improvised from empty cans.

"Be a little more cheery for you," he explained casually, almost too casually, Nan thought.

She hid a smile, shrewdly guessing the true purpose of the additional candles. "It's about time we had a good look at each other," she commented a bit wickedly.

Lee flushed, bent hastily over the improvised fire-place, but not before Nan caught the admiring gleam in his eyes. In a moment he had the fire crackling, a pleasant, homey sound above the dreary moaning of the wind. Still on his knees he reached for a battered coffeepot and began measuring water into it from a canteen. The firelight was full on his face, a lean, darkly tanned face, with strongly cut, almost stern features. Nan suspected that the bright sunlight would reveal glints of red in the dark hair that showed under his dusty sombrero. He might be thirty, she guessed, a little under—or over. He got to his feet, long, and lean, and hard, and after a critical glance at the coffeepot now nestled against the cherry-red embers, slowly turned and met her interested gaze. Nan had the uncomfortable feeling that those direct, hard, cold eyes were piercing her through and through—were absorbing her every detail, physically and mentally. She felt oddly limp, a bit frightened, until the slow, lazy smile came, a singularly warming, boyish smile that softened the stern features and put friendly laughter into the gray-black eyes.

"Hungry?"

His matter-of-fact tone broke the momentary tension. Nan nodded.

"Famished!" she declared.

Lee grinned and vanished again into the darkness beyond the glow of the candles and when he returned he found that the girl had slipped off her *chaps* and sombrero. She looked startlingly young—and lovely—between the soft-flaming candles. Lee bent quickly over the fire, his face inscrutable. Nan smiled demurely at his broad back.

"What is it to be?" she wanted to know, "pork and beans, or just plain beans—and pork?"

"Wrong—both times." Lee was raking the embers into a compact red heap. "Mesquite House does not serve such plebeian fare to its guests."

Nan bent her head for a peep into the can he was

holding. "Rabbit!" Her eyes sparkled. "I'm going to *like* Mesquite House!"

Appetizing odors filled the air—the savory smell of broiled rabbit, the redolent aroma of coffee, fragrant flapjacks, hot from the pan. They sat opposite to each other, cross-legged, on a piece of canvas Lee spread on the ground, the food between them on tin plates. Candles and fire threw weird lights and shadows; and encircling them like an impenetrable black wall was the dark night. It was the strangest meal she had ever eaten, Nan thought. She had the feeling that they were alone in a vast dark world filled with fearsome demon creatures ready to devour them if they dared to leave their tiny illumined haven. The moaning of the wind was the desert's chant of death. She shivered. But for the man opposite to her she would have been deep under the hissing, crawling sands.

II
Mesquite House

Lee was eyeing her with frank curiosity. "You must be new to our desert country," he surmised.

Nan's look questioned him.

"An old-timer would have read the signs—known a sandstorm was blowing up," he explained.

"It's all so different, here," she confided. "I'm not used to this fierce, blazing land—the grim, barren mountains that seem to encircle one like gigantic pinnacled walls—the savage bristling cactus—the eternal dryness—"

"You're from the South," he guessed again. He grinned. "I'd gamble you're from the land of swamps and alligators—"

"It's my accent," laughed the girl. "Yes, I'm from the Florida 'Glades country, where there are swamps and 'gators and turtles and mangroves and coconut palms—and sometimes a hurricane that seems to rip the world to pieces."

"Not much like the desert," admitted Lee. "You'll get used to it, though, if you stay long enough. One learns to love the desert; it has its own charms." His voice lowered and for a brief moment the girl felt that she was listening to a prophet who saw deeply into unborn years. "The desert will not always be a land of eternal dryness," he told her dreamily. "Some day the desert will bloom—be a land of happy homes."

"You sound utterly mysterious," she declared. "By

what magic could water be produced to make your desert bloom?"

Her smile was tinged with wistfulness—a hint of doubt. "Perhaps I *will* grow to love it—in time I'll be staying long enough to know all its moods."

Nan saw his deepening interest, and, after a momentary hesitation, "I suppose if it hadn't been for Los Posos I'd never have thought of coming out here to live," she explained. "The old family plantation was done for—nothing left but a mortgage; so when I learned that my great-uncle William had bequeathed Los Posos to my father years ago it seemed like an act of Providence."

If the girl had been observant at that moment she would have wondered at the startled look in Lee's eyes. She put down her coffee cup and smiled at him. "It was rather strange about great-uncle's will. I happened to find it locked away in an old desk after my father's death. Father evidently thought it wasn't worth troubling about. You see, great-uncle William was my grandfather's younger brother—and a bit wild, they said. He left the old home years and years ago and was never heard from again. At least," she added, "I never heard of him until I chanced to find his will bequeathing my father or his heirs a cattle ranch lying on the edge of the Colorado Desert in faraway California."

Lee nodded, his face expressionless. "Rancho Los Posos," he said curtly. "Yes, I've heard of the place."

"Los Posos means *The Wells*," explained Nan. "You see there are old Spanish settlements down in South Florida and I picked up the language from my nurse. I brought Teresa and her husband, Diego, with me to Los Posos," she added.

"I speak Spanish myself," Lee informed her. "My grandmother was a Spanish-Californian," he explained. He stared at her thoughtfully. "So you're going into the cattle business on Rancho Los Posos?" His tone was dubious. "I gather you haven't been on the ranch long—"

"Three weeks," Nan told him. "There's not much there, except a log house and ranch buildings—and some lovely old shade trees around the wells, cotton-woods and willows and sycamores. The wells really are a series of flowing springs and make quite a little creek that disappears into the desert sands after it leaves the canyon."

"I've been there," Lee said, a bit gloomily, the girl thought. "Haven't had any trouble, I suppose. I mean—nobody has objected to your moving in on the old place?"

Nan shook her head. "Why should anybody object?" she wanted to know. "I'm the owner of Los Posos!" She frowned prettily. "I *was* a bit surprised to find the old place in quite good condition," she went on. "I rather suspect that some cow outfit has been using the ranch buildings but as yet only one rather curious thing has happened. Teddy and I thought that maybe somebody was having a little fun with us."

"Teddy!" There was a hint of sharpness in Lee's voice. "You mean your husband—"

"I mean nothing of the sort," dimpled the girl. "Teddy is my only brother—and living relative—and he'll soon be twelve years old." She laughed affec-tionately. "Teddy is really my one big reason why I was glad to come out here. He's inclined to be delicate and I was glad to get him away from those swamps. I felt that this western country would build him up—and he's absolutely wild to be a really, truly cowboy. He vows he's going to be a cattle king."

Lee's face, that had grown more and more stern the past few moments, softened as he watched the color kindle on her smooth cheeks, the sparkle in her eyes; he gave her his slow, warming smile.

"You're a pair of kids—babes in the woods," he chuckled.

"I'm not a kid!" Nan declared indignantly. "I'm twenty-three, if you must know!"

He was suddenly grave again. "What was this curious incident you mentioned—that Teddy and you thought was some sort of joke?"

His tone vaguely disturbed her, brought back the pucker between her eyes.

"It happened about a week ago," she related slowly, "and if it was a practical joke, it was also a horrid one. Teddy found it fastened to the corral fence—a large sheet of paper—a warning for us to leave Los Posos."

Lee's face hardened. "Was it signed?" he wanted to know.

"No. All it said was—'*We give you one week to clear out. There'll be no second warning.*'" Nan eyed her host with some apprehension. "Does it sound like a joke—to you?"

He shook his head. "I don't think it is a joke, Miss Page," he said reluctantly.

The girl gave him an aghast look. "But—but who would want to drive us away from Rancho Los Posos?" she cried. "Why—the place really is mine—and Ted's!"

"How much land do you claim is taken in by the ranch?" queried Lee. "And are you certain that your great-uncle William is not still alive?"

"That's a double question," pondered Nan. "I'll answer the last question first. There was a letter with the will I found—and a deed—I mean several deeds. The letter said that he—I mean great-uncle William— believed he had not long to live, which was why he was sending the will and the deeds to my father." Nan paused and looked at her listener thoughtfully. "That letter was written twenty years ago; and great-uncle William has never been heard from since. Wouldn't you think he is dead—from that fact?"

"The law would grant that he is," admitted Lee.

"Now for the deeds enclosed with the letter," continued the girl. "One was the sort of paper a home-steader gets from the federal government and the others were from homesteaders who had sold their land to him—about a thousand acres and taking in the wells or springs known as Los Posos."

"I'd like to have a look at those papers, some time," Lee said briefly.

Nan nodded. "The thousand or so acres of deeded land takes in most of a little valley lying in the Chocolate Mountains and known as *El Valle de Los Posos*, the Valley of the Wells," she went on, "but that is not all the ranch. Great-uncle William's letter explicitly said that the ranch had grazing rights to at least twenty thousand acres of free range back of the Chocolate Mountains—some of it spreading over into Arizona." She paused, a bit breathless. "Doesn't it seem as if I—Ted and I—own Rancho Los Posos?"

"It would seem so," Lee agreed gloomily. "Those water-rights are valuable," he pointed out significantly. He mused for a moment. "So you have never heard from your great-uncle William again—nor if he died from some illness—or—"

The girl was looking at him with widened eyes. "You mean—that he—he might have been—been killed?" she asked in a low, horrified voice.

"*Los Posos* represents what every cattleman covets—water," Lee said, "and what men coveted in those days when your great-uncle William possessed Rancho Los Posos, they fought for—tooth and nail—"

"—*and murdered for,*" whispered the girl. She drew a deep breath. "It would seem that the years have not changed the ruthless law of fang and claw, you mean, Mr. Cary." Her eyes were very bright. "You mean that I should be warned—that I should leave this country— give up Los Posos!"

"I think the notice left on your corral fence meant all that it said," answered the young man reluctantly.

"I don't care!" flamed Nan. "I'm not giving up Los Posos. The ranch is mine—Ted's and mine! No cowardly threat is going to frighten us away from what is ours!"

Lee rolled and lit a cigarette. Nan watched in silence while he replenished the fire from the pile of mesquite roots and removed the remnants of their supper. The cheery crackle of the fire was a pleasant sound against the background of the moaning wind that continued to buffet their arboreal haven. Nan's thoughts flew to the log ranch-house at Los Posos. Teddy and the others would be frantic. They would have no idea where to look for her. She fervently hoped they would not attempt a search. The thought of Ted being caught out in that fury of sand and wind terrified her. Another thought disturbed her. The warning notice left on the corral fence had given them one week to "clear out." The week would be up the next day. At all costs she must be back at the ranch to meet and defy her unknown enemy.

Lee looked at her, seemed to sense her agony of spirit. "Nothing we can do—until the storm breaks," he said in his quiet voice. "You might as well make yourself comfortable." He squatted on his heels on the opposite side of the fire and smiled at her over his cigarette.

Nan leaned forward, chin propped on clasped hands, and attentively studied the keen bronzed face now clearly lighted by the leaping flames. There was a tiny scar on his left cheek, she noticed. It was not disfiguring, she decided, in fact it added distinction to the dark, somewhat haughty features. She suddenly realized that the man was still a complete mystery. All she knew of him was his name, and that his grandmother had been a Spanish-Californian.

"I'm completely ashamed," she told him. "The talk has been all of myself. I'm not the only human being in the world who has troubles."

The gray-black eyes twinkled. "You won't find me in the least interesting," he assured her.

"But really—I'm consumed with curiosity about you—and why you should be living here, in this weird place," challenged the girl. She laughed softly. "You've been a marvel of patience, listening to my life's story—and—well, I'm a good listener, too—"

"It does seem peculiar," admitted Lee. "Perhaps the explanation is that I'm in hiding—a fugitive from the law—a man with a price upon his head." He grinned cheerfully. "Is *that* what you suspect?"

Her candid eyes appraised him coolly. "My verdict is that you are not in hiding from anything to be ashamed of," she finally announced. "You dress like a cowboy but I'm not at all sure that you are one."

His smile was enigmatic.

"I do think that you have some extraordinary purpose that forces you to take every precaution." Nan gestured around. "The fact that you are so careful to conceal the entrance to Mesquite House proves that you don't want people to know of your presence here."

"Perhaps I'm a prospector," suggested Lee.

"That might explain the mystery," mused the girl. "Is there any gold in them thar hills?"

"Plenty of gold in these desert hills," he admitted, "but there are other things in the desert a man might search for."

"How stupid of me!" she exclaimed. "Of course— you're some sort of naturalist, looking for snakes and tarantulas and bugs—or some sort of scientist interested in desert plant life—"

Lee interrupted her. "I'll put you out of your misery," he whispered mysteriously. "I'm searching for something that nobody save myself knows is here."

"You're too provoking!" declared Nan. She made a face at him. "You can keep your secret!"

"I warned you that I'm a most uninteresting person," countered the young man, unabashed.

"You think I'm horribly rude—trying to pry into your life," she mourned.

"Not at all," he assured her soberly. "It's only that I'm afraid you'd laugh at me—scoff—as others have."

"I'm sorry—" Her voice was repentant. "You have been a soldier, haven't you?" she went on. "In the days of plenty, I went to a girl's school in Switzerland"—she smiled faintly—"my first beau was a German University student. He was quite vain of his duelling cuts."

Lee fingered the scar on his cheek. "Memento from San Juan Hill." He grinned, tossed his cigarette into the fire and listened a moment to the blustering gale. "Looks like an all-night sojourn here for you—"

Nan stared at the fire. "I'm not going to be silly about it," she said quietly. "I'm lucky to be here—instead of out there—where you found me." She shuddered. "What *does* worry me is the thought of Teddy and Teresa and Diego—and old Baldy Bates. They'll be just about crazy with anxiety—"

"Baldy Bates?" Lee's tone was curious.

"Baldy is my one lone cowhand," she explained. "I picked him up in Abilene. We drove from there in a real old-time covered wagon and Baldy was teamster, pathfinder and generalissimo of the expedition." Nan laughed. "He's quite a character. Teddy adores him, and he really is an experienced cowman. I'd planned to keep him on as foreman of the Los Posos outfit—to-be—"

Lee nodded. "Sounds like a good man," he decided. "You'll not need to worry about Teddy and the others—with an old-timer like him to look after them."

"You *are* comforting," Nan told him gratefully, "but there's something else that quite terrifies me. We were warned to get out in a week—and the week is up tomorrow—"

"We'll be there," interrupted Lee grimly.

Nan gave him a puzzled look. It was the second time he had used the expression. "What do you mean by *we*?" she wanted to know. Her accompanying smile softened the sharpness of the question.

"I mean what the word implies," he said simply. "I'm going with you"—he hesitated—"as a friend; if you can trust a man whom you must regard as a mysterious unknown."

She was on her feet, cheeks flushed, eyes starry as she met his steady, almost challenging look. "I have already been trusting you, haven't I?" She smiled, held out her hand impulsively. "I'm content to keep on trusting you, Mister Lee Cary."

For a brief moment her firm little hand lay in his. He grinned contentedly. "It's a lot less trouble to call me just plain *Lee*," he suggested diffidently. "All my friends do."

Nan laughed, withdrew her hand. "It's quite unusual, on such short notice," she declared, "but then, the circumstances are more than unusual—they're fantastic. If I'm to call you just plain Lee— then I must be just plain Nan to you."

"*Plain* Nan?" His eyes twinkled

She gave him a rueful smile. "I feel positively ugly," she declared. "All this sand in my hair and clothes! I'm a real plain Nan, today!"

Their laughter bridged over the momentary embarrassment; and Lee said, with seeming irrelevance, it struck the girl, "Lot of smoke trees over in Los Posos Valley. Or maybe you don't know what a smoke tree looks like—"

"Oh, but I do!" Nan protested. "They're beautiful! We have lots of them in Los Posos."

"You'll think them even more beautiful in the Spring—when they bloom," Lee told her. "They have an elfin ultramarine blossom—great clustering masses that billow in the wind like clouds of blue-gray smoke." He began to rhapsodize on the wonders of Springtime in the Colorado Desert, described for her the gorgeous flame-like flowering of the ocotillos, the jeweled golden mantle of the green palo verde trees, desert verbena, solid masses of pink and lavender, and other splendors of the desert in bloom. Nan sensed that he had a purpose in it all, a purpose that she was unable to fathom. She waited patiently, not without real pleasure; he talked easily—drew a vivid picture of a scene she saw he knew well, and loved. Finally he came back to the smoke trees.

"The name is quite identified with the Chocolate Mountain country back of your place, Smoke Tree Range old-timers call it." He spoke casually, but Nan felt that he was guardedly probing her.

"It's a lovely name for a cattle range." She puckered her brows at him. "I've the oddest feeling that you're leading up to something that concerns me."

His answer, which was a question, increased her bewilderment.

"Ever hear of the Smoke Tree outfit?"

Nan shook her head.

"The Smoke Tree is the biggest cattle outfit in the country."

"You're trying to tell me something," complained the girl, "but I can't guess!"

"Maybe the Smoke Tree outfit doesn't like neighbors in Los Posos," Lee said in an odd voice. He stared somberly down at the fire's red embers. The flames had died down and his face was again lost in the shadows thrown by the flickering candles.

"So—you think that the big, big giant is going to devour the wee little girl who has so foolishly dared to trespass? Is that what you mean, Lee?" Nan's voice was worried.

"I've been doing a lot of thinking, since you told me about that threat. I'm afraid I can't see any other meaning." He shrugged his shoulders. "No sense in making wild guesses. Tomorrow will tell the story."

Nan felt rather than saw his slow, warming smile. "I'll build up the fire for you," he said in his usual placid tone. "The nights get cold out in the desert." He piled knotty roots on the embers and poked them into a cheery blaze. "Not much of a bed for you," he mourned, eyeing the rumpled blankets spread over the straw.

With an effort the girl forced herself to a show of gaiety. "It's a gorgeous bed!" she declared brightly. "Don't you dare criticize the comforts of Mesquite House. I'll sleep like a top!"

Lee grinned at her disbelievingly, but was obviously grateful. "You have the stout heart of a true pioneer," he applauded. He took up one of the candles. "All that I can say is—no sense in useless conjectures. The bright dawn of tomorrow may show another picture."

Nan eyed him doubtfully. "But what about yourself?" she worried. "Where will—will you sleep? And why give me *all* the blankets?"

"I'll keep company with the horses," he told her with a chuckle. "Won't be the first time I've slept in a stable. Got more straw out there—and saddle blankets are warm—" His voice died away and he became a vague shadow pushing into the surrounding wall of darkness, the flickering candle a tiny twinkling star that suddenly vanished around the bend of the passage tunneling the mesquite. His voice came again from out of the dense blackness.

"Good night, Nan . . . Page . . . *buenas noches!*"

"*Buenas noches*—Lee," she called softly.

She blew out the remaining candle and dropped wearily to the pallet and pulled up a blanket. She was certain that she would not sleep a wink, despite her gay boast. The fire crackled, sent out weird lights and shadows, and presently died down. Nan watched, wide-eyed, until the glowing red embers slowly faded—and suddenly there was only darkness, the melancholy moan of the ravaging wind, the sinister slither of crawling sand. Her eyes closed; she slept—and dreamed that she was again out there in that savage wind-assailed tangle of cactus—that a monstrous giant was towering over her—reaching to seize her with huge, hideously clawed hands.

III
Smoke Trees

Nan awakened with a start of surprise. It seemed incredible that she actually had been sound asleep. She sat up, winking her eyes and stared around with renewed interest. Sunlight filtered in through the branches; the pleasant twitter of a wren came to her ears; the storm was over—the desert again at peace, aloof and still and mysterious under the cool blue of the dawn. Nan threw the blanket from her and sprang to her feet. There was no sign of Lee Cary; the ashes of the fire were cold. She stared down the passage to the bend that led to the "stable." Something white was dangling from a mesquite twig—a piece of paper. She ran to it, sensing it was a message. She could use the water remaining in the canteen, read the brief penciled scrawl, and she would find a piece of soap in a coffee can by the tin washbasin. He had gone with the pack-burro to Lone Palm Canyon for a fresh supply of water from the spring and in the meantime if she felt domestic Nan could start the fire and slice some bacon that she would find hanging from the "kitchen ceiling." He'd be "back soon," finished the note.

Nan hesitated; she was in a fever of impatience to be on her way to Los Posos but the thought of a refreshing wash was too great a temptation. The water in the canteen was sufficient for two full basins. With a quick motion she pulled the dusty flannel shirt over her head and shook it thoroughly, then luxuriously scrubbed arms and shoulders and face. In five minutes she was dressed again and running a pocket comb through her short red-brown curls. She felt immeasurably refreshed and ready to be "domestic." It was at this point that Nan discovered a flaw in her thoughtful host's program—there were no matches.

"If that isn't like a man!" she scolded aloud. "As if a girl carries matches!" Nan giggled. After all, she *was* wearing overalls, she reflected, and might reasonably be expected to carry matches like any cowboy. She poked disconsolately among the various cans, all tightly covered against bugs and pack-rats. Pack-rats were such pilferers. More than one bar of soap had mysteriously vanished from the ranch-house kitchen before she had learned about the creatures. There was everything save matches—coffee, flour, sugar and what-not—even wild desert honey.

Reluctantly she gave up the search. She had wanted to be helpful—do something in return for what he had done for her. The stamp of hoofs gave her an idea; she *could* look Linda Rosa over—saddle her. She hurried down the passage to the "stable" where the red mare greeted her with a soft nicker.

Nan knew about horses; the Palomino tied across the way from her own Linda Rosa drew her eyes like a magnet. She knew that she was looking at a perfect specimen, a king among Palominos. An unusually valuable horse for a man living the life of a desert rat, Nan reflected.

A brief inspection informed her that Linda Rosa had suffered no hurts from the storm; in fact the condition of her glossy hide showed that Lee Cary had done quite a thorough job of grooming. Deeply touched by the thoughtfulness, Nan's gaze sought for her saddle.

It was hanging close to another saddle at which she stared with widened eyes. A magnificent saddle such as she had never seen before, of fine hand-carved leather and rich silver mountings, a saddle worthy of the great Palomino—a strange saddle to be owned by the occupant of the humble desert abode that had sheltered her from the storm.

She examined it more closely, noticed that the high silver horn was decorated with some sort of design, obviously intended to represent a tree with odd cloud-like little curlicues drifting from its branches.

A troubled look shadowed the girl's face; she went quickly over to the sleek Palomino. Ignoring the friendly liquid eyes the big horse turned to her, she carefully scrutinized the small mark neatly burned into the glossy skin The design was similar to the one on the saddle horn. Dismay—and fear—crept into Nan's deep blue eyes.

"The Smoke Tree!" she exclaimed aloud.

Nan felt as if she had been struck by a bolt of lightning. She stood like one paralyzed, staring with disbelieving eyes at the mark which she knew must be the brand of the man whose herds roamed Smoke Tree Range. What was Lee Cary's connection with the Smoke Tree outfit? She wildly asked herself the question. There must be a connection or why would his horse and saddle wear the Smoke Tree brand?

Wretched doubts assailed the girl. Lee Cary knew for a fact that the Smoke Tree outfit was back of the threat to drive her from Rancho Los Posos—perhaps had himself been the man who had posted the vicious warning to the corral fence. His talk about Smoke Tree Range—about the ruthlessness of covetous cat-

tlemen—was a subtle attempt to frighten her. His
kindness was a sham, a shameful cloak of villainy.

With breathless haste she saddled the red mare.
Lee Cary would not find her cooking breakfast when
he returned from Lone Palm Canyon.

IV
Two at the Gate

"Ain't many *hombres* been skelped an' live to tell of it," rumbled Baldy Bates reminiscently from his seat on the corral fence, his long gaunt frame hunched forward, elbows on knees, high boot heels hooked over a split rail. He glanced down slyly from the corner of a faded blue eye at the boy sitting in a like position by his side.

"Oh, Baldy! Were you *really* scalped by the Indians?" Young Teddy Page looked up with awed eyes at the old cowboy. "Is that why you never take off your hat? And why they call you *Baldy*?" Teddy wriggled excitedly. Like the veteran puncher he wore a sombrero and flannel shirt and loosely knotted bandanna and leather chaps over his overalls.

Baldy eased his lanky person more comfortably on the hard fence-rail and leisurely rolled a cigarette. Teddy watched the performance admiringly, impatient for the deft flick of match against thumb-nail. It was a trick he himself had been practicing unsuccessfully in secret. He regarded Baldy Bates as the most extraordinary of mortals' and yearned to emulate him in all things. There was no end to Baldy's accomplishments. Baldy always wore two huge ancient six-guns with sinister notches on their black butts. Those notches were wont to enthrall Ted's imagination—they told grim tales of sudden death meted out to ruthless desperadoes. Baldy could draw his six-guns faster than the eye could follow and send an empty tin can rolling

along the ground with a staccato fusillade of bullets;
he could rope and tie a steer, and, according to Baldy's
own modest statement, he could ride any "onery
critter" that ever wore saddle. Ted never wearied of
Baldy's thrilling, hair-raising tales of the roaring days
of the old Chisholm Trail when daring riders of the
rangers drove countless herds of romping longhorns
up from Texas to distant northern markets.

The match snapped into flame against the veteran's
horny thumb-nail; Baldy inhaled luxuriously, blew
twin spirals of smoke from hairy nostrils, a feat that
never failed to fascinate his young admirer.

"I was trail-boss with the ol' Circle C outfit," he
began. "Long time ago it was too, sonny—afore yuh
was born—or Miss Nan was born—" The grizzled
cowpuncher shook his head, a faraway look in his
still keen, faded blue eyes as memory roved down the
long lane of the years. "I mind it like it was yesterday;
thar'd been the dangest 'lectric storm I ever saw—an'
I shore have seen some bad ones—great yeller balls of
fire rollin' 'long the ground an' blue sparks playin' tag
on them thousands of horns. A black night of rain an'
thunder an' lightnin'."

"Did the herd stampede, Baldy?" cried the boy
excitedly. "Gee whiz! Wish I'd been there with you!"

"Shore the critters stampeded," chuckled the ex-trail
boss, "the hull five thousand of 'em. Took us two days
to gather 'em up ag'in. Waal, we shoved 'em crost the
Cimarron—had to swim 'em, an' the next night we
made camp at Buff'lo Crik—"

"Did you lose any cow-critters when the herd stampeded, Baldy?" Ted broke in anxiously.

"Not more'n a hundred or two," reassured the
old man a bit impatiently. "Waal, we made camp at
Buff'lo Crik like I said an' that night a bunch of

Comanches jumped us—thought to git our remuda away from us—"

"How many broncs did you have in the remuda, Baldy?" the boy wanted to know.

"I was tryin' to tell yuh 'bout them Comanches," complained Baldy a bit testily. "How'm I goin' to tell you how I was skelped if yuh keep cuttin' in on my trail?"

"Gee whiz, Baldy! I just wanted to know about the remuda!"

"The ol' Circle C allus carried plenty broncs on a big drive," Baldy assured him. "Reckon we had all of three hundred broncs in the remuda that drive. Waal, as I was tellin' yuh, them redskins jumped us—"

"Were they painted warriors—with war bonnets, Baldy?" asked Ted eagerly. "Did they gallop round in circles and shoot arrows?"

A sad expression crept into Baldy's faded blue eyes, the despairing look of a hopelessly defeated man. "Don't yuh aim to know how I was skelped, Sonny?" he reproached.

"Sure I do!" protested Teddy. "Show me the place, Baldy—the place on your head where the Indians scalped you."

"No!" said the old cowboy hurriedly. "Tain't a fitten sight for yore young eyes, Teddy. Man nor woman ain't never seen the place whar my ha'r was lifted from—"

"Baldy Bates! Aren't you ashamed—making up such fairy tales! You know you haven't been scalped!"

The grizzled puncher's booted feet slid to the ground. "Shucks, Miss Nan, Ted kinda likes to hear me talk of them ol' days." He grinned sheepishly at the girl smiling from the other side of the corral fence.

"You're a dear old fraud," laughed Nan. "I saw your head the other day when your hat blew off. The only thing you've lost is your hair."

Baldy's drooping mustaches twitched. "Mebbe I'm some mixed up 'bout thet skelpin'," he admitted. "Come to think of it, 'twas ol' Brazos them Injuns skelped thet night at Buff'lo Crik." He grinned shamelessly at Ted, who was eyeing him doubtfully. "Shore is a true story, Sonny—on'y it was Brazos an' not me them redskins skelped."

"Well," decided the boy loyally, mollified by the explanation, "it might have been you they'd have scalped, Baldy, only I reckon you worked your old six-guns too fast." He paused, looked at his old friend shrewdly. "I'll bet it was you saved Brazos from being killed when they scalped him."

Baldy Bates was silent, his gaze fixed on nowhere in particular, from which Nan correctly surmised that while her aged cowhand liked to indulge a picturesque imagination there were true tales he could tell—tales of heroism an innate modesty forbade the telling. Her thoughts went to more serious matters.

"Noticed anything suspicious, this morning, Baldy?" she queried anxiously.

"Ain't found no more of them papers stuck up," Baldy reassured her. His kindly leathery face was suddenly a hard, grim mask. "Shore would like to meet up with the coyote was prowlin' round last week."

"I bet you'd have pulled your old six-guns and filled him with plenty lead, Baldy," declared Teddy enthusiastically. He looked at his sister. "Gee, Nan, wish you'd let me have a *real* six-shooter for my holster— 'stead of this old wooden thing!"

Nan's look was horrified.

"I'm big enough," insisted the boy. "I'm going on twelve—and Baldy says I'm all he-man! Gee whiz—wish I had a little old twenty-two for my holster!"

"Perhaps soon," relented the girl. "On your birthday."

Teddy let out a delighted whoop, then was suddenly grave as he read the real worry in his sister's eyes. Despite his scarcely twelve years, Ted Page keenly felt his responsibility as the man of the family.

"I've been cutting sign for tracks, the way Baldy showed me," he told her importantly. "Been all round everywhere and down the creek. Reckon no *hombre* 'll come prowling round Los Posos and me not know it, Nan."

His sister smiled faintly. "Be careful with your grammar, Teddy," she begged.

"Aw, cowboys don't use good grammar," scoffed the boy.

"You're going to be one cowboy who will," she promised. "And remember, Teddy, you're going to be a *cattle king*—not a cowboy."

"Gee whiz—that's right," agreed her young brother, impressed. "I reckon cattle kings have got to use good grammar."

Baldy Bates nodded. "Shore do, Sonny," he affirmed sagely. "Take *me* now. If I'd been brung up to talk good grammar mos' likely I'd have been kingpin of the ol' Circle C down in the Panhandle." He was staring fixedly at a low distant ridge as he spoke and the girl sensed a sudden stiffening of the long gaunt frame.

"What is it, Baldy?" Her voice was sharp with apprehension. "You've seen something!"

The old man silently gestured and now Nan saw the horsemen silhouetted against the skyline—five riders—moving slowly along the ridge. In another moment they had dropped from sight into the shadows of a gully. The girl's face was pale. She looked at Baldy despairingly.

"Then it's true!" she said in a low voice. "They really mean to run us off the ranch—"

"Mebbe you an' Teddy best go into the house," suggested the old man. His seamed, weather-bitten face was like granite. "Reckon it's up to me to do the talkin', Miss Nan."

She shook her head, the color back in her smooth cheeks. "You are the one who will go into the house," was her surprising answer. "I'll do the talking for Rancho Los Posos."

Baldy gaped at her, lugubrious face set in frozen lines of horror.

"Men don't leave the fightin' to wimmen whar I come from!" he protested with growing indignation. "No, ma'am, Miss Nan, mebbe I've done plenty I could be hung for, but leavin' a lone fee-male in the lurch ain't never been chalked up 'g'inst Baldy Bates." The old cowboy glared at her. "Reckon I kin still throw plenty hot lead with the best of 'em!" He patted a low-slung six-gun.

"That is just why I don't want you around when those men come," Nan quietly pointed out. "You'd be only one against five armed men—"

"Wouldn't be the first time I've been one 'g'inst more'n five *hombres* lookin' for trouble," Baldy told her crossly.

"You'll obey orders!" flared the girl. "I won't risk gun-play!"

The look in her eyes told Baldy that further open rebellion was useless. Muttering to himself the old man stalked away, the rowels of his huge spurs rasping the dust. The door of the little log cabin that was his bunkhouse slammed behind his tall, stoop-shouldered frame.

Nan felt that her decision to face the enemy alone was the one sane thing to do. The presence of belligerent old Baldy Bates with his bristling display of guns could only result in tragedy, with the stanch old cowboy sacrificing his life for no purpose. She looked at Teddy thoughtfully.

"I'm not going into the house!" said the boy defiantly. "You can't make me leave you! I own Rancho Los Posos, too. You told me I did!" He jerked the wooden gun from his holster and brandished it. "Gee! Wish I had my little twenty-two—'stead of this old thing! Wouldn't let any old gang run us away if I had my little old twenty-two!"

Nan smiled affectionately. "You can stay with me, Ted," she assented. "You're the man of the family—you have a right to stay—only please throw that thing away. They might think it's a *real* gun—"

Teddy obeyed willingly enough. His expression betrayed that he had conceived a violent disgust for the make-believe six-shooter. Of what use was an imitation gun when trouble brewed? For that matter of what use was anything imitation? Teddy was learning rapidly.

Nan walked slowly toward the gate near the small barn. She failed to observe Baldy's head peering out like an old turtle from the bunkhouse door. He emerged stealthily and darted into the cottonwoods lining the little creek that flowed from the springs. He carried a big Sharps' buffalo gun. With the silence of an Indian he went swiftly down the tree-lined creek which meandered past the barn some two score yards from the gate.

The minutes dragged interminably. Nan leaned pensively against the tough willow post that held taut the barbed-wire gate. She had changed into a simple blue print dress since her return in the early morning hours. She had encountered Baldy, accompanied by Teddy and old Diego Pinzon, some three miles from the

ranch; had merely explained that she had been forced
to seek shelter from the sandstorm. She was curiously
reluctant to relate the full story of her strange adventure, her meeting with Lee Cary.

The sun told her that it was nearing midafternoon
and still no sign of the horsemen they had glimpsed on
the ridge. Nan gazed about her, absorbing the details
of the home she had planned to make for Ted and
herself—the home that her adventuring pioneer great-
uncle William had carved from the wilderness. He had
fought for it too, she realized; perhaps had died for
it. The girl shivered. Perhaps somewhere in the grove
of trees, surrounding the log house that he had built,
was his unmarked grave. She eyed the old house with
respect. It was well and sturdily built of solid spruce
logs, obtained possibly from the timbered heights of the
distant Santa Rosa mountains. He had planted vines
that the eternal flowing wells had kept alive through
the years until they covered the old building with a
softening, gracious mantle. Nan knew that Spring
would fill the air with incense of honeysuckle. Her
gaze idled down the creek, past the horse corral where
the red mare was dozing in the warm sun. Teddy's
pinto was drooping nearby, and Baldy's big roan, the
one he had brought with them from Abilene. Farther
down the little valley, in a green meadow fed by the
creek, browsed the dozen or more horses of the ranch
remuda and the modest beginnings of the Bar-2—the
brand Teddy and she had so happily devised. Was it all
to be nothing more than a dream, she wondered? Her
thoughts reverted to the previous night. Had that been
a dream, too? Had she really passed the night in that
strange abode of wandering Indians and desert rats?
Was there really such a person as Lee Cary? As if from
afar she heard Teddy's excited whisper.

"Nan! They're coming! All five of 'em!"

Nan's gaze leaped down into the valley. Five riders were approaching; horses shuffling at a running walk. She watched with dilated eyes, her face suddenly pale. Teddy looked at her, caught hold of her cold hand.

"Don't be scared, Nan! I won't let 'em hurt you!" Teddy's voice was fiercely gruff "Wish I had my little old twenty-two!" he added.

Nan bent quickly and kissed the earnest, tanned face, blessing the manly instinct to protect her. She threw a glance at the bunkhouse, saw that the door was closed. Baldy was obediently remaining in seclusion according to orders, she reflected. Another glance told her that old Teresa and Diego were standing in the kitchen door. They were wondering what was about to take place—were anxious.

"Teddy," she said quickly. "Run and tell Teresa and Diego to keep out of sight. Tell them it's my orders!"

The boy ran off and Nan's gaze went back to the nearing horsemen. A tall man on a roan horse was in the lead. Her heart skipped a beat. Lee Cary! Lee Cary was heading the invaders! A second look told her that she was mistaken. That slouching rider was not Lee Cary, she realized. Also Lee would be riding the Palomino. She glanced again at the bunkhouse, to assure herself that old Baldy was obeying orders. The door was closed, she saw with relief. If she had looked past the barn toward the creek, Nan might have detected the grim visage of Baldy Bates peering from a thicket of palo verde—seen the glint of sunlight on the menacing barrel of his long rifle. Fortunately for her peace of mind the girl's gaze was concentrated upon the approaching horsemen, now less than a hundred yards from the gate.

Teddy rejoined her, breathless from his dash to the house and back. He had no intention that she face danger without himself by her side. Nan looked at him, saw that his face was pale and tense. She knew that it was time that she draw to the full upon her own reserve of courage. She smiled down at him, reached for his hand.

Together they waited at the gate, staring in silence at the nearing riders. They could plainly see the face of the tall man on the roan, a harsh, beak-nosed face with cold, mirthless lips. A rifle was tucked in saddle boot; he wore two guns buckled to lean waist. Behind him in twos rode the four men, each of them heavily armed. They came on more slowly now, eyes wary, watchful, as though fearing an ambush—five hard-faced men. Nan's breath quickened. The menace in those fierce, scowling faces was unmistakable. Grim purpose was bringing those five riders to Rancho Los Posos. The clatter of their horses' hoofs sounded in her ears like titanic thunders of doom.

V
The House of His Ancestors

Lee methodically unloaded the cans of fresh spring-water and stripped the pack-saddle from the burro. Fleecy cloud-drifts were melting into the blue horizon above the low hump of the Bullion Mountains; there was a tang in the cool air that spoke of distant rain-drenched hills; and a subtle, evanescent freshness in the moisture-laden westerly wind, an elusive sweetness of newly washed earth. Lee's heart quickened; he was disturbingly aware of an odd thrill of expectancy.

"Paloma," he informed the diminutive white burro; "my plans for the day do not include your further services." He rubbed a long, attentive ear affectionately. "Browse where the spirit wills—yet wander not too far from call." He spoke in liquid Spanish.

The burro rolled soft dark eyes at him, switched a stubby tail and sauntered leisurely away. Lee grinned. He knew that when he again needed the faithful Paloma she would be found in nearby Lone Palm Canyon, where the browsing was good, the water sweet.

No sound came to him from the main gallery in the heart of the huge mesquite. Apparently the girl was still asleep, Lee decided. He dragged the heavy cans of water into the passage and proceeded to the stable with the pack-saddle. The Palomino greeted him with a friendly nicker. Amazement and consternation brought Lee to an abrupt standstill. The red mare was gone!

His astonished gaze roved about the little brambled chamber, grasped the significant fact that the girl's saddle was also missing. The mare, then, had not broken loose and strayed. She had been ridden away! Lee dropped the pack-saddle—went swiftly up the passage. One glance was sufficient—tumbled blankets, cold, gray ashes. Nan Page had fled the place without so much as a "thank you" for his hospitality.

His face hardened. He had not thought her capable of such crudeness. Not even a note of explanation. The fact that she was worried about the ranch and was in haste to return, could not excuse her callous treatment of him. That she had found his own note was evident. It was lying where she had dropped it near the cold ashes. Anger surged through him.

Another angle presented itself. Lee turned it over in his mind thoughtfully. He was finding it difficult to picture Nan Page in so ungracious a role. There was a reason—*had* to be a reason explaining her extraordinary flight—and that reason could only be—*fear*. Lee frowned, went slowly back to the Palomino.

"Buck, old fellow," he grumbled, "if you could talk you could tell me what frightened her—" He broke off, comprehension widening his eyes as he stared at the brand on the Palomino's sleek creamy skin. He bent down, scrutinized the ground intently. The imprint of Nan's small high-heeled boots was unmistakable. With a muttered exclamation Lee went quickly to the big silver-mounted saddle and again closely studied the ground beneath. The imprints of the girl's boots were plain enough. She had examined the saddle, the horse, seen the telltale brand of the Smoke Tree. Relief and chagrin spread over the young man's face. To know that the girl was not guilty of an unpardonable rudeness rolled a load from his mind; to know further it had been *fear of himself*—a fear inspired by the mark of the Smoke Tree on his own equipment, that had sent her away in terror, filled him with dismay. After his veiled comments regarding Smoke Tree Range it was only natural for the girl to take alarm at the sight of the sinister emblem on his own belongings.

Lee scowled. He had been a fool to give her a chance to learn of his connection with the Smoke Tree outfit.

"Buck," he told the Palomino grimly. "We've got a heap of work cut out for us today!"

He swung the saddle down and threw it over the sleek back, slipped into leather chaps and buckled on spurs and guns.

He rode at a steady pace that ate up the miles. The fast Palomino needed no urging; tough and tireless and sure-footed, the big horse took the rough going as it came, climbing like a cat and plunging and sliding down slippery descents; leaping boulders and narrow gullies. Lee did not spare him; he knew the enduring qualities of the great silver-maned stallion. And as he rode, swaying easily in the saddle to the rocking motion of the horse, his thoughts were with two people. One was the slim tawny-haired girl with the fearless dark blue eyes—she whom the fierce desert winds had flung so strangely into his life. For her sake he was daring to face the proud and arrogant old man who was lord of the vast domain known as Smoke Tree Range. Lee's own haughty face set in hard lines. Their last meeting had not been pleasant, he recalled.

The desert lay below them, for the last hour the trail had wound up the canyon. He could see on the right the serrated ridges of the Chocolate Mountains—the twin peaks of the Coyotes on the left; the canyon walls fell apart and soon the Palomino was moving at a swift swinging trot down hill—down into a long wide valley

walled by rugged ramparts. They crossed Moonlake—
now dry, its mud-caked surface gleaming like smooth
yellow crackle-ware. Chimney Peak swung into view,
a great, lofty pinnacle that seemed to touch the blue.
Below, on the swelling breast of the foothills at the end
of the valley, other details now caught the eye—ancient
gray walls nestled among the trees—the great house,
proudly standing on the heights and surrounded by
the lesser buildings and the corrals of Smoke Tree
Ranch. Cattle grazed quietly along the slopes. He could
hear the bawling of calves, the awesome challenge of a
range bull. Lee's spurs touched the Palomino's satiny
sides. The horse leaped into a swift gallop.

On a broad balcony of the house on the hill was an
old man in a big armchair. One foot, swathed in ban-
dages, rested upon a low stool; a stout stick of polished cherry-red manzanita leaned at his elbow. He
was, perhaps, between seventy-five and eighty years of
age with a thick shaggy mane of white hair and deep-
set gray eyes under beetling grizzled brows. His nose
was high, set in a thin eagle-keen face and he wore a
frosted pointed beard under bristling mustaches. A
fine, strong face, save for the stamp of arrogance that
marked the haughty features. He was not unlike an
arrogant old eagle watching from proud heights the
doings of a crawling world.

He straightened in the big chair, gaze intent on the
distant horseman breasting the slope. Presently he
lifted a brass telescope from a mahogany box on the
small table by his side and leveled it. A curiously exultant gleam flared in the cavernous eyes and slowly,
methodically, he replaced the telescope in the box, in
which also reposed a long-barreled Colt six-shooter.
From another box he took a cigar which he lighted with
great deliberation. A close observer might have noticed

a slight tremor in the lean brown fingers that held the match. Again his gaze sought the approaching lone horseman, and, leaning back in the chair he continued to watch, thin, haughty face an inscrutable mask.

A grinning Mexican mozo met Lee at the gate which he ran to open. Lee threw him a smile of thanks and spurred to one of the stables where a second grinning mozo greeted him.

"*Buenas dias, Senor!*"

Lee returned the salutation in Spanish and swung from the saddle.

"Remove the saddle, Pio," he instructed in the same tongue. "Rub him down well and a mouthful of water to cool his throat. Saddle him again as soon as he is dry for we ride far and fast."

"*Si*, Senor," promised the mozo. "A horse of horses, this one! Never has the Smoke Tree bred a greater, Senor!"

"Buck is *all* horse," agreed Lee in English, then in the same tongue he asked abruptly, "Gil Hawken around, Pio?"

Pio rolled the whites of his eyes, glanced apprehensively at a squat, bow-legged cowboy who had suddenly appeared in the doorway of a bunkhouse across the yard.

"I asked you if Gil Hawken is around," reminded Lee, a rasp in his voice. "What's got your tongue, Pio?"

Pio licked dry lips, darted another nervous look at the watching cowboy. The latter gave a hitch to his gun-belt and started across the yard toward them. Pio turned a scared face to the frowning young man.

"I fear to talk, Senor," he said rapidly in Spanish. "This man who comes is a bad one. He would have my life if I speak of things that I should not—"

Anger glinted in Lee's eyes. "Pio"—his voice was purposely loud "I asked you a question. Where is Gil Hawken?"

A Texas drawl broke in. "Pio ain't answerin' questions, mister—not if he's got good sense, he ain't."

Lee whirled on high boot-heels and coolly stared at the runty cowboy, an up-and-down appraisal. The latter returned the look with cold unwinking eyes.

"Who may yuh be, mister, ridin' in here so high an' mighty—an' askin' for the foreman of the Smoke Tree?" For a moment the man's gaze studied the brand worn by the Palomino. Surprise flitted across his vicious face; and then, with growing impudence. "How come yuh forkin' a Smoke Tree bronc?" He leaned forward, balanced on the balls of his feet in the attitude of a gunfighter, hands hovering over the butts of the guns carried in either low-slung holster.

Lee eyed him silently for a moment. "Who are you, fellow?" His voice was a soft, lazy drawl, his gaze that of one who is examining a particularly loathsome object. "You must be new 'round here on the Smoke Tree."

"Take up that slack in yore lip an' speak yore bus'ness here!" snarled the runty cowboy. "I got a hair-trigger temper, feller!"

Lee shrugged dusty shoulders and proceeded to roll a cigarette. "I'll say one thing," he observed wearily; "you've been badly brought up. No manners at all." He touched a match to the cigarette and inhaled deeply. "I was asking Pio where I could find Gil Hawken. Perhaps *you* can tell me."

Unnoticed by them the tall old man, leaning heavily on his stout manzanita stick, was watching from the corner of the veranda. One observing him closely would have sensed a wistfulness in the proud, cold face, a hint of hope in the deep-set eyes.

"Perhaps *you* can tell me where I can find Gil Hawken," repeated Lee in a chill voice.

A sneer distorted the man's thin, mirthless lips; his crouch became more pronounced, the poise of hands over gun-butts more ominous.

"Stranger," he said in a thin, deadly voice, "I shore warned yuh plenty. Shore I know whar yuh kin find Gil Hawken—but I ain't answerin' yore question. I'm givin' yuh ten seconds to git outer here—"

His voice died in a strangled gurgle as Lee's hand suddenly darted out and seized him by the collar of his flannel shirt and before the man's paralyzed hands could go through the motions of drawing his guns Lee had plucked them from holsters and thrown them aside.

"Now!" he said, still in the same quiet voice, "we'll see if you won't answer questions—" He shook his victim with the wholehearted enthusiasm of a terrier shaking a rat; slapped him right and left on the face and finally lifted him off his feet and flung him down on the hard ground. "Where is Gil Hawken?" he asked again, softly.

The cowboy lay breathing heavily and moaning and spitting blood from bruised mouth. "Gil—an' some of the outfit done rode over to Los Posos," he gasped.

"What are they doing over there in Los Posos?" demanded Lee. His eyes flamed and instinctively the man flung up a shielding hand.

"Went to run off some damned nesters!" he panted.

Lee turned a contemptuous back on him. "Hurry, Pio!" he told the goggle-eyed mozo. "A quick rub-down—and have Buck round by the side gate in ten minutes!" Not deigning another glance at the groaning and thoroughly broken cowboy, he turned on his heel and made swiftly for the big ranch house.

The tall old man on the veranda limped slowly back to his chair; an extraordinary pride—and elation burned in the deep-set eyes; bristling mustaches twitched with a grimly exultant smile.

"A Cary!" he muttered. "Aye—the Cary blood *won't* be denied!" He sank awkwardly into his chair and rearranged swathed foot on the stool. "But by the blood that's in him the lad's got to bend to my will—"

There was a quick, firm tread of advancing feet, the rasp and jingle of spurs, and Lee stood before him. The old man looked up at him coldly.

"So you're back, eh?" His tone was mildly amused, triumphant. "Kind of reckoned you'd come to your senses—"

Lee glared down at him. His face was pale, his eyes black with suppressed fury.

"I've come to see you about that girl down in Los Posos!"

"What girl? Don't know of any girl down in Los Posos," returned the old man, indifferently. "Leave those things to Gil Hawken, now, grandson. Gil's business to run off those nesters—"

"She's not a nester!" declared the young man fiercely. "You've got no right to threaten her—terrorize her!"

"I leave those things to Gil Hawken," repeated the old man mildly. "Gil told me there were some nesters down there on the old rancho and reckoned he'd run 'em off."

"The day of big cattle ranches is done," declared Lee. "The time is coming when thousands of prosperous homes will fill the hills and valleys you now claim as range for Smoke Tree cattle—and the desert, too," he added with a defiant look at his grandfather, "the desert, too, *will* become a land of plenty—"

Old Jim Cary glared at him with suddenly bloodshot eyes. "You—you young fool!" he grumbled, "I'm losing patience! College ruined you—filled your head with crack-brained nonsense."

"You cattlemen can't go on hogging *all* the land," Lee said positively.

"Fool! Away from here! Out of my sight—and stay out of my sight until you come to your senses!" stormed his grandfather.

"I'm not leaving until we settle about this Los Posos business," Lee told him quietly.

"You've had my answer!" fumed old Jim Cary. "I never interfere with my foremen about nesters. Gil Hawken will do what is right—run 'em out—"

"Not this time, he won't!" His grandson's tone was grim.

"*I'm* master here," rasped the old man.

"You forget something," said Lee softly. "Your rights as master of Smoke Tree Range come from my grandmother's father, Senor Felipe Torres, who in turn became owner through the royal grant of a king of Spain to his ancestor. My rights in Smoke Tree, through Don Felipe's daughter who was your wife and my grandmother, are quite equal to yours."

Old Jim eyed him silently. He knew there was justice in the statement. He had been a penniless young Texan, a cavalry captain in Scott's invading army during the Mexican War. Taken prisoner, young Captain Jim Cary had been rescued from a firing squad by the pleas of lovely Senorita Carmela Torres who had fallen in love with the dashing young Americano. The war at an end with the signing of the Treaty of Guadalupe Hidalgo, Carmela became the bride of Jim Cary and the young couple had been given the old Smoke Tree Rancho in distant California. Yes, there *was* justice in Lee's statement that his own rights were too strong to be ignored.

"What do you want, then?" queried the old man, finally.

"I want Gil Hawken ordered to leave Los Posos strictly alone," was Lee's answer.

Jim Cary lifted his heavy manzanita stick and pounded the floor. "No!" he roared. "As long as I live— no nester will possess a foot of Smoke Tree land!" He fumbled in the long mahogany box and pulled out a checkbook and pen and ink.

Lee watched wonderingly, and with impatience. He was frantic to be on his way to Los Posos. Jim Cary opened the checkbook; his pen scratched.

"Here," he said gruffly. "Maybe this will ease your sensitive conscience if you believe wrong is being done."

Lee took the piece of paper; saw that it was made out to bearer in the sum of ten thousand dollars.

"What's it for?" he wanted to know in a puzzled tone.

"For the girl you spoke of," barked the old gentleman testily. "First time in my life I ever offered to buy a nester out," he grumbled.

"She won't accept it," declared Lee. "She's not the kind you can buy out. She's a fighter, grandfather."

Old Jim Cary eyed him shrewdly. "Trying to tell me you're in love with this girl?" he wanted to know.

Lee gave him a startled look. "Why—why, I hadn't thought about it that way," he stammered. He tossed the check onto the table and turned away. "I'll not stand idle and see Gil Hawken do her harm!" he flung back at his grandparent.

He was gone and soon old Jim Cary heard the drumming beat of shod hoofs as the big Palomino sped into the west toward Rancho Los Posos. Again the look of pride burned in the old man's deep-set eyes. He sat for a moment crumpling the check between his fingers, watching horse and rider drop with bullet speed down the long slope. Presently he touched a bell. A mozo slid into view.

"Pedro," ordered Lee's grandfather, "tell Slinger Cole I want to see him at once."

He waited, gaze following the distant horseman. Slouching footsteps aroused him. He straightened up, quickly took the six-shooter from the mahogany box and placed it on the table by his side. The squat cowboy Lee had manhandled came hesitantly toward him. Behind him, in the doorway, waited the watchful-eyed mozo.

"Slinger," said old Jim Cary in a chill voice, "the young man you insulted a few minutes ago was my grandson. I'm glad he did what he did. In his place I would have shot the gizzard out of you." His pen scratched a moment. "Here is your pay to the end of the month. Now get off this ranch and stay off. If I catch you within twenty miles of the ranch I'll have you hung to the nearest tree handy. Now get out!"

The man took the proffered check and slunk away sullenly. The old lord of Smoke Tree range leaned back in his big chair with a grunt of satisfaction and reached for the long brass telescope. There was still time for another glimpse of the Palomino's rider before he disappeared into the gloom of the gorge. And presently Lee Cary's grandfather was dozing peacefully, the drumming of the Palomino's hoofs still in his ears.

VI
Trouble at Los Posos

Surprise was visible on the hard faces of the five riders as they drew rein; tense expressions relaxed and to a man they gazed with wide-eyed approval at the attractive bare-headed young girl coolly waiting at the gate. It was seldom they were privileged to gaze at a pretty girl of her quality—and Nan was undeniably pretty and winsome with her bright tawny hair and simple blue print dress. She stood proudly erect, skirts fluttering in the rising midafternoon breeze and revealing the graceful lines of lissome body. No wonder the hard eyes of the horsemen softened with admiration and pleasure at the picture she made.

The tall, beak-nosed leader on the powerful roan smiled down at her doubtfully.

"You livin' here, Miss?"

"This is my home," she returned in a level voice. "What is it you want?"

The man seemed nonplused. "Is yore pa 'round? Reckon our bus'ness is with him—"

"You can state your business to me," Nan informed him in the same quiet tone. "My brother and I own this place." She indicated the wide-eyed Teddy close by her side.

The roan's rider stared at her silently for a moment, the friendly smile gone from harsh-visaged face; saddle-leathers creaked as the men at his back shifted uneasily and exchanged quick, dismayed glances.

"What yuh mean—you an' the kid ownin' this place?" queried the tall leader gruffly.

"I mean exactly what I said," answered the girl coolly. "My brother and I are the owners of Rancho Los Posos and you can state your business to me."

"It ain't pleasant bus'ness," muttered the man. "Wasn't expectin' you'd turn out to be a girl."

Nan smiled sweetly, waited for him to continue.

"Don't yuh know this is Smoke Tree land?" A scowl darkened the man's face.

Nan sensed that he was deliberately whipping up his fury. She shook her head, still smiling. "If you are a Smoke Tree rider you should know that this is not Smoke Tree land," she told him gently. Her glance rested on the roan for a moment. "I see that your horse wears the Smoke Tree brand."

He gave her a thin-lipped smile. "You're talking to Gil Hawken, Miss," he informed her, "foreman on the Smoke Tree outfit."

Nan's smile was gracious. "I'm Nan Page," she returned, "and this is my brother Ted. I hope the Los Posos and the Smoke Tree will be good neighbors," she added in a friendly tone.

Hawken seemed taken aback by her friendliness. A laugh came from one of the riders. The tall foreman turned in his saddle and gave the offender a malevolent look. "No more of that from you, Sandy," he said menacingly. His gaze went back to the girl, seemed to absorb her from head to foot. Nan felt the color suddenly hot in her cheeks. He continued to stare at her, a growing insolence in his smoky devouring eyes.

"Reckon yuh'd make a right nice neighbor—anywhere else but here." His tone was amused. "Right pretty, for a nester—" He winked round at the grinning faces.

"I'm afraid you are becoming insulting," Nan said icily.

Hawken leaned forward, face blackening with whipped-up rage. "Don't yuh know yuh're trespassin'—that yuh're a nester?"

"We're not trespassing and we're not nesters!" she flung at him haughtily.

"Los Posos belongs to the Smoke Tree," Hawken said savagely. "Yuh're a nester. If yuh was a man we'd take yuh out and hang yuh to yonder cottonwood."

"If I were a man you'd probably be getting the worst beating of your life," flared the girl. "Take your men and go, Mr. Hawken!"

The foreman laughed mirthlessly. "Shore spunky, ain't yuh?" he sneered. His face hardened. "I left yuh a warnin' to leave. Why ain't yuh out of here?"

"We're not leaving," defied Nan. "Los Posos belongs to my brother and me and you can go and tell your boss, whoever he is, that I'm not afraid of him or his ruffians." Her eyes sparkled. "Now get out of here! Get off this ranch!"

Hawken scowled. "Open that gate, kid!" he suddenly ordered Ted roughly.

Nan's hand went to her startled brother's shoulder. "You coward!" she blazed. Hawken gave her a wolfish grin, spoke sharply to one of his men. The latter spurred up to the gate and leaning from saddle jerked the rope fastening loose. A rope hissed through the air and in a moment the wire gate was snatched wide open at the end of the lariat. The girl uttered a faint cry—sprang to the opening, arms extended to bar entrance.

"You're not coming in!" she gasped. "You're not— you're not!"

For answer Hawken slid from his saddle and seized her arm. Ted flew at him.

"Leave my sister alone! Leave Nan alone!" Half crying with rage and fear the boy belabored the tall foreman with tightly clenched fists. One of the grinning riders swung a rope and Teddy was jerked off his feet.

"Tie the brat up!" ordered Hawken, with an oath, one big hand still clasping the girl's arm. He looked at her with grim amusement. "The Smoke Tree don't waste time with nesters," he sneered. "If they don't get out when we tell 'em, we burn 'em out."

"You coward!" she said with quiet scorn. "Let go of my arm!"

Hawken's face bent toward her. There was an ugly gleam in the cruel smoky eyes, an avid light that sent a cold prickle of terror through Nan. For the first time she was conscious of real fright. Instinctively she shrank.

"Shore one little wildcat," grinned the man. His low laugh was sinister. "I like 'em onery. Makes it interestin'."

"You're hurting me," the girl said in a low voice. She glanced at Teddy, helpless on the ground in the coils of a rawhide lariat. The boy's face was turned toward her piteously; she saw that his terror was all for her—not for himself. Nan's heart sank; her knees suddenly seemed to turn to rubber. "Oh, you cowards—you cowards!" she choked.

Hawken regarded her thoughtfully, the same frightening light still in his eyes. "Mebbe we ain't burnin' yuh out today," he said with a leer. "Mebbe we kin fix things for yuh to stay—awhile. What yuh say, bright eyes?"

For answer Nan's free hand swung up. "Beast!" she panted and struck the leering face with all her strength. Hawken only laughed; the flame in his eyes became more pronounced. Out of the corner of her eye the girl glimpsed Diego and Teresa running toward them from the house. The old nurse was shrieking and waving her arms.

One of the riders jerked a gun from his holster and fired. Diego halted.

"Go back! Go back!" screamed the girl.

Diego came to a standstill. Teresa was not so obedient. She continued her shrieking approach.

"Murderers—dogs!" she screamed in Spanish. She came at a waddling, painful gait, for Teresa was of vast proportions and a sufferer from rheumatism.

"Keep the fat old fool away!" Hawken snarled to Fargo.

The latter grinned, moved toward the oncoming Teresa, swinging his rawhide rope. A rifle roared from the palo verde thicket down by the creek. Fargo staggered, went down on his face. Old Teresa puffed past the prone figure without so much as a glance.

"Murderers—dogs!" she continued to scream in Spanish. "Take your vile hands from my sweet lamb!"

For a moment the Smoke Tree men stared with stunned eyes at their fallen comrade.

"Elevate yore hands pronto," boomed a voice from the palo verde thicket, "an' turn the gal loose, mister, or you'll shore git the next bullet. I ain't missin' at this range—"

"You'd better do what Baldy says!" shrilled Teddy excitedly and struggling with his bonds. "Ol' Baldy 'll shoot the daylights out of you if you don't mind him!"

With a muttered imprecation Hawken jerked Nan between himself and the rifle menacing from the palo verde thicket. The terrified girl felt his gun pressing into her back.

"Tell him to drop that gun!" he said fiercely, "and keep that old woman away—if you want to live—"

Nan read death in the savage face. Frantically she waved Teresa back, at the same time faltering out her peril to Baldy.

"He—he'll kill me, Baldy, if you don't obey—"

Reluctantly the rifle menacing from the thicket lowered from view.

"Don't hurt Baldy!" she begged. "He was only trying to do what any real man would do—protect Teddy and me!"

"Tell him to come out of them bushes—and to keep his hands high," snarled Hawken. His gun pressed into her back.

Slowly Baldy obeyed the summons—emerged from his ambush, hands lifted above his head, his seamed, leathery face a study of horror and dismay. A Smoke Tree man ran with drawn gun and scrape of dragging spurs to meet him and in another minute the grizzled puncher was relieved of his two ancient six-shooters.

"If Fargo's dead—we're hangin' yuh," Hawken promised curtly. "Mebbe we're hangin' yuh anyway—"

The gaunt prisoner shrugged his stooped bony shoulders. "He' ain't dead, that hombre," he mildly told the glowering foreman. "Didn't aim to do more'n crease the coyote's skelp for him—knock him senseless—"

A Smoke Tree man, Sandy, swore softly. "Reckon the onery ol' buzzard shore kin place his shots like he claims," he admired. "That bullet on'y knocked Fargo plumb senseless for a moment. See, fellers, Fargo's sittin' up—wonderin' what's give him a headache!"

Fargo was staggering to his feet, cursing luridly and tenderly rubbing his creased scalp. His marveling comrades eyed the veteran cowboy with vast respect. It was a feat they could appreciate.

Hawken relaxed his hold on the girl. She gave him a look of such sheer horror and loathing that the man had the grace to lower his insolent eyes. A deep flush stained his dark face.

"Don't hurt Baldly!" she begged. "He was only trying to do what any real man would do—protect Teddy and me!"

Hawken looked at Baldy thoughtfully. The old man's skill with a rifle had impressed him. Baldy was a man the Smoke Tree could use.

"Mebbe we'll give yuh a chance to save yore neck," he told the old cowboy. "Mebbe I can fix it for yuh to join up with the Smoke Tree outfit, feller."

"Mister"—there was profound scorn in Baldy's voice—"yuh're shore talkin' through yore hat! I'm on the Bar-2 payroll, meanin' this here Los Posos ranch."

Hawken's rage revived. "Tie the old buzzard up," he ordered curtly. "He's goin' with us." He looked at Nan. "I'll be round to see yuh in a day or two," he told her. "We'll talk things over. In the meantime you can do some thinkin'."

"What do you mean?" she asked, white-faced. "And won't you turn my brother loose? What harm can a little boy do to a lot of big armed men?"

"The kid's going with us," grinned the foreman.

Nan uttered a cry and ran to the boy and began to tear at the rawhide rope. Old Teresa panted up, brandishing fists at the grinning men. Hawken rasped out an order; a Smoke Tree man pushed them aside roughly—jerked Teddy to his feet and swung him up to one of the riders; the latter's hard arm clamped the boy firmly. Teresa began to scream.

Force against these brutal men was futile, Nan realized. She had thought to defy the power of the Smoke Tree. She knew now that she could not. Teddy was more precious than any other thing life could offer. She had lost the fight—lost Rancho Los Posos.

"We'll go," she told Hawken in a stifled voice. "Please don't harm my brother! We'll go!"

"I'm not afraid of them, Nan!" cried the boy defiantly from his perch on the Smoke Tree horse. "Baldy and me'll escape, you bet!"

There was a derisive laugh from the riders.

Nan shivered under the look in the tall foreman's eyes. He smiled, as if pleasantly confident of the outcome.

"No rush for yuh to leave—for a few days," he said. "I'll be round, like I said, an' we'll talk it over. Yuh can't stay on Los Posos for good. The Big Boss won't stand for nesters, but mebbe we can fix it for yuh to live in Coldwater—if yuh're reasonable. Real nice town—" He smiled again, eyes absorbing the girl's slim loveliness. "I'm leavin' Fargo here to sort of keep a eye on things 'til I git round to see yuh. Baldy," he added, "yuh're forkin' Fargo's bronc. Climb up thar, feller. An' one of you fellers rope the buzzard to the saddle good an' tight."

Nan was trembling. "Please don't take my brother away!" she begged brokenly. "Oh, how can you be so cruel—wicked!" She held out her arms imploringly. "Teddy!"

The boy began to struggle against the hard clamping arm that held him to the saddle. "Let me down—let me down!" he sobbed. "Baldy!"

But old Baldy Bates, now securely roped to Fargo's horse, had no answer. He stared gloomily into the far horizon, his long lugubrious face the picture of despair. Teresa was on her knees, muttering prayers in Spanish, a little silver cross in her work-worn fingers. And a prayer, too, came to Nan's lips as she stood there among those cold-eyed, callous riders. She scarcely heard Hawken's voice.

"I'm taking the kid to help yuh make up yore mind. Never seen a girl I fancy like I fancy you. We could git along fine—if yuh act reasonable—git married by a preacher if yuh want it that way." He swung up to the roan horse. "I'm takin' the kid to help yuh make up yore mind," he repeated.

The last of his speech went unheeded by the girl. She was gazing down the canyon, her lips parted, a heaven-born hope suddenly in her eyes, gazing with a wild, exultant singing of the heart at the horseman storming up the trail. She knew that great golden horse—knew the tall rider!

The others now heard the drumming beat of hoofs. Eyes turned quickly.

"Hell!" exclaimed a surprised voice. "That's Lee Cary's Palomino!"

"—and Lee Cary forkin' saddle," muttered another voice.

They fell silent, threw uneasy glances at their foreman. Hawken's bold face was a frozen mask, save for the watchful, smoldering eyes fixed upon the approaching horseman. Nan sensed that the man's single emotion was deepest hate for the Palomino's rider. His henchmen feared, but he hated. The thought was reassuring. She had fled from Lee Cary with mistrust in her heart for him. The reaction of these Smoke Tree men at the sight of him seemed to deny that he had any connection with the ruthless owner of Smoke Tree Range—was proof that he was innocent of any complicity in the outrageous attempt to evict her from Rancho Los Posos.

The big golden stallion slid to a halt, nostrils blowing, sides heaving. The Smoke Tree men threw admiring, respectful glances. They were of the breed that loved a good horse; dimly they divined that the mighty Palomino had made a miracle run across many miles of rough country; that only the stout heart in him could have made possible so swift and gallant an ascent of the last long slope.

For a long moment Lee stared silently at the tall Smoke Tree foreman. The look of cold rage on the haughty face made the girl gasp. No wonder the riders had shown fear at his approach. His gaze went to the man holding Teddy on his saddle.

"Put the boy down."

Nan felt her spine tingle. There was the shocking impact of a high-powered bullet in the low, quiet voice. The cowboy turned pale. Silently he allowed the boy to slide to the ground. Teddy stood for a moment, wavering giddily on his feet, wide eyes fastened on the Palomino's tall rider, then he ran to Nan, clasped her hand tightly. Lee spoke again, gestured at Baldy, bound to Fargo's horse.

"Turn that man loose."

A rider spurred close to Baldy's side, hand reaching out to jerk off the binding rope. Hawken's furious voice halted him.

"Keep yore hands off that rope, Sandy! I'm boss of this outfit!"

Sandy hesitated, glanced uncertainly at Lee. The latter's face was impassive. "Turn him loose," he repeated in the same flat, chilling voice.

Gil Hawken's gun flashed from holster. "I'm boss of this outfit!" he said again, in a voice hoarse with blind rage. "Mind yore own damn business, Lee Cary! You ain't got authority over me!"

Lee seemed not to hear him. "Turn that man loose, Sandy," he said again. "I won't tell you a third time—"

Sandy darted a rebellious look at the foreman, reached out a hand and jerked the knot. In a moment Baldy was coolly shaking off the rope. Sandy grinned at him. He was the youngest of the Smoke Tree men, a freckled-faced, sandy-haired youth.

"I like yore brand of talk, mister," Baldy chuckled to Lee. "It's a lingo these *hombres* shore *sabe* plenty."

Lee turned his attention to the angry Smoke Tree foreman. There was murder in the latter's eyes. He lifted his gun. Nan held her breath. Oh, why didn't Lee draw his own gun? Was he going to let that man shoot him down, she wondered despairingly?

Two times Hawken lifted the gun, dark face convulsed with insane range. Some power stronger than his own mad desire seemed to paralyze his trigger-finger. With an oath he suddenly re-holstered the weapon. Relief turned the girl giddy and for a moment the Palomino and his rider wavered crazily before her eyes—loomed suddenly colossal. She could see nothing but that golden horse—the tall, implacable eyed rider. As from afar she heard his quiet voice.

"Get out of here, Gil Hawken. Let's see your dust. And don't come back!"

"You ain't got authority over me," muttered the man sullenly. "I come to run these nesters off the place an' I aim to do it." Hawken was regaining his usual cool poise. His insolent eyes sparkled. "Yore grandfather ain't likin' nesters on Smoke Tree land—"

Nan felt suddenly cold. Then Lee was the grandson of the dread owner of the Smoke Tree! No wonder he had been reluctant to talk of himself that night in the mesquite! She looked at him miserably—met his unhappy eyes.

"Yore grandfather ordered me to run this outfit out of Los Posos," continued Hawken, vaguely divining he had scored a hit. "I take my orders from Jim Cary, mister—not from his no-count grandson."

"You're a liar," Lee said very softly, and leaned forward, one hand hovering over holstered gun.

Hawken seemed content to let it pass. "Yuh can ask

him yore own self," he sneered. "I'm ridin' now, but tomorrow 'll find me back—" He flung a meaning look at the girl.

"He's worse'n a liar," loudly opined Baldy Bates. "He's all pizen snake." The old man was sheathing his recovered six-guns. "Carry plenty hot lead for pizen snakes when they git in my way," he added grimly.

"He was mean to Nan!" shrilled Teddy. "He pinched her arm—made her cry!"

The Palomino seemed to soar through the air. Lee catapulted from his saddle in a dive at the man on the roan horse; the two men crashed to earth, locked in each other's arms. One of the Smoke Tree men gave a yell, jerked at his gun. A six-shooter roared deafeningly and the gun dropped from the rider's hand. He stared with shocked eyes at a suddenly bloody wrist.

"Elevate pronto!" boomed Baldy's voice. "Up with 'em, fellers! I crave to make me some buzzards' meat!"

They obeyed, hard eyes raking the old man with poisonous looks.

"Git their smoke-pots, Teddy," rumbled Baldy. "Yore turn to ride the coyotes!" The veteran cowman grinned joyously at white-haired Diego Pinzon who came panting up, unable longer to resist the screams of his distressed wife.

But Nan would not allow this; she clung to Ted, and it was old Diego who emptied the holsters.

"No call for us to go on the prod at that," muttered a Smoke Tree man, the freckled-face Sandy. "Ain't carin' much for this dirty business if you ask me. Shore hope Gil gets the tar whaled out of him."

Nan was appalled at the stark fury of the two battling men—and conscious, too, of a fierce satisfaction. The Smoke Tree foreman would get the beating she would have given him had she been a man. Not for a moment did she doubt the outcome of the conflict being waged so desperately before her eyes.

The two men were fairly evenly matched, with Hawken perhaps the heavier and tougher. Once on his feet he bored in with the ferocity of a charging bull, arms swinging pile-driver blows. Lee fought coolly, content at first to avoid his opponent's rushing attack. It was soon apparent that he was the better boxer. Again and again his left jab found its mark—left red smears on Hawken's face. The sight was too much for Nan; she hid her face against Teresa's comforting shoulder. Nor did she look again until Teddy's shrill, exultant yell informed her that the affair was ended.

"He licked him! He licked him good!" jubilated the boy. "Gee, Nan, that nice man licked him!"

Nan looked around, saw that Hawken was getting groggily to his feet and that Lee had turned his back on him—was walking toward them. The Smoke Tree man's face was a bloody smear, one eye was closed; the other glared murderously at the man who had whipped him. With a muttered imprecation he jerked at his gun. Nan's scream warned Lee. He whirled, gun leaping from holster and spurting flame. Hawken's forty-five spun from his hand, exploding in the air as it fell. The Smoke Tree foreman's swart, bleeding face was a study of shocked incredulity. He stared disbelievingly at his paralyzed fingers.

"Some shootin'!" murmured an awed voice from one of the riders. "Knocked the gun clean out of Gil's hand before he could pull trigger!"

Lee sheathed his smoking Colt, watchful eyes on the man who had attempted to shoot him in the back.

"Pick up your gun and get out of here with your outfit, Hawken." His tone was bleak. "And keep it in your thick head that Rancho Los Posos is the property of Miss Page and her brother. Now get going!"

Hawken sullenly retrieved the six-shooter and climbed stiffly into his saddle. "Yuh ain't heard the last of this, mister," he said thickly. Black rage gleaming from swollen, slitted eyes, he spurred away.

The four Smoke Tree riders hesitated, looked longingly at their confiscated guns. Lee read their thoughts, motioned for Baldy to return the weapons. The latter grudgingly obeyed.

"I'm advisin' yuh to leave 'em home—next time yuh come Los Posos way," he grumbled. "Now hightail it pronto—let's see yore dust."

Hoofs dug into the ground and the five Smoke Tree riders swung away, went rocketing down the trail. Lee watched them for a moment, then turned and looked at Nan. His expression was cold, unsmiling. She sensed that her abrupt flight from Mesquite House had deeply hurt him. She colored, started to speak—found she had no words. It was Teddy who broke the tension.

"Gee, mister! You sure can throw lead! Reckon you've got Baldy Bates faded all right!"

There was the unmistakable light of hero-worship in Teddy's admiring eyes. Lee smiled at him, the slow, friendly, warming smile that Nan had come to know. The boy continued importantly. "I'm Ted Page—and she's my sister Nan. And this is Teresa and Diego— they've always lived with us; and Baldy Bates is our foreman. He used to drive longhorns up the Chisholm trail and fight Indians and shoot buffaloes and everything. Nan and I are partners in the cattle business," he added. "Reckon I'll be a cattle king when I grow up."

"I'm betting you will," averred Lee gravely, "I'm betting you'll make a first-class cattleman. I'm Lee Cary," he introduced. "I hope we'll be good friends."

There was a challenge in the look he suddenly gave the girl, a hint of reproach.

Nan gave him a timid, uncertain smile, a mute plea for mercy in her lovely eyes, then with a little cry of concern she ran to him. "Lee, your face is bleeding!" She dabbed at the cut cheek with a wisp of handkerchief, whispered, *"Forgive me, Lee—for running away!"*

VII
A Wolf in Sheep's Clothing

Coldwater possessed all the drab features of the average desert hamlet. Dejected frame buildings lined the abbreviated dusty street. There were the usual number of saloons, including the more ornate Desert Bar with its sun-blistered red front; there was the two-story frame Coldwater Palace Hotel with its equally blistered white-washed walls and dingy sign-board swinging over the warped veranda steps announcing ROOMS 25¢ & UP . . . MEALS TWO BITS; and there was Ma Kelly's boardinghouse, an ancient adobe structure roofed with age-mellow red tiles. It stood somewhat aloof at the far end of the street and half-hidden behind graceful palo verde and feathery tamarisk trees that were fed by eternally bubbling springs. It was there that a footsore, weary, thirsting Franciscan padre had rested and bestowed grateful blessing—and the name of Agua Frio—on the place that had refreshed him with cooling water and shade. The passing years, the war with Mexico, the coming of the gringo with his covered wagon, had gradually dimmed the memory of that valiant pioneer of the Cross. Agua Frio became Coldwater, a few humble 'dobe huts, at first the abode of Indian converts, then a lively rendezvous for gay young blades of spur and reata—and later a tough border town, a drab place. The good padre perhaps wept to see the change in the desert oasis he had named and blessed with humility and gratitude; or perhaps sturdy faith fixed resolute eyes on the little cross of carved wood resting on Ma Kelly's bosom. He had fashioned the little cross from a green twig, a piece of palo verde, while resting in the shade of its cooling branches. It was still fastened to the trunk of the same palo verde when the widow Kelly found it a century or more later.

The discovery of the little cross profoundly affected the Widow Kelly. She felt that it was a sign from Heaven, bidding her to make her home in Coldwater. There beckoned the abandoned old adobe, nestled among green trees by the side of flowing springs. She moved in, little dreaming that in the distant years to come Ma Kelly's Adobe Inn would be the mecca of travelers from far countries. In those days Ma Kelly was content to run a little boardinghouse where she served absurdly big meals for absurdly small prices, and sometimes for no price at all; and if some lonesome young cowboy was homesick he could be certain of a motherly welcome from Ma Kelly. Her heart was as big as the wide world; there was always room for one more chick to mother.

Wirt Stoner was the antithesis of the plump and wholesome Ma Kelly, as different as the hard, tawdry red front of his saloon and dance-hall was different from the picturesque adobe boardinghouse nestled among the green trees. Their distrust of each other was mutual. Ma Kelly had small use for the cold-eyed proprietor of the Desert Bar and was not averse to frankly expressing her low opinion of him. Wirt Stoner was more subtle. Few knew of the hate he bore for the buxom widow. Stoner's ways were dark and devious. Ma Kelly would have been astonished to know that Wirt Stoner was behind the various offers from certain strangers to purchase her homestead. She would have rested less easily under her red-tiled roof had she been aware that the saloon man secretly coveted the flowing springs of water in her yard.

The several springs rising in Ma Kelly's back garden were the main source of the town's water supply. They gushed unceasingly from unknown depths, crystal clear and ice cold. The flow formed a tree-lined stream known as Kelly's Creek that meandered through the town finally to sink again beneath the burning sands.

Wirt Stoner, and Jake Kurtz, had sunk deep wells, from which old-fashioned wooden windmills pumped water sufficient for their needs into huge wooden tanks that stood on twenty-foot towers behind their respective places of business. Those few residents who could afford the cost piped their water from these tanks; but for the most part Coldwater supplied its needs free of charge from Kelly's Creek. Stoner's tank was painted a rusty red; Jake's water-tower, like the front of his prosperous General Merchandise Emporium across the street from the Desert Bar, was a bright green, kept fresh by a semi-annual coat of paint. The rotund storekeeper took enormous pride in the business he had started from a peddler's wagon.

Sunset fires flared above the rim of the low-lying Bullion mountains—made billowing golden gossamer veils of the dust flung up by the hammering hoofs of Smoke Tree horses. With shrill yips and a salvo of guns the outfit, headed by Gil Hawken on his roan, roared up the street and drew rein in front of Wirt Stoner's saloon and dance-hall. Jubilant and noisy, the cowboys swung from saddles. It was Saturday—a month's pay in their pockets called for action. Stoner's black eyes glittered as he sat in his private room, listening to the clatter of spurred boots, the swelling chorus of voices demanding immediate liquid refreshment. Other cow outfits would be storming in with gold to spend. Roulette and faro, the wiles of his dance-hall sirens, would transfer much of that gold to his own pockets before the long night was done.

Voices came to him through the small window open to the cooling evening breeze. The saloon man glowered. Ma Kelly, and the Dutchman across the street, were having their usual Saturday night gabfest. Saturday nights always brought an influx of ranchers and cowboys and prospectors with money to spend, which meant late hours for Jake and kept him from occupying his usual place at Ma Kelly's dining-table. As the storekeeper was her star boarder, Ma Kelly made a point of taking him his favorite dish of corned beef and cabbage, and a pot of steaming coffee.

The friendship between Ma Kelly and the genial proprietor of Coldwater's General Merchandise Emporium was a source of growing annoyance to Wirt Stoner. He suspected Jake Kurtz of ulterior motives in cultivating the goodwill of the owner of the springs coveted by himself. The corpulent moon-faced storekeeper was shrewd—a hardheaded, farsighted man—a dangerous competitor for the Adobe Jim property.

Wirt Stoner's expression was suddenly thoughtful as he continued to watch the couple across the street. Ma Kelly was not uncomely—in fact was decidedly attractive—still sprightly and vivacious, with warm Irish eyes and raven hair only lightly touched with gray. The speculative look in the saloon man's eyes grew more pronounced. Why not follow the example of the wily Jake Kurtz? What he had failed to gain by direct action he might win with the wooing words of a lover. Stoner smiled, complacently twirled the waxed points of his black mustache. The fat Dutchman would soon be out in the cold once Wirt Stoner's hat was in the ring.

Wide-brimmed black Stetson adjusted at a rakish angle on glossy black head, he sauntered through his private door into the street, on conquest bent.

A sturdy, red-headed young cowboy was talking to Ma and Jake. Stoner recognized him as a member of the recently arrived Smoke Tree outfit. A harum-scarum youngster, Sandy Wallace, and one of the reasons why Ma Kelly had small use for the owner of the Desert Bar. The reckless, freckle-faced Sandy was overfond of the place and its doubtful pleasures. Of all her "boys," Sandy Wallace was her favorite and his association with the Smoke Tree's hard-faced and hardened riders grieved the widow. She feared a repetition of what had happened before—a promising lad gone wrong.

"You come home with me, Sandy-boy," Stoner overheard her say; "'Tis as nice a dish of corned beef and cabbage I've ever made you'll have for dinner."

"Why, Ma, I sort of aimed to play 'round with the fellers for a spell . . . promised Willie Sims an' Slim Kendall of the Lazy Y I'd meet 'em over at Stoner's place." Sandy grinned "Shore will crave me one of yore soft-sleepin' beds come mornin' I reckon."

"I know a young feller likes to have his bit of fun," admitted Ma. "I ain't one to preach, Sandy—only 'tis a poor place for the likes of you—what with the liquor an' gamblin'—and them painted hussies—"

"Aw, Ma," grumbled the youth, reddening, "I ain't no booze hound nor nothin'—"

"You've got a month's pay burnin' holes in your pocket," Ma Kelly pointed out severely. "It will be gone before mornin', Sandy, unless you leave some of it with me. Them cardsharps of Wirt Stoner's 'll strip you clean."

"Won't git into a game with 'em," grinned Sandy. "Was aimin' to play some draw with Slim an' Willie Sims—

just friendly like we always has when we git together."
The young cowboy's face hardened. "Reckon my horns
is growed plenty, Ma. I can take care of myself!"

"You shouldt be zenzible undt do like Ma advise,"
put in Jake Kurtz solemnly. "Safe your goot money."

"Mind yore own business, Dutchy!" retorted the
youth. He swung away, strode across the dusty street
and vanished behind the red swing-doors, unobserving
in his boyish anger of the elegant person of Wirt Stoner
lounging indolently near the entrance. The latter's trim
mustache twitched in a faint smile of derision—and
secret satisfaction. So the young fool thought he had
grown his horns—could take care of himself! But the
boy was coming along, apparently had cut loose from
Ma Kelly's apron-strings. Which last thought was the
source of Wirt Stoner's satisfaction. He had certain
plans for Sandy's future. The young cowboy possessed
qualities that would make him useful. Wirt had many
irons in the fire. There was always work for a man who
could obey orders.

Hiding her disappointment, Ma Kelly gave Jake
Kurtz a warm parting smile and came tripping across
the street, a basket on one arm, free hand holding up
her sweeping skirts from the dust and displaying a
pair of trim ankles that Jake paused to admire slyly
as he turned to enter his store. With a twitch at his
black bowtie, Wirt moved down the board sidewalk,
planning to intercept his quarry. Ma Kelly apparently
had no eyes for him. She came blithely on, pausing
in the middle of the street to let a covey of whooping
cowboys dash past. For a moment she was lost in lifting
clouds of dust. The incident was an opportunity made
for him, Stoner decided. He darted toward the dust-
enveloped widow, hat in hand, and gallantly seized
her arm.

"Those boys need a good bawling out," he apologized; "no manners at all—throwing dust on a lady like you, Mrs. Kelly—"

Ma Kelly weakly fanned at the choking yellow cloud, then recognizing her would-be rescuer she brushed his hand aside. "I'd rather have their dust—than the touch of your hand, *Mister* Stoner!" was her retort. She flounced indignantly on her way, chin in air.

Stoner's gaze followed, angrily. The woman had publicly rebuffed him, left him standing like a fool in the middle of the street. Without looking he knew that the cowboys were grinning at his discomfiture. For a moment he was tempted to abandon his plan to captivate the owner of the coveted springs. But Stoner was not easily turned from his purpose. Choking down wrath—and dust—he hastened to overtake the widow. Ma Kelly came to an astonished standstill as he paused by her side, black Stetson in hand. His smile was ingratiating.

"You are not very friendly, Mrs. Kelly," he reproached.

"It's smart of you to guess the truth so quick," responded the widow brusquely.

"I want to talk to you—"

"I'm not so clever as you," she retorted. "I can't guess what about, Stoner. I'm in a hurry to be lookin' after things at the inn," she added frigidly.

"It's about young Sandy Wallace," purred Stoner. "I think you're interested in the boy—"

"Indeed an' I am," averred Ma Kelly, sudden anxiety sharpening her voice. "What's wrong? Is it some trouble the lad's in, I'm askin' you?"

"I'd like him to stay away from the Desert Bar," Stoner told her. "He's young—easily influenced." The gambler shrugged elegant shoulders. "I run a decent place but you know—a—a dance-hall is not a Sunday school, Mrs. Kelly—"

She sniffed scornfully. "Sink of iniquity, you mean!" she exclaimed. "Haven't I begged the lad again and again to keep away from your nasty place! Why don't you shut the door in his face, I'm askin' you?"

"I'll have a talk with him tonight," promised Stoner. "That's what I wanted you to know, Mrs. Kelly. You see," his smile hinted of sadness, a longing in his heart, "you see, dear Mrs. Kelly—I—I want to be your friend."

Disbelief was rampant in the shrewd look Ma Kelly gave him. "Stoner," she said with a shake of her head, "did you ever hear the story of the wolf that put on sheep's clothing?" Scorn chilled her warm Irish eyes. "I'm thinkin' you're up to some devil's mischief, Stoner. And you can put *that* in your pipe and smoke it—you old wolf." She flounced away.

Stoner stared after her angrily, chagrined by the widow's canny insight. With a stifled oath he strode back to his place of business.

VIII
Sandy Wallace Meets a Lady

A lone rider was advancing up the street, the rose-tipped black wall of the Bullions at his back, a gorgeous setting that made startlingly vivid the proud beauty of the silvery-maned golden stallion—the statuesque grace of the tall man in the silver-mounted saddle. Wirt Stoner loosed an admiring exclamation. Like many of his type, he was something of a sybarite—a lover of barbaric splendor. He lifted a hand in friendly salutation.

"Hello, Lee!" he greeted, "climb down from that high-stepping bronc and have a drink on the house. Gil Hawken and a bunch of the boys are inside."

Lee threw him a curt nod. "Sorry, Wirt. Busy, tonight—" The Palomino paced on down the street—came to a halt in front of Ma Kelly's white picket gate.

Stoner watched uneasily. What business could Lee Cary have with the Widow Kelly? He was suspicious of any man who had business with the owner of those bubbling springs. He pushed thoughtfully through the red swing-doors.

The long bar was already crowded with noisy, thirsty patrons. Stoner's roving gaze fastened on Gil Hawken, chatting with a dark-haired girl. She was strikingly handsome, obviously a high-caste Mexican—or Spanish. She wore a deep wine-colored dress covered with jet beads that shimmered with every movement of her sinuous body, and a Spanish comb, set with brilliants, sparkled in shining black hair piled high on her shapely head. The abbreviated skirt revealed red silk stockings and high-heeled red slippers. Stoner's eyes narrowed as he watched the couple, otherwise his expressionless face offered no clue to his thoughts. He proceeded slowly down the length of the bar, paused behind the Smoke Tree foreman.

"Want to talk to you, Gil," he said softly, and disappeared into his office.

Hawken flashed a startled glance at the closing door, drained his glass and grinned down at his companion. "What's up, Juanita?" he wanted to know. "Wirt shore looks awful solemn."

The dark beauty lifted an ivory shoulder. "*Quien sabe?*" she laughed. "The mind of Senor Stone is deep—like the sea beyond the mountains. Who knows what is in the mind of that man?"

Hawken eyed her suspiciously. "There's times when I think yuh could tell me plenty," he grumbled. "You keep them pretty lips shut awful tight, Juanita, when it comes to answerin' questions. I was thinkin' me an' you was good friends—"

"Fooleesh!" The girl laughed softly, tapped his swarthy cheek with her fan. She grew serious, added in Spanish, "But go quickly! He likes not to be kept waiting!"

The Smoke Tree man glowered. "Only one *hombre* I take orders from," he muttered. "You know who he is, Juanita—"

"*Si!*" her voice lowered. "*El Capitan!* Si—he is a man to be obeyed—that one. His anger destroys those who do not obey." Again her fan lightly tapped Hawken's dark face. "And so does the anger of Wirt Stoner destroy—"

"I'd shore like to know what's in yore mind," muttered the Smoke Tree foreman uneasily. He frowned down at the cool smiling eyes, turned abruptly toward the office door.

The girl watched him go, a satirical light in her dark eyes. "Ox!" she murmured, "a stupid ox—that one—and dangerous." Her gaze idled round the long room, encountered the eager eyes of a red-headed youth sitting alone at one of the small tables. Juanita's full lips parted in a smile; the little fan clicked open, and, waving it languidly she undulated to an adjoining table.

Sandy Wallace could scarcely believe his luck; a second look told him that there was more than invitation in those dark eyes smiling at him over the little fan. He read a command, subtle, graciously given, but none the less imperious. Puzzled, but willingly enough, he moved over to the girl's table.

"You look a nize boy," she greeted him with a cool little nod. "Too nize for thees malo place, no?"

The young cowboy flushed. "Ain't gettin' yore meanin'," miss," he told her bluntly. "I can take care of myself."

The dark eyes studied him intently under lowered lashes, fan waving gently. Sandy's discomfort grew. Girls had played small part in his young life; they made him feel shy, awkward; and this languorous beauty was a type strange to him. He began desperately to wish that he had refused the invitation of those luring, commanding eyes. With an effort he nonchalantly produced cigarette papers and tobacco. The girl's hand went inside her low-cut bodice, drew out a flat enameled silver case.

"Try one of these," she smiled; "they come from Mexico." Her low, liquid voice had a pleasant foreign intonation.

"Don't care if I do," muttered the embarrassed cowboy. He took one gingerly; a match appeared in the long white fingers, sputtered into flame and she leaned toward him across the little table. Sandy was aware of a strange baffling perfume. He tingled from head to foot.

"Permit," she murmured and touched the light to his cigarette; with the same match she lit one for herself *"Habla usted Espanol?"* she wanted to know.

"Shore I do," Sandy told her. "Most all the boys speak some Spanish. Kind of handy when we git south of the border lookin' for strays." He puffed with relish on the cigarette that had come from Mexico City. "Shore good!" he admired.

She smiled faintly, blew a wisp of smoke from red lips, continued to study him with absorbing eyes. Sandy dared an appreciative look. "How about a drink, Senorita?" he ventured, with a nonchalance he was far from feeling.

The girl shook her head. "Nize girls no dreenk in place like thees," she said. She leaned toward him and again the heady fragrance of her sent a pleasant tingle down Sandy's spine. "What ees your name, nize boy?"

He told her, and added with offended dignity, "Reckon yuh got me wrong, Senorita, callin' me a boy like yuh does. I'm mos' twenty!"

She laughed softly at that. "You no like that I call you nize boy?" A shadow passed over her expressive face. "But one is yong so leetle time—and old—so long!" Her eyes twinkled. "Ver' well, I will not do it again—beeg Americano mans!"

Sandy glowered a moment, not at all certain that he had won his point. He looked at her more boldly, was reassured by her admiring smile. She was only a girl—a dance-hall girl, at that, or why would she be in Wirt Stoner's place? If he were a man he'd make a play for her, talk about how pretty she was, make her think he'd known lots of girls in his time. Girls liked to be told pretty things, he'd heard the fellows say.

"Ain't given me *yore* name, yet," he reminded with a grin.

"You can call me Juanita, nize beeg Sandee." She looked at him provocatively over her little silver-and-jet fan.

"Are yuh Gil Hawken's girl?" he asked bluntly. "Seen him talkin' to yuh—"

The smile left the girl's face and she shook her head. "I am no man's girl," she replied in a low voice.

"Ain't seen yuh here before," went on the young cowboy. "Reckon yuh'll be right pop'lar with the boys. Yuh've got the other gals faded for keeps."

"*Gracias, Senor Vaquero,*" laughed Juanita, "but I no stay here ver' long time." She leaned toward him again. "You work for the Smoke Tree Rancho, no?"

"Top-hand rider an' bronc buster," he boasted.

The awe in her eyes exhilarated Sandy. He wished Willie Simms and Slim Kendall would make their promised appearance—see him conversing so intimately with the gorgeous Juanita. He could fairly envision their pop-eyed amazement, their envy! She was leaning toward him again, rounded elbows on the table, lovely chin cupped in the palms of her hands.

"Then you know the Senor Lee Cary—if you work for the Smoke Tree—" There was an odd, breathless note in her voice that made the cowboy vaguely wonder.

"Shore I know Lee," he admitted. Sandy paused recalling the affair at Los Posos. His honest, freckled face glowed. "*Shore* I know him," he repeated, almost reverently. "A he-man—that *hombre*!"

The girl seemed pleased. "Tell me more about the Senor Lee Cary," she begged. "He ver' 'andsome, no?"

Sandy Wallace deliberated. He was wont to judge a man by his deeds rather than by his looks. "Reckon a gal would say Lee's right smart lookin',", he finally decided. "Don't see much of him at the ranch," he confided. "Lee and the big boss—ol' Jim Cary—don't git along none too good—"

Juanita seemed disturbed; she drew down her brows, was lost in thought. The cowboy looked at her curiously. She had worked around to Lee Cary rather cleverly, he vaguely realized. The girl had deliberately cultivated him for the purpose of questioning him about Lee Cary. Sandy was inclined to be resentful.

"You knowed all the time that I work for the Smoke Tree," he accused her sulkily. "Usin' me for a pumphandle, I reckon."

She gave him a quick, disarming smile. "I like you, Sandee," she murmured. "You mus' not be cross with Juanita—"

The youth's momentary resentment subsided, and after a moment, he said, "I'm guessin' there's somethin' on yore mind, Juanita. Somethin' that's got yuh plenty worried—"

The girl nodded, her expression suddenly tense. "Sandee—you know the man they call *El Capitan*, no?" She watched him closely.

The youth gave her a startled look. What could be her interest in *El Capitan*—notorious border desperado and cattle rustler—the mystery man of the Smoke Tree country?

"Reckon most folks have heard of *El Capitan*," he answered. "Nobody knows who the *hombre* is, or where he hangs out, or if he's Mex or American. There's talk that if yuh join up with him yuh git a knife or a bullet in yore back if yuh don't obey orders." Sandy scowled. "A bad *hombre*—a devil—that *El Capitan*."

Juanita was silent, eyes downcast. Sandy watched her uneasily. Her questions perplexed him. Was there some connection between Lee Cary and the notorious *El Capitan*?

"What yuh drivin' at, Juanita?" he demanded. "What yuh talkin' about Lee Cary and this here *El Capitan* all in the same breath for?"

She looked up at him. "Sandee, I want you to do me a beeg favor." Her voice faltered. "*Please*, Sandee! It is ver' important—"

The pleading in the lustrous dark eyes was unmistakable—irresistible. The young Smoke Tree man gulped. At that moment he would have braved any peril for her sake.

"Ain't nothin' I wouldn't do for yuh, Juanita," he declared. "If there's some *hombre* been usin' yuh rough I'll fill him with plenty lead if yuh say so."

"Not that, Sandee," assured the girl, gently; and the kindly look she gave him made the youth suddenly feel very young—not at all like a tough, hard-riding cowboy out for a good time. "I like you, Sandee," she repeated, softly. "You are nize and so brave and true. My heart tells me I can trus' you." Her hand fumbled inside her bodice for an instant and drew out a small envelope. "I want you to geeve thees letter to the Senor Lee Cary—ver' queek as you can do." She slid the envelope across the table. "Promise, Sandee!"

The cowboy's big freckled hand closed over the letter, transferred it to a vest pocket. "I promise, Juanita," he assured her briefly.

"Thank you, Sandee," she whispered, and rising swiftly, she moved gracefully away, her smile flashing back at him.

The young cowboy watched her go, his face set in new stern lines. He felt very much a man at that moment. Had not a lady in distress appealed for his aid—entrusted him with a mission?

IX
Ma Kelly Talks

Lee turned the Palomino over to a short, wrinkled mozo and made his way to the kitchen in the rear wing of the inn. Savory smells greeted him as he pushed through the screen door.

"Hello, Ma!" Lee grinned at the widow who was investigating a big steaming kettle with a long-handled fork. "I'm in luck," he sniffed hungrily, "no corned beef and cabbage like yours!"

Mrs. Kelly turned a startled, flushed face. "Lee Cary!" Her voice rose excitedly and thrusting the fork at the Mexican woman by her side she swooped with a swish of crisply starched skirts toward the tall young man smiling at her. "If you ain't a sight for sore eyes!" Her plump arms went round Lee's neck and she gave him a hearty kiss. "Where have you been keeping yourself all these months?" She had known Lee since he was a small boy. "I was thinking of sending Cisco out to the ranch to ask if anything was wrong!"

"Well, Ma, been busy about something I'm keeping under my hat," he explained. "How are things with you, Ma?" Lee's eyes twinkled "You look younger and sweeter every time I see you," he declared. "If Jake Kurtz doesn't wake up he'll be sorry—too late."

"Young impudence!" The widow laughed, not displeased. "Jake is too busy with his store to have time for lovemaking." Mrs. Kelly's pleasant face sobered. "I've a heap of worry on my own mind," she added. "It's that glad I am to see you, Lee! I've questions to ask you."

Lee chuckled. "I'm here to ask *you* a few questions," he confessed.

"I'll answer them if I can, but not 'til you've had a bite of supper," Mrs. Kelly said firmly. "Inez," she called, "set out a plate for Mr. Cary; and don't you be sparin' with the corned beef and cabbage—"

"I'll eat out here in the kitchen, Ma—"

"You're welcome, lad. I'll join you in a bite my own self," the widow decided. "Inez, you can take my place in the dining room and see that the folks is satisfied. I've only five at the table, tonight," she told Lee. "One of them is a new man—such a nice feller he is. Jake eats at the store Saturday nights—and three of the boys that was stayin' with me have got jobs out of town."

"A good thing for you." Lee smiled. He was aware of Mrs. Kelly's generous ways with her "boys."

"Oh, the lads always pay me in good time," she said placidly. "It don't do a lad no harm to know he's welcome at Ma Kelly's whether he's money in his pocket or not. And what is it that's on your mind, Lee?"

"You've been here in Coldwater a long time," Lee said reflectively. "At least twenty years—"

"Twenty-two—last Spring," admitted the widow. "'Twas the year them murderin' redskins killed poor Terence, God rest him! He was freightin' supplies for the mines out of Bisbee when them Injuns got his scalp." Mrs. Kelly dabbed at her eyes with a corner of her apron. "We'd been married less than three months," she recalled.

Lee was distressed. "I'm sorry—"

"Oh, you needn't mind!" protested the widow quickly. "I'm all over it now, lad. 'Twas a long time ago." She looked at him curiously. "But why are you wantin' to know how long I've been in Coldwater?"

"I was wondering if you ever heard of, or knew a

man named William Page. He homesteaded some land out Los Posos way about twenty years ago."

"Bill Page!" Mrs. Kelly's eyes widened with interest. "Indeed and I knew Bill Page well. 'Twas Bill who put me onto this bit of land. He said the day would come when I'd make me a fortune out of the springs." The widow's smile was wry. "Bill Page was one grand optimist, I'm thinkin'—for all the fortune the springs have made me. Twenty-two of me best years wasted here in the desert—and me a young widow scarce twenty-two when I come."

"I wouldn't call them wasted years," Lee argued. "You have made a fine place out of the springs—"

"I've not the fortune—and I'm still a widow," she retorted.

"You're a widow because you'd never say 'yes' to a man," laughed the young man. "Why, there's not an eligible man in the Smoke Tree country who hasn't thrown himself at you. You were the prettiest widow in ten counties—and still are," he added gallantly.

"There hasn't been one of them worth trading my independence for," declared Mrs. Kelly with a toss of her head. "Thanking you for the kind words all the same, Mr. Cary." She chuckled. "You've the blarney tongue of me own Terence," she accused. "Terence was a rare one to say the sweet things to a woman, God rest him." Her momentary gloom fell from her and she beamed contentedly round the roomy, comfortable kitchen. "They've been happy years and I love the old place—even if the fortune didn't come."

"Listen," Lee said earnestly, "you have a fortune in the springs—and don't you ever let them get away from you!"

She regarded him thoughtfully, a hand fingering the little faded green cross at her throat. "It's what Bill

Page said to me the day he drove me here to look at the place," she said soberly. "I mind the day well; it was when I found the padre's cross fastened to the old palo verde. I took it for a sign that Bill Page was speakin' the truth."

"He told you the *gospel* truth," Lee declared. "Don't you let any man talk you into selling Adobe Springs."

"It's the very same business that's on me mind," confessed the widow with a worried frown. She shrugged plump shoulders. "But it can wait, Lee. What is it you're wanting to know about Bill Page? Poor fellow—he's been gone these many years."

"I want to know when you last saw him—anything you can tell me about him—"

Mrs. Kelly reflected. "He was in mortal fear the last time he came to see me," she recalled. "He told me his life had been threatened."

"What else did he tell you?" Lee's face was pale. The widow hesitated.

"Well," she said reluctantly, "you know how your grandpa always hated 'nesters'—"

"William Page was no nester," interrupted Lee. "He homesteaded land rightfully open to entry—bought up a few abandoned quarter sections that gave him control of Los Posos."

Mrs. Kelly seemed doubtful. "He was running his cattle on Smoke Tree range," she pointed out.

"Most of that country is free range—open to any cowman," Lee argued.

"Your grandpa didn't think the way you do," Mrs. Kelly said grimly. "To his way of thinking there was no free range—only Smoke Tree range."

Lee stared at her unhappily. "You—you think that Page was—killed?"

"All I know is that I've never seen him again from

that day to this—nor heard of him," she told him sadly.

"You—you think my grandfather was responsible for his disappearance?"

"I wouldn't think Jim Cary would knowingly have a hand in a killing of that sort," the widow said quickly. "Jim Cary would order his men to run squatters off—burn 'em out, maybe—but I wouldn't say he'd be party to a cold-blooded killin'."

Lee was silent, his face troubled.

"It is sure queer for you to be askin' after the man after all these years," ruminated Mrs. Kelly. "What are you after, Lee? Los Posos is all Smoke Tree land again—like it was before Bill Page went and built his log house at the wells." She sighed. "A pretty home he was makin' out there. It was in my mind that he was maybe plannin' to marry a wife."

"Meaning yourself, ma'am?" Lee eyed her quizzically.

"Well"—the comely widow colored—"Bill Page was a fine, upstanding man for all he was near twice my age," she said with a noncommittal smile. She went on: "Don't you be frettin' too much about what happened to him, Lee. While it was true he had some trouble with some of the cowmen, there were others Bill Page had reason to fear more than he did your grandpa."

"You're sure of that?" Lee's tone was relieved.

Mrs. Kelly nodded. "Now I think of it—there was a fellow awfully set on owning those wells. Like as not 'twas him that made away with poor Bill—and then let Jim Cary take the blame." Her eyes narrowed thoughtfully. "This fellow I'm speakin' of had a way of insinuatin' things about your grandpa—would talk of how mean Jim Cary was to folks that moved in on the range."

Lee pondered. "Why didn't this man you speak of move in on Los Posos—after Page disappeared?" he mused.

"Scared of Jim Cary, most likely." Mrs. Kelly's expression was thoughtful again. "Lee! I'm thinkin' we've stumbled on the answer. Wirt Stoner—he was a young fellow then, but awfully sharp—was crazy to get hold of Los Posos. I'll bet 'twas him that did away with Bill Page!"

Lee's look was incredulous. "That's a serious accusation," his tone was grave. "It's dangerous to accuse a man of a crime—unless you have proof."

"I wouldn't put it past Stoner." The widow's mouth tightened.

"You mean the Wirt Stoner who lives in this town?"

"The same Wirt Stoner," affirmed the widow. "He's lived here ever since, and done well, what with his fox brain and unscrupulous ways."

Lee was dubious. "The fact that Stoner has never attempted to possess Los Posos does not prove he killed Page—"

"He lost his nerve," Mrs. Kelly declared, reluctant to abandon her theory. "I'll bet your grandpa suspected the truth—warned Wirt Stoner to keep off Los Posos, or hang for murder. Old Jim Cary has his own way of doing things. Maybe he kind of thought Bill's heirs would show up some day and figured to hold the land for 'em. You can never tell what's in Jim Cary's mind!"

Jim Cary's grandson regarded her with thoughtful eyes. "Ma," he said slowly, "I believe you have answered my question one hundred percent."

"It's an answer to questions I've been askin' me own self," she replied. "But you haven't told me yet why you're wanting to know about Bill Page."

"You suggested that his heirs might show up some day," reminded Lee. He grinned at her sudden excitement. "Well—your prophecy was good. The heirs of William Page have arrived at Rancho Los Posos."

"Land sakes!" marveled the widow. "After all these long years!" Her brown eyes were very bright. "It sounds too good to be true," she added doubtfully. "Maybe it's a trick of Wirt Stoner's. Some sly scheme to get his claws on the place." Mrs. Kelly's misgivings grew apace. "It would be easy enough to fake up some heirs," she worried. "How do you know these folks are the true and lawful heirs of Bill Page?"

"There's not the least doubt!" Lee's tone was positive. "I'm convinced they are the heirs."

"You seem some interested in 'em," observed Mrs. Kelly with a shrewd smile. "One of these heirs is a girl—I'm thinkin'."

"Her name is Nan," Lee informed her. He reddened. "A nice girl! You'll like her. She's as plucky as she is—is good-looking. I want you to be her friend."

He gave the hugely interested widow a brief account of Nan and Ted and of Gil Hawken's attempt to eject them from the ranch.

"How come you was on the spot so handy?" inquired his intrigued listener curiously. "You must have known what Hawken was up to, I'm thinkin'."

Lee related a carefully expurgated version of his first encounter with Nan in the desert. He was reluctant to divulge the details of that night under the sheltering old mesquite tree.

"From what she told me about the mysterious warnings posted to the corral fence I suspected trouble was in the wind," he explained.

"And you suspicioned 'twas the Smoke Tree back of the dirty business," surmised Mrs. Kelly. She shook her head. "I wouldn't have thought old Jim Cary would act that mean to a pair of young innocents like them Page children!"

"He claimed to know nothing of the affair. Said he left such matters to Gil Hawken."

"That Gil Hawken man!" Mrs. Kelly tossed her head scornfully. "I've no use at all for the likes of him!" She gave Lee a shrewd look. "Hawken and Wirt Stoner are as thick as thieves. Wouldn't surprise me at all if Stoner is back of the nasty business."

"Gil Hawken works for the Smoke Tree," Lee mildly reminded.

Mrs. Kelly sniffed. "Gil Hawken is no good," she said. "Workin' for the Smoke Tree wouldn't stop him from schemin' dirty tricks with Stoner." Her tone grew curious. "What did your grandpa say when you told him 'twas the Page children Hawken was all set to chase away from Los Posos?"

"He doesn't know their name."

The widow's eyes widened. "You mean to say you never told him their name was Page!" She shook her head. "Of all the dumb things, Lee Cary! If your grandpa had known the name was Page he'd have acted mighty different."

"How was I to know that who they were would mean anything to him?" grumbled the young man. He grinned guiltily. "Anyway I was so darned mad that afternoon I didn't stop to go into details about them," he confessed.

"Well," mourned Mrs. Kelly, "it's a pity you didn't tell him."

"I'll tell him, you bet," promised Lee. "Don't you worry, Ma—"

"Running a cattle ranch is a man's job," Mrs. Kelly went on. "Your grandpa should pay the Page children what he thinks Los Posos is worth to him. It's no place for a young innocent lass like this Nan Page."

Lee thought a bit ruefully of the check for ten thousand dollars he had flung back at old Jim Cary. But hard on the heels of his half regret came the conviction that Nan would never have accepted the check. She wanted Los Posos—not money. He tried to explain his views of the situation to the widow.

"When you meet Miss Page you will see she's no ordinary girl," he declared.

"Hark to the lad talk," scoffed Mrs. Kelly. She chuckled. "The young woman has got you hypnotized, I'm thinkin'."

"Now don't get romantic, Ma." Lee grinned.

"I hope I'll never be too old to enjoy a bit of romance," was Mrs. Kelly's fervent wish. "But I'll not be plaguin' you, lad." Her face sobered. "Just the same, the girl would be a heap better off with good money in her pocket than with a run-down old ranch that is mostly desert. It's no life for a young lass, and with all these border rustlers on the rampage these times she'll lose her cows quick as she can raise 'em. Even an old-timer like Jim Cary is kept on his toes fightin' off cow thieves."

Lee's face was noncommittal. Border cattlemen were resigned to occasional depredations, philosophically accepted sporadic rustling along with the dry years and low prices as all part of the game. Although he took no active part in the affairs of the big ranch Lee was aware that the past few months had seen a marked revival of the ancient pastime of cow stealing. In answer to old Jim Cary's sarcastic comment that he was beginning to believe that Smoke Tree cows were becoming too modern to raise calves any more, Gil Hawken would sulkily complain of the growing boldness of Mexican raiders from below the adjacent border. It was Lee's own private belief that the steady drain was the work of a cleverly organized gang captained by a shrewd, crafty brain. The raids were too skillfully planned to be charged against any ordinary desperado.

Mrs. Kelly was harping on Wirt Stoner again. "I wouldn't put it past the man to be mixed up in Hawken's dirty work with the Page children," she proclaimed emphatically.

"Why do you suspect Stoner?" Lee pushed his chair back from the table and fumbled in a pocket for cigarette papers.

"Stoner will not let any heirs walk off with that ranch—not if he can stop 'em," the widow said flatly. She shook her head. "No sir! Not after him waiting all these years for Jim Cary to—to die—"

Young Cary's eyes narrowed. "What has my grandfather got to do with it?" His tone was blunt.

"Don't tell me you're *that* dumb!" fretted Mrs. Kelly. "Wasn't I just tellin' you that Stoner knows your grandpa suspects he killed poor Bill Page and has warned him to keep away from Los Posos—or dance on air from a Smoke Tree rope?"

"All your suppose-so," argued Lee. "We really don't know that Stoner killed Bill Page—"

"You ask your grandpa!" flared the widow. Her cheeks were pink. "I'll bet he'll tell you I've hit the mark fair and square!"

"I'll do that," Lee promised. "I'll pin him down to the question." He grinned. "Some detective!"

"Your nonsense!" laughed the widow.

"You've been reading Sherlock Holmes," Lee insisted. His eyes twinkled.

"Such nonsense!" Mrs. Kelly dimpled. "It's nothing but plain, every-day common sense—and knowing a few facts. Wirt Stoner is set on owning Los Posos because of them flowing wells. He's crazy about water. I've heard the man talk. He has a notion that water-rights in this country are gold mines." She gestured disdainfully. "The man is loony!"

"Perhaps I'm loony, too," muttered the young man opposite her.

Mrs. Kelly ignored the interruption. "Wirt Stoner is *daffy* about water! I've heard him rant!" She chuckled. "Only when he was kind of lit up—toward sundown. Almost every evening he's a way of dropping in on Jake and making an offer for Jake's store. Jake always gives him the laugh."

"Wants to buy Jake's place?" Lee's tone was thoughtful.

"I'm not finished talkin' about Stoner, yet," Mrs. Kelly told him. "Maybe it'll take some thinkin' before you get a notion of what's in my own mind. I'm tellin' you that Wirt Stoner is daffy about water—springs—creeks—flowing wells—anything that spells *w-a-t-e-r*—"

"Perhaps"—Lee's tone was noncommittal—"perhaps he is not so daffy as you seem to think—"

Mrs. Kelly eyed him shrewdly. "I've heard that your own head is filled with queer notions about making the desert bloom like a new Garden of Eden," she accused.

"We're talking about Stoner," Lee reminded. "I gather from your talk that Stoner wants Los Posos and is plotting with Hawken to run the Page children off the ranch. Is that your argument?"

"While Jim Cary lives, the man we're talking about is afraid to make a move," Mrs. Kelly averred. "Stoner is after Los Posos ranch, Lee. The minute your grandpa dies, Wirt Stoner plans to make himself owner of Los

Posos. He's not going to sit twiddlin' his thumbs and let any heirs step over the threshold of that log house Bill Page built. Not if he can scare them out of the notion."

"Sounds plausible," admitted Lee. He reached for a match, touched the spurt of flame to cigarette. "Don't talk wildly," he warned. "Talk means less than nothing—only trouble—without proof to back up—words—"

"I've no proof," Mrs. Kelly shook her head—"no proof to back up a word I've told you, Lee. It's only my feelin's," she confessed. "There're reasons why I don't like that smooth-tongued saloon-keeper." The widow's lips set tight. "No matter what you think of my reasons, I'm tellin' you it's a mercy that Jim Cary hasn't been murdered before this day," she told Jim Cary's grandson. "You listen to me, lad, warn your grandpa to be on the watch for a sneakin' killer. Stoner'll not wait forever for Jim Cary to die!"

Lee's face was white—and hard. He did not choose to tell Mrs. Kelly that more than one mysterious attempt had been made to end the reign of the old Master of Smoke Tree Range. Two gunshots from ambush . . . and Jim Cary was still lame from an injury caused by a loose saddle-cinch. The leather girth had been deliberately sliced! Lee's examination of the girth had convinced him that his grandfather's nearly fatal spill was not the rider's fault. Jim Cary had put the attack down to the growing boldness of border rustlers. Lee was not so sure that his grandfather was right. Mrs. Kelly's keen analysis of the suave proprietor of the Desert Bar Saloon uncovered another and startling angle to the mysterious affair.

The widow was eyeing him sharply. "You're thinkin' I'm a false alarm," she sighed.

"Tell me some more about Stoner," he urged. "You've

given me something to think about. I've an idea that Stoner has had spies on my trail. Nabbed a man the other day watching me through a telescope. He got away—but left the telescope behind him in his hurry."

"I'll bet you hurried him with a bullet or two," guessed Mrs. Kelly.

Lee grinned. "Has Stoner been bothering you?" he wanted to know.

"It's what I was wanting to talk to you about," Mrs. Kelly confided. "I've been that puzzled about things and it's only when you started asking me about Bill Page that the answer came to me." She nodded. "It's all as clear as daylight. Some time back Wirt came to me and asked if I'd sell him the Adobe Inn—offered me a house in Bisbee for the place. I turned him down cold and since then there's been half a dozen strangers droppin' in and making me offers."

"All of them from Mr. Stoner, eh?" Lee grinned

"I was that dumb I never guessed they was acting for him," confessed Mrs. Kelly. "Not 'til we got to talkin' about Bill Page. It come to me all of a sudden. Stoner wants my Adobe Springs the way he wants Los Posos."

"You control every drop of water in this town," Lee pointed out.

"There're the two wells Stoner and Kurtz sunk," she reminded.

"Water means life—here in the desert," Lee went on. "Your springs flow enough water to irrigate many hundreds of acres. Some day there'll be a real town here. You'll be a rich woman."

"Maybe you're right, Lee." Her mouth tightened. "Don't you worry about me sellin' the springs—not after all these years!"

Lee was suddenly anxious. "If what you think of

Wirt Stoner is true—you are sitting on dynamite," he worried.

"Stoner wouldn't dare harm me," she scoffed. "I've too many good friends in this country. My boys, bless their reckless kind hearts, would have a rope round the spalpeen's neck in no time at all."

Lee looked dubious as he recalled the scene at Los Posos. Nan's peril had been real enough that afternoon, he pointed out to the widow.

"She was new here," Mrs. Kelly told him "The lass was without friends—savin' for the chance that made her acquainted with you. It's different with me. Stoner wouldn't dare lay a finger on me. Like I said, there'd be a hundred hard-ridin', fightin' young fellers like wolves on his trail."

"Not including Jake Kurtz," Lee added with a sly grin. He snubbed out his cigarette and got to his feet. "Well, ma'am, if I eat any more corned beef and cabbage I'll not be able to fork my saddle for a week—"

"You're not leavin' so soon," she protested. "There's a nice room for you, lad. What's your hurry?"

"I'll be back later," he promised. "Thought I'd ramble up the street and look in at the Desert Bar." Lee's smile was a trifle grim "Had it in my mind to tell Wirt Stoner that I'm one of your best friends."

"It's a bad time to go foolin' round that nasty place," she demurred uneasily. "A Saturday night—and all the scum of the border carousin' there and no place at all for a decent young man like yourself."

"It's business that takes me," Lee answered briefly.

Mrs. Kelly sighed. "Oh, well, if you must!" She brightened up. "You can do me a favor, then," she went on. "If you see young Sandy Wallace I wish you'd try and bring him back with you for the night. He's a good lad—for all the bad company he keeps."

"You don't think much of the Smoke Tree outfit," grinned Jim Cary's grandson.

"Most of 'em are Gil Hawken's hand-picked ruffians," sniffed the widow. "If you was mindin' your grandpa's business for him you'd know more of what goes on at the ranch."

Lee's smile was enigmatic. "You think I'm a loafer, ma'am?"

"Indeed I don't!" she denied, flushing. "You're a bit of a mystery to most of us, and there's been some talk about what you're up to. 'Tis even said you're huntin' for a lost gold mine—or buried Indian treasure." Mrs. Kelly shrugged her shoulders. "I tell 'em it's none of our business."

"Lady," Lee's smile was mysterious, "if I succeed in what I'm trying to put over, it will be tremendously your business—the business of every decent man and woman in Coldwater."

"Lee!" she gasped. "If you ain't the provokin' young feller! I'll not close me eyes this night long for wonderin' what it's all about!"

Lee chuckled. "I'll tell you something else. I'm in Coldwater for *two* reasons. One was to ask what you knew of Bill Page and to tell you about the arrival of his heirs. The second reason is that I'm here to meet a man coming in on the morning stage. He'll stay with you while he's in town. Treat him well, lady. He's got a lot to do with making a success of my plans."

"I'll treat him like a prince," promised the Adobe Inn's proprietor. "And what might the gentleman's name be?" she inquired curiously. "If it ain't another deep secret."

"Dawson," Lee told her. "His business with me is secret—but not his name."

Mrs. Kelly gaped at him. "You don't tell me!" she

finally sputtered. "Why 'tis the name of the nice feller I spoke of a while back. He's in the dining room this minute—if he ain't finished and gone to his room—" She laughed. "He came in on the morning stage all right—only 'twas yesterday morning. A big, tall gentleman with an accent that could come from no place but the old country!" Mrs. Kelly wiped her eyes with a corner of her apron. "I thought he was some sort of bug-huntin' professor," she confessed.

"Dawson is one of the most distinguished men of his profession," Lee assured her. He hesitated, looked longingly in the direction of the dining room, on fire with eagerness to meet the man upon whose expert opinion so much depended. Mrs. Kelly's recently voiced suspicions had made him uneasy. If it were true that Wirt Stoner was responsible for the mysterious disappearance of Bill Page, it was also apparent that Nan Page and her young brother were in grave peril. In fact his own grandfather was in peril—and the widow Kelly. Lee felt that Mrs. Kelly's shrewd reasoning had startlingly uncovered a sinister trail that he must relentlessly follow.

He reached for his wide-brimmed hat and turned to the screen door. "Well, lady—I'm heading up the street for a look-see." He grinned at her. "*Hasta la vista!*"

"Keep an eye open for young Sandy Wallace," she reminded. "Bring the lad home if you can."

"May have to knock him on the head to do that," chuckled Lee as the door swung behind him.

X
A Saturday Night in Coldwater

The lights broke through the darkness suddenly, as the spring-wagon crawled over the summit; they were like stars, Nan thought, winking from the black rim of the world. She saw Baldy Bates' dolorous face peering round at her.

"Coldwater," he announced, briefly.

They jolted down the slope, the high wheels of the spring-wagon grinding with a hissing sound through coarse sand and rattling noisily over the stony, washboard stretches. It was scarcely a road—little more than an old-time cattle trail at best. Nan marveled that Baldy could follow its twisting course through the moonless night.

It was their first trip to Coldwater, over an unknown and now dark road. The drive in from the ranch had seemed interminable. A broken tongue had delayed them for an hour while Baldy fashioned a makeshift affair from a sapling alder his search discovered in a nearby dry-wash. They should have made Coldwater by sundown instead of having nearly ten miles to go when overtaken by nightfall. The makeshift wagon-tongue, the pitch darkness, had kept them from moving scarcely faster than a walk. Nan was thinking they would be forced to make camp under the stars. Those softly glimmering lights were pleasant reassurance.

Teddy, on the front seat with Baldy, was suddenly wide-awake. "Gee, Nan!" he jubilated, "if the store's open when we get to Coldwater can I buy my Winchester twenty-two pistol tonight?" He wriggled excitedly.

"I thought you were asleep, Ted," smiled his sister from the backseat.

"I wasn't really asleep," protested the boy. "I was only sort of taking forty winks to pass the time away."

Baldy Bates chuckled. "Yuh'd have fell off the seat if I hadn't hung onto yuh tight. Yuh was plumb fast asleep, mister. Reckon yuh was dreamin' 'bout that twenty-two," he added dryly.

"I was, sort of," confessed Ted. "Dreamed I was popping coyotes and jackrabbits with my twenty-two." He shook his head dubiously. "Need a rifle for coyotes and jacks. I want a Winchester—or maybe a Flobert—"

"We'll see what the man carries at the store, Ted," promised the girl. She was feeling very kindly toward her young brother. Teddy had carried himself like a real man that exciting afternoon of the raid.

He looked back at her with shining eyes. "I want a Winchester," he declared; "a repeater—" The boy's spirits soared; he began to observe hitherto unnoticed beauties of the desert night.

"Gee, Nan!" he exclaimed. "The stars look close enough to touch! I reckon there's a trillion billion stars up there! What's the name of that one, Nan?"

"Jupiter," informed his sister; "and over there, low against the horizon is Orion's Belt. The stars are beautiful, tonight, Ted," she added. "The thin desert air makes them seem so close."

"That thar feller that don't show up so bright is the Pole Star," interposed Baldy. He pointed his whip. "Yuh should Pam the Pole Star, Teddy. Ev'ry cowboy's got to know whar to locate the Pole Star—then he can figger which way is North an' won't git lost."

The road improved as they neared the town; the horses broke into a gentle jog, while Nan and Ted continued their absorbed study of the glittering canopy spread so gorgeously above them. Ted learned about the Big Bear and the Little Bear and how to locate the North Star, and a lot of things he had not known about stars; and in a few minutes, or so it seemed to them, the spring-wagon was rattling up Coldwater's wide, dusty street, past dimly lighted windows, past the decrepit Coldwater Palace Hotel, to the brightly lighted green front of the Coldwater General Merchandise Emporium.

Ted hopped down, all eagerness to be inside the store. Nan looked at Baldy.

"You'll come back?" she queried. "I'll want you to see about that barbed wire for the new pasture."

The old man nodded. "Be back soon's I've located a feed stable for the broncs," he promised. He gazed with ill-concealed longing at the red swing-doors of the Desert Bar Saloon across the street. "Mebbe I'll drap in yonder for a spell," he added tentatively. "Mebbe I can line up a good cowhand—like we planned."

Nan hid a smile. "Well, Baldy," she commented dryly, "you're certainly old enough, and wise enough, to know what you're doing." She climbed out and smilingly took the bag Baldy reached down to her.

"No call to worry, ma'am, about me," he assured her. "A mossyhorn like me savvys how to take care of hisself most any place." Baldy's gaze had wandered across the street again. "Seems like all the cow outfits in fifty miles is in town tonight by the looks of them broncs—" He broke off and continued to stare fixedly at a group of horses drooping at the tie-rail in front of the saloon.

"I suppose the dreadful hotel we passed will be

crowded," worried the girl. "I have my doubts about that hotel, Baldy. It shrieks of bedbugs."

"Yes, ma'am." Baldy's tone was gruff. "Seems like we picked a wrong time to come to this cow-town," he muttered.

Nan sensed by his tone that something had disturbed the old man. "What makes you say that?" Her own gaze roved to the drooping cow ponies at the tie-rail opposite. "*Baldy!*" Her voice was panicky. "Isn't that strawberry-roan the same horse Gil Hawken was riding—that day—"

"Shore is, ma'am," muttered Baldy. He shook his grizzled head pessimistically. "Addin' up the figgers we git Gil Hawken and his onery Smoke Tree outfit come to town."

"Oh, Baldy!" Nan looked at him with dismayed eyes. "What *shall* we do?"

Baldy seemed surprised. "Why, ma'am, reckon we'll do what we come to town to do."

"I don't like it," she fretted. "There'll be trouble if we run into those men. You keep out of that saloon," she added sharply.

"Never was one to hide in the bushes," rejoined the old man tartly. "Best way to meet trouble is to put on yore own war paint."

"You'll keep out of that place," declared Nan firmly. "What chance would you have against all those terrible Smoke Tree men?" Her tone was suddenly pleading. "Please, Baldy, I know you're not afraid. You must think of us. What would Ted and I do if you get killed?"

"Mebbe yuh're talkin' smart sense," admitted the veteran cowman, mollified now that his courage was not questioned. "Mebbe it ain't jest the right time for a showdown with them coyotes—with you and the boy in town." He stared down the street for a moment. "I'll put up the team at the O.K. stables—yonder." He kicked the brake loose and rattled away in a cloud of dust.

For a moment the girl was tempted to call him back, announce their immediate departure from the town. The thought of an encounter with Gil Hawken appalled her. The Smoke Tree foreman was not the sort to forget the stinging defeat of his plans that afternoon at Los Posos, she reflected dismally. Gil Hawken would seize any opportunity for revenge. Nan shivered. Stanch old Baldy Bates would not protect her, could not fight the Smoke Tree outfit single-handed.

With an effort she fought down her growing panic. She was of a race that did not run when danger threatened. The thought stiffened her courage.

She found Teddy already earnestly discussing guns with the storekeeper. Jake Kurtz greeted her affably. "The young man says he buys from me a rifle, yah?" His eyes twinkled "A Winchester twenty-two, he says, and a twenty-two six-shooter—"

Nan laughed. "We want to buy a lot of things," she informed him, and deciding on the spot that she was going to like the beaming-faced storekeeper. She glanced at her young brother who was gazing with fascinated eyes at the small rifle in Jake's hand. "Is that a good gun, Ted?"

"Gee, Nan! It's a *real* Winchester!" Teddy's face glowed. "Mr. Kurtz says they don't make 'em better!"

Jake nodded. "A goot gun," he affirmed with the gravity he sensed the occasion demanded. "You buy it, yah?"

They purchased the little Winchester, and a twenty-two six-shooter and a huge quantity of cartridges.

"He'll need lots of target practice," Nan explained to Jake. "I don't suppose a box will last him a week and we won't have time to be running into town every other day for fresh supplies of ammunition." She smiled faintly. "Los Posos is too far away."

The rotund storekeeper widened surprised blue eyes at her. "Los Posos? Himmel! Los Posos is Smoke Tree range!"

"So some people seem to believe," rejoined the girl with a little shrug of her shoulders. "The truth is, Mr. Kurtz, Rancho Los Posos belongs to my brother and me."

"You don't tell me!" gasped the amazed storekeeper. "Always I think it belong to old Jim Cary of the Smoke Tree! So you buy from Jim Cary, yah?"

"We did not!" Nan's smile was cool. "We inherited Los Posos from my grandfather's younger brother, William Page." She eyed the astonished storekeeper thoughtfully. Perhaps the man had known her uncle, she reflected. She asked him.

Jake shook his head. He had never even heard of William Page.

"It's a long time ago, since he was last heard of from Los Posos," Nan confided. "Twenty years or so—"

Jake shook his head again. "I have not been here so many years," he explained. "Only ten years ago I come to Coldwater—joost a peddler with a wagon." Jake's honest face glowed with the pride of achievement. "From a peddler's wagon I build up this so fine store," he told his new customers. "Yah, I am sole owner of the Coldwater General Merchandise Emporium."

Nan's gaze roved approvingly over the well-filled shelves. "It's a splendid store!" she praised. "I see that I can get everything we need from you—"

"Not in San Diego, or Los Angeles—or any place—

can you buy more cheap as from me," Jake assured her earnestly.

"I hope you are right," Nan laughed. "Money is none too plentiful with us," she confided. "We have to count the pennies."

Jake Kurtz furrowed thoughtful brows at her. "I tell you somet'ing," he suddenly suggested, "to goot customers like you the Emporium sell on credit." The portly storekeeper nodded vigorously. "Yah, when a customer so nice like you buy from me—the credit is goot."

Nan shook her head. "I pay cash, Mr. Kurtz. Thank you all the same for your kindness." She gave Jake a warm smile. "You're nice!"

"To give credit is sometimes goot business," he argued.

Nan was firm. "Cash," she repeated. "That's our slogan. Isn't it, Ted?"

"We can save money now I've got my Winchester, Nan," declared the boy. "I can shoot rabbits every day for dinner—and doves and wild geese and ducks. Baldy says there'll be plenty wild geese and ducks in the Winter!" Teddy's eyes sparkled. "I'll bet there's plenty deer back in the hills, too. Baldy says he's seen tracks—"

"Daniel Boone, aren't you?" Nan's affectionate smile froze; she stared with suddenly dilated eyes at the two men framed in the doorway. The smaller, more elegant man, she had never seen before; but there was no mistaking the tall, dark-faced Gil Hawken.

The Smoke Tree man met the girl's look with an impudent smile. "Look who's here!" His tone was ironic. "If it ain't the purty little squatter gal come to town. Wirt, meet Miss Page of Los Posos. She's the gal I was tellin' yuh about. Figgers to run cattle on

Los Posos." The foreman leered. "Shore is ambitious-homin' in on Smoke Tree range, huh, Wirt?"

Stoner removed his immaculate Stetson with a flourish. "Welcome to Coldwater, Miss Page," he greeted suavely. "We are honored." His glittering black eyes absorbed her from head to foot.

Nan hesitated; she desperately longed to announce that she had no desire to make the acquaintance of any friend of Gil Hawken. With an effort she crushed the impulse. The situation was perilous, required careful handling if she would avoid an immediate and perhaps fatal clash with Hawken; and the presence of his smooth-tongued friend might prove the bridge to safety for the moment. She sensed power—and authority—in the man.

Her smile was friendly. "It's our first visit to Coldwater," she said pleasantly. "My brother and I had some shopping to do."

"Nan's bought me a *real* Winchester!" announced Ted, "and a twenty-two six-shooter." He flashed a defiant look at Gil Hawken.

"You must let me show you a few tricks with them, some day," Stoner smilingly suggested. "I'm supposed to be right smart with a six-gun."

"Can you shoot from the hip?" Teddy wanted to know. "I want to learn how to shoot from the hip—like Baldy Bates. He's a *dead shot*—most good as old Buffalo Bill."

"Baldy must be a shooting *hombre* if he's as good as Buffalo Bill," admired Stoner. He looked at Nan. "So you're going to run cattle on Los Posos?"

"That is our intention," admitted the girl. She was fervently hoping that Hawken and his friend would leave before Baldy Bates arrived. The thought of a surprise encounter between implacable old Baldy and the Smoke Tree foreman chilled her to the marrow. Guns would smoke!

"You're a nervy young lady," Stoner told her bluntly. "You'll have some job, bucking old Jim Cary. That old Smoke Tree wolf is rough on squatters."

"I prefer not to discuss the matter." Nan's voice was icy.

Stoner's lips lifted in a fleeting smile that showed a gleam of perfect white teeth under his black mustache. "My advice—friendship—might be helpful," he suggested. "It is possible I can force Jim Cary to recognize your claim to Los Posos, providing you can furnish necessary proof. In the meantime let me know if there is anything I can do—any little service."

Nan suddenly felt that she thoroughly distrusted the man. He was too smooth; and when he smiled there was no accompanying friendly light in his cold, unwinking eyes. They made her think of a snake. Jake Kurtz, too, she guessed, had no liking for Stoner and his companion. The storekeeper's manner was anything but cordial.

"You're most kind," she forced herself to murmur. "I'm sure there is nothing." She pretended to look at her list. "I think Mr. Kurtz can manage to supply all our needs this trip."

"The town is full, tonight," Stoner went on. "The hotel will be jammed." He regarded her thoughtfully. "Have you secured your rooms yet?"

Nan shook her head. She was frankly nervous. Baldy Bates was due any moment. She desperately wanted to see Hawken out of the store before Baldy's return. The list blurred before her anxious eyes.

Stoner seemed worried that she had neglected to arrange for hotel accommodations. "Not a chance that Meeker will have a room left by now." He frowned.

"Tell you what I'll do, Miss Page—I'll send over and have Meeker save two of his best rooms for you and your brother. Meeker is a good friend of mine. He'll be glad to do me a favor—even if it means throwing a few cowpunchers into the street." Stoner's cold-eyed smile glittered briefly at the storekeeper. "Jake knows that people in this town usually jump at the chance to do me a favor, eh, Jake?"

"Yah," grunted Kurtz sourly. "Meeker—he do anything you say." His face reddened; he eyed the saloon man impatiently. "What you want, anyway, Wirt. All this talk when I am so busy! I want to close the store joost so quick as Miss Page buys her supplies from me."

The outburst seemed to amuse Stoner. "You'll make Miss Page believe you don't like me, Jake," he reproached.

Hawken broke in. "Was aimin' to git some ranch supplies from yuh, Jake," he explained. "Guess thar's no sense waiting 'til you git finished with Miss Page. Can drop in Monday." He threw the girl a mirthless grin and turned to the street.

Stoner staged a more formal exit. "Been a pleasure to meet the owners of Rancho Los Posos," he assured them. "I shall look forward to a visit some day. And about those rooms, Miss Page, I'll attend to the matter at once. Meeker will take good care of you." With a parting nod he followed Hawken out to the sidewalk.

Nan was unable to repress a little sigh of relief. "I'm afraid I don't like that man," she frankly confessed. "I really don't know why! It was nice of him to see about the hotel." She looked at Jake shrewdly. "What is wrong with him, Mr. Kurtz? I can see that you don't feel very friendly toward him."

"It is somet'ing that I cannot yet explain," Jake said with some reluctance. He shook his head. "Some day we will know what is wrong with him. He is powerful in this town and can make trouble if he don't like you. Yah—it is not goot to talk about him. He has spies." Jake shook his head ominously. "People who get in Wirt Stoner's way do not live long. Always there is an accident. Yah, there is much mystery about him."

"You didn't seem afraid of him," reminded the girl.

"Always I sleep with one eye open, maybe," chuckled Jake. "I have not'ing Wirt Stoner wants. Maybe some day I have what he wants—then goot-by, Jake Kurtz."

"I think that is terrible!" exclaimed Nan. "Is there no law in this town?"

"Wirt Stoner is the law," grunted the storekeeper. "You want it I grind the coffee, Miss Page? Or maybe you haf a coffee-grinder—"

Nan said that she had a coffee-grinder. "I'll take one of those hams, as well as the side of bacon," she added with a little laugh. "I'm not sure that we'll want rabbit for breakfast *every* morning, even if Ted does become a mighty hunter."

"Yah," chuckled Jake. "Coffee undt ham undt flap-jacks a goot breakfast make."

Nan nodded pleasantly, if a bit absently. She was thinking of the memorable night under the sheltering old mesquite tree, when a tall, brown-faced young stranger had served her with broiled young rabbit and fragrant coffee and flapjacks. She had not seen Lee Cary again, since the afternoon of the raid. There was a mystery about him, too, she reflected. He had asked her not to divulge the secret of the mesquite tree.

Nan found herself wishing she could see Lee Cary again. He was in her thoughts constantly. Lee had saved her from peril twice. She would have died in the desert the night of the sandstorm but for him; and he had come again to her rescue the following afternoon. She never would forget the picture of him storming up the canyon on his fleet golden horse— that terrible fight with Gil Hawken.

"Nan!" Teddy's voice interrupted her reflections. "Do you think Mr. Kurtz will give me this Winchester almanac? See, it's got a picture of Daniel Boone with his long rifle!"

"You bet I gif it you the almanac," called Jake from behind his counter. "To a goot customer like you that buys from me a Winchester rifle undt a six-shooter, I gif him always a almanac."

"Gee!" Ted eyed his treasure gleefully. "You're awful nice, Mr. Kurtz! Next time we come to Coldwater I'll bring you a couple of jackrabbits for your dinner— maybe."

"A couple of rabbits will be good," beamed the gratified storekeeper. "Ma Kelly—she will a fine rabbit pie make for me." Jake's expression was suddenly thoughtful. "Himmel! So dumb I am!" he muttered. "You will not go to that hotel, Miss Page," he announced firmly. "You undt Teddy will go to Ma Kelly's place."

"Who is Ma Kelly?" queried the girl, smiling at him. "She sounds nice and homey—"

Jake nodded vigorously. "Ma Kelly—she is goot woman," he declared enthusiastically. "Her place is clean with beds so soft—undt her food—ach! Her food it is fit for a queen. I am a boarder with her," he added.

"Sounds nice and homey," repeated Nan. She shook her head dubiously. "I'm afraid we must go to the hotel this time, Mr. Kurtz, now that Mr. Stoner is going to so much trouble to arrange for our rooms."

"That hotel! It is not a goot place for a girl like you," grumbled Jake. "You must not go there. Ed Meeker— he is only Stoner's hired man. I do not trust him."

"You mean Stoner is the real owner of the Palace Hotel?" Nan was surprised.

"Yah. Wirt Stoner is the real owner," admitted Jake with a cautious glance at the street door. "Tonight the hotel will be filled with men who get drunk at his saloon." He gestured at the brilliantly lighted Desert Bar across the way.

"Oh, so he is a saloon-keeper, too!" Nan stared doubtfully across the street. The prospect of the crowded, noisy hotel was not enticing.

Jake eyed her anxiously. "You will to Ma Kelly's nice place go, yah? I will mein self take you joost so quick I close the store."

"It would not be fair to Mr. Stoner," argued the girl. "I'd hate to seem rude," she hesitated—"and after what you have hinted about him, I'd rather not offend him. It might make trouble for you."

"You come with me to Ma Kelly's place," insisted the storekeeper. "I am not afraid of Stoner!"

"No," decided Nan firmly. "Thank you a lot, Mr. Kurtz, but I really think it is best for us to go to the hotel. It isn't worthwhile offending Mr. Stoner." She smiled brightly. "Ted and I won't be entirely alone. Baldy Bates will share Ted's room, I suppose." Nan laughed. "If you want to know who Baldy Bates is, you can ask Ted."

"Baldy carries two big forty-four guns," Teddy informed the storekeeper, "and he carries a Bowie knife in his boot and I reckon he's killed more Indians and rustlers and buffaloes than any *hombre* out of the Panhandle. It's true—'cause he told me himself."

The prowess of the redoubtable Baldy Bates failed

to arouse Jake's enthusiasm. "I do not like it you go there," he muttered disappointedly. In gloomy silence he selected a ham.

"Nonsense, Mr. Kurtz!" scoffed the girl. "What harm can possibly come to Ted and me in that hotel?"

Nan's amused laugh belied her own secret misgivings.

XI
"Out of the Mouths of Babes—"

Dust drifted in the street, flung from the churning hoofs of hard-ridden horses. The riders were Lazy Y men, Lee's casual glance informed him. One of them, a long-legged youth with unruly straw-colored hair and a snub nose, threw him a friendly grin as he reined in front of the saloon. Lee recognized him for a former Smoke Tree man.

"Hi there!" greeted the cowboy, "seen my ol' buddy 'round, Lee?" He swung from his saddle and fished tobacco and cigarette papers from the pocket of a gaudy pink shirt. "Should have hit town two hours back," he grumbled; "reckon that red-headed galoot's done lost his month's pay by now—and me aimin' to trim him like he done me last month."

"Sandy is somewhere round, I heard," Lee said. "How are things with you, Slim?"

"Fine as silk," blithely assured Slim Kendall. He beckoned to one of the riders, a stocky, bow-legged dark youth. "Hi, feller! Sandy's in town. We'll shore trim the maverick plenty if he ain't broke already."

Slim grinned at Lee. "You remember Willie Sims, don't yuh? Gil Hawken fired him from the Smoke Tree same time he fired me."

Lee nodded pleasantly at Willie. He had liked him and the voluble Slim and their dismissal from the Smoke Tree had been something of a mystery to him.

"Why did Hawken fire you?" he questioned them. "What got Hawken down on you boys?"

The youthful punchers exchanged quick looks. "Reckon Gil kind of didn't like us," was the long-legged Slim's somewhat vague explanation.

"Told us we wasn't salty enough," muttered the chunky Willie Sims. He spat disgustedly.

Lee suppressed a smile. From his own very thorough knowledge of cowboys he judged that Willie Sims and Slim Kendall were extremely salty specimens of the breed. Each wore formidable six-guns in low-slung holsters, and the resolute courage stamped on the hard young faces was unmistakable. They were natural-born fighting men, the Simon-pure product of a rigorous calling.

"Sounds like Gil Hawken was hard up for an excuse," he sympathized.

"Willie an' me figger he couldn't trust us," blurted Slim.

Lee was puzzled. "You mean he thought you loafed on the job?" he wanted to know.

"Naw! Gil figgered we was too nosey about the rustlin' been going on," sneered Willie. "Didn't like it none when Slim got to jokin' about *El Capitan* one day. Slim wanted to bet him that *El Capitan* wasn't no Mexican—"

"To hell with Gil, anyway!" interrupted Slim Kendall sulkily. He was obviously nervous. "Let's mosey into Wirt's place and locate Sandy before his cash is gone." He gave his friend a warning look.

Willie evidently got the message; he seized eagerly on the subject of Sandy Wallace. "The cards that onery redhead held last time we played!" he moaned. "Seems like every time I was holdin' kings he'd slap down a fistful of aces—the lucky stiff!"

With friendly grins and invitation for Lee to join them at the bar, the twain clattered across the boardwalk and vanished behind the red swing-doors. Lee's gaze followed them regretfully. He knew that the next night would find them homeward bound, pockets empty, a trifle bleary-eyed and headachy, their brief holiday over and another stretch of long days and nights of arduous work to be done before payday replenished purses with the means to repeat the performance. The occasional visit to town was the cowboy's one relief from the monotony of life on the range. There was no other outlet for pent-up exuberance and with few exceptions most of them chose to celebrate well if not wisely, as long as the money held out. Slim and Willie were typical of the breed. Restless and reckless, there was no vice in them. They worked hard and played hard—were staunchly loyal to the man who paid their wages, and despised traitors and four-flushers and enthusiastically hated those who violated their iron code of chivalry toward a good woman.

Lee recalled his halfhearted promise to drag Sandy Wallace back to Ma Kelly's motherly care for the night. The prospect irked him. He supposed he would have to do the same for Willie and Slim. They were special protégés of Mrs. Kelly's, too. The thought of playing nursemaid to a trio of lusty, rebellious young cowpunchers was not agreeable. The performance would call for shrewd diplomacy.

The frown deepened on Lee's brow as he mulled over his brief talk with the two Lazy Y men. They had been decidedly evasive in explaining why Gil Hawken had discharged them from the Smoke Tree payroll. Something to do with rustling, and the elusive, mysterious *El Capitan*. Willie Sims was on the verge of divulging some interesting angles when interrupted by the more nimble-minded Slim. It was plain that the tall, blond cowboy was reluctant to disclose the true reason for their dismissal from the Cary ranch. Fear of Hawken's vengeance, perhaps, or a natural disinclination to talk too freely in the presence of Jim Cary's grandson. A man who talked too much usually got himself into trouble.

Two men came out of the store across the street. For a moment the flickering light of the big kerosene lamp was full on their faces. Lee was conscious of suddenly taut muscles. The taller man was Gil Hawken, whom he had not seen since the afternoon of the fight. His companion was Wirt Stoner, he saw.

They came ploughing through the dust, Stoner talking in a low voice to his big companion who seemed in a sullen mood from the ugly look on his face. They pushed through the swing-doors without observing Lee standing back in the shadows. His glance went across the street, to the store; he could see Jake Kurtz wrapping groceries—caught a vague glimpse of a girl's profile. He was startled for an instant; there was something familiar about that head. He could have sworn it was Nan Page. He stared again. The silhouette vanished. Lee hesitated, half of a mind to cross over to the store. Instead of surrendering to the impulse he turned to the saloon. It was absurd to think that Nan Page would choose a late Saturday night to do her shopping in a tough cow-town like Coldwater. She was too intelligent for such foolhardiness.

A sudden ominous hush brought him to an abrupt standstill inside the swing doors. It was the usual Saturday night assembly—pleasure-bent cowboys for the most part, with a sprinkling of miners and Mexicans and border riffraff, cold-eyed professional gamblers and scantily-clad entertainers.

A low, bitter voice cut like a steel blade through the silence. The speaker was Sandy Wallace, crouched slightly away from the bar; hands hovered over holstered guns.

"I'm repeatin' it, Gil Hawken, yuh're as low down as they make 'em! A skunk is shore a gent 'longside of yore kind!"

"Yuh're plumb full of redeye," jibed the Smoke Tree foreman. "Yuh ain't responsible for yore talk." He leaned sideways against the bar, a half-emptied glass in his right hand. With a contemptuous grin he drained the glass and started to lower it to the wet near-mahogany.

"Keep yore hand like yuh've got it—holding that glass," warned Sandy. "Yuh're listenin' while I talk." His chill blue eyes bored the older man menacingly. "Yuh ain't firin' me, mister. I'm quitting the Smoke Tree here and now. I ain't takin' orders no more from a *hombre* that treats a gal like yuh done the other day over at Los Posos. If I knowed what yuh was up to I shore wouldn't have rode with yuh on that party."

Hawken was plainly at a disadvantage with his gun hand still grasping the whisky glass; nor did he dare drop the cigarette from his free hand and reach for his other gun. His eyes sent out furtive signals. Slowly, as though pushed by an invisible hand, the surrounding bystanders pressed back from the danger zone. Slim Kendall's gun leaped from holster and covered the barman who was slyly reaching for his concealed six-shooter. With a muttered oath Joey's hand reappeared, lay passive with its mate on the wet bar. Wirt Stoner's pale face peered from his office door—jerked from view as another gun leaped into the steady hand of Willie Sims. The two former Smoke Tree men were backing up their buddy's play in deadly earnest.

The redheaded Sandy grinned mirthlessly at the visibly frightened foreman. "Ought to plug you," he declared.

"You're loco," Hawken told him hoarsely. "You'll have a rope round yore neck before I'm cold—if yuh pull trigger—" Again he sent out a covert signal.

"Go for yore gun, then, you yeller hound!" The young cowboy sneered. "I'll give you a break, feller!" Sandy's laugh was contemptuous. "I'll bet there's a rope dangling for you—when folks learn some things about you."

"Damn you!" frothed the foreman. "What you aim to insinuate?"

"You know the answer better 'n I do," sneered Sandy. "Well—are yuh goin' for yore gun? Or are yuh ready to say yuh're sorry you was rude to a lady the other day?" The cowboy's voice was ominously polite. "I'll take yore message to her myself," he promised.

Lee was edging slowly in from the doorway. The reckless redhead was too confident, he realized uneasily. The barroom was full of Smoke Tree men—handpicked by Hawken for their readiness to pull trigger on any and all occasions—cold-eyed gunmen who would seize the first opening to make an end quickly of the matter, including Sandy and his two loyal friends. He dared not speak with the voice of authority as the grandson of the outfit's boss for fear of throwing the boy off his guard. An instant's inattention would find a half score guns emptying lead at the trio.

As Lee moved cautiously toward a point between Sandy and a group of men he had been alertly observing, the swing-doors pushed open behind him. He flashed a backward glance, glimpsed the tall, stoop-shouldered figure of Baldy Bates framed in the entrance, saw the veteran ex-trail driver's ancient forty-fours leap into big, gnarled hands. Instantly his attention went to the group of Smoke Tree men sitting at a table behind Sandy Wallace. Three of them were on their feet, jerking at their guns. One he did not know, but the squat, bow-legged man with the swarthy face he recognized as Slinger Cole. Close by the latter's side crouched Fargo, his left arm in a sling, the result of Baldy's bullets the afternoon of the fracas at Los Posos. A knife flashed in the hand of a fourth man, a slit-eyed half-breed.

Almost as fast as the pictures registered, Lee's own two guns were blazing and from behind sounded the heavy roar of Baldy's six-shooters. The long barroom rocked with thunderous explosions; a terrified girl screamed, went limp in the arms of her cowboy partner; the air was suddenly reeking with acrid gun smoke. And as suddenly there was a silence as terrifying as the momentary uproar. Men stood tense, fearing to let even the sound of their breathing start a blast of lead in their direction; a girl began to sob hysterically, pushed frantically from the crowded little dance-floor.

"My Gawd! I want out of here! I'll never come back to this hellhole—so help me!"

The smoke cleared. Lee found Baldy by his side.

"Saw them *hombres* all set to throw lead at yuh!" gasped the old man. "I shore got that Fargo coyote proper—this time!"

Lee somberly eyed the limp bodies sprawled by the card-table. The Smoke Tree outfit had lost three of its men—for the knife-throwing half-breed was among the dead. Slinger Cole was slumped in a chair, cursing softly and nursing a numbed wrist. The shambles made Lee feel a bit sick. He knew that his own bullet had shot Slinger's gun from his hand. Whose deadly aim had downed the half-breed and the unknown puncher, he was not sure, but suspected Willie Sims. The chunky young cowboy's guns were both smoking.

Lee's stern gaze fastened on the ashen-faced Hawken. "Your fault, Gil," he accused grimly. "I saw you signal Slinger and the bunch back there. You planned for that Mexican breed to knife Sandy in the back. It's a pity Sandy didn't fill you with lead while guns were smoking."

"I couldn't pull trigger!" almost sobbed the red-headed cowboy. "The yeller skunk wouldn't go for his gun!" He sheathed his own weapons dejectedly. "Guess I ain't a shore-enough killer," he bemoaned.

"It was a mistake," muttered Hawken, haggard eyes on the three limp bodies. "The boys figgered the young fool aimed to git me cold. They'd a right to start their guns smokin'."

"Fargo and Slinger were trying to get Baldy Bates and me," contradicted Lee. "No mistake about *that*, Gil."

"Hell!" exclaimed the foreman in a startled tone. "What would they want to kill *you* for, Lee?"

"I had to use Slinger rough the other day," explained Lee. "He thought the mix-up gave him a chance to pay off the score."

The foreman was his blustering self again. He scowled at the wounded gunman. "That true, feller?" he demanded. "Was yuh aimin' to git Lee—like he claims?"

Slinger Cole snarled a profane denial. "Kind of lost my haid when that long-legged ol' buzzard come bustin' in from the street," he said sullenly.

Baldy Bates bristled. "Referrin' to me, mister?" His tone was acid and his glance flickered at the still forms lying on the floor. "Fargo figgered the way Slinger done about you," he told Lee. "The coyote aimed to git even with me for that bullet I put through his arm the other day."

Wirt Stoner came in hurriedly from the office,

followed by an elderly shaggy-bearded man who stood in the doorway and blinked red-rimmed eyes at the scene. He wore a low, flat-brimmed, greasy hat, and soiled red shirt, belted by an equally soiled blue overalls tucked into high boots. An unkempt and unlovely specimen of the desert rat prospector, Lee's sharp appraising glance decided, and perhaps the one man in that sordid room who was not visibly armed. He stared with lazy curiosity for a moment, puffing at a short blackened corncob that protruded from untidy whiskers. Then like a man who wishes to avoid trouble he abruptly swung back into the office and closed the door. Lee vaguely speculated. Was it Wirt Stoner's quick, warning frown that had caused the unprepossessing stranger's hasty retreat, or was it the sudden appearance from the street of a weazened little man with a sheriff's star pinned to his open vest?

There was a weary sag to the sheriff's thin shoulders. He was hot and tired and dusty from a long, grueling ride.

"What's goin' on here?" His tone was resigned. "Seems like every time I come to Coldwater there's gun-play—"

Not waiting for an answer he went quickly to the prostrate bodies. "Looks like a slaughter house," he grumbled after a brief scrutiny. He eyed round at the tense faces.

"Talk up, somebody," he urged. "What's the trouble? Who started the shootin'?"

Lee knew Sheriff Day for an honest, fearless officer— and long a stanch friend of his grandfather.

"Plenty of witnesses here who can testify that it's self-defense, Sheriff," he said quietly.

Sheriff Day nodded thoughtfully. "They were bad

eggs," he stated, with another brief look at the slain men. He stared pointedly at Gil Hawken. "Those *hombres* should never have been on the Smoke Tree payroll. They're killers—with records a mile long."

The foreman reddened.

"Ain't got the time to look up the records of ev'ry jasper I hire," he said in a surly voice. "The Smoke Tree ain't a Sunday school, nohow."

The sheriff snorted, gave his mind to more immediate matters.

"All right, Lee," he said, "I'm listenin'. You tell me what you know about this killin'."

Lee explained briefly, touching lightly on the quarrel between Sandy Wallace and Hawken, much to their relief. It was plain that his testimony was not displeasing to Wirt Stoner. There was a furtive gleam of satisfaction in the latter's black eyes as he attentively listened.

The little sheriff pondered for a minute. "Sounds like they had it coming to them," he finally decided. "Nothing for me to do about the matter." He looked at Stoner. "Have the bodies removed, Wirt. I'll send the coroner down from Palo Verde in the morning." He turned to the street door, dusty shoulders sagging wearily. "Want to see you a moment," he muttered as he pushed past Lee.

"I'm about done up," he confided as Lee joined him on the sidewalk. "Been on another wild-goose chase after that infernal *El Capitan*. Was tipped off his gang of renegades had been seen in Wild Horse Canyon." The sheriff's voice was despondent. "Been on a lone trail for twenty-four hours and got nothing for my trouble. I'm growin' too old for a sheriff's job, Lee."

"I wouldn't say that, Sheriff," protested Lee.

Sandy and his two Lazy Y friends had followed Lee

from the barroom, evidently deciding they had had their fill of the saloon for one Saturday night. Slim and Willie exchanged looks, and the blond cowboy said softly:

"Mebbe this here *El Capitan* jasper wouldn't be so hard to find if yuh was to look closer to home."

"Huh!" The Sheriff eyed Slim intently for a moment. "What you mean by them words? Givin' me some free advice?"

The cowboy grinned. "Jest a idee," he said. "You savvy how it is, Sheriff. Sometimes yuh go lookin' for a stray all over the range an' then find the critter feedin' in the home pasture."

Sheriff Day nodded his gray head thoughtfully. "I get you, boy." He laughed softly. "Out of the mouths of babes and sucklings—" He turned to a raw-boned buckskin gelding and climbed stiffly into the saddle. "Well, so-long, boys—and save your lead for *El Capitan*."

They watched in silence as the grizzled officer rode at a jog down the street. Lee eyed his young companions. "Ma Kelly will be pleased to see you," he told them pointedly.

"You called the turn," chorused Slim and Willie; then in a surprised voice, Slim said, "Doggone! Where's that onery redhead gone to now?"

"I'll get him," Lee said sharply as the two punchers swung with one accord to the saloon door. "You boys beat it to the Inn."

Grumbling a bit, the twain went on their way. Lee turned to the swing doors. Baldy Bates was missing, too. He wanted to see Baldy. The latter met him at the entrance, a contented expression on his long face and telltale foam on his drooping mustaches. Lee scowled at him.

"Thought an old-timer like you would have more sense than let Miss Page come to this town on a late Saturday night," he complained.

"Break-down made us late," explained the old man placidly. "Would have been in town early if we hadn't busted the wagon-tongue. At that," he added, "Miss Nan's the boss of the ranch. Ain't for me to order her 'round."

Lee's gaze went across the street. The store was dark. Only the glaring kerosene lamp—and Jake underneath, reaching up to the chain of the snuffer.

"Knew where she's staying the night," he inquired.

"Said something about bunking down in that thar hotel," Baldy said. "That's whar she spoke of goin' when I left her yonder at the store, to go put up the team at the O.K. stables." He grinned sourly. "Was to meet her an' Teddy at the store—but was some dee-layed."

"The hotel is no place for her," grumbled Lee. He was staring across the street. The big kerosene lamp suddenly winked out. "Jake's heading over here," he added. "We'll find out from him where she went."

The storekeeper approached cautiously, pausing as he neared the rough board sidewalk.

"That you, Mr. Cary?" His voice was timorous.

"Yah—it is you. Thought it was you standing there under the lamp." He came up, breathing fast and obviously excited. "Himmel! Lee! What was all the shootings about?"

"All over," Lee replied laconically. "Sheriff's given the town a clean bill of health—and gone on his way." His voice lowered. "Where are Miss Page and the boy, Jake?"

The storekeeper gestured unhappily. "They go to the hotel," he informed them. "I do not like it they go there, Lee. I try make her go over to Ma Kelly's place—but no—she not listen to my advice—"

"Why?" Lee's tone was curt. "Why wouldn't she go to the Inn?"

"Wirt Stoner—he come over and tell her that he get nice rooms for her at the hotel," grumbled Jake. "Miss Page think she make him mad with me if she don't go." He gestured hopelessly. "So she go—undt I can say not'ing to stop her."

"I'll see what I can do, Jake. You run along and tell Mrs. Kelly she may have guests in a few minutes."

"Yah!" Jake's tone was relieved. "Goot idea you get her away from the Palace." He hurried away.

"Baldy!" Lee eyed the old man reflectively. "You hop over to the hotel. If it's not too late I want to see Miss Page. Tell her to wait up for me. I'll be there in a few minutes—just as soon as I locate Sandy Wallace."

Baldy faded silently into the darkness. He moved with the noiseless stride of a stalking Indian, Lee noticed. A valuable and canny man, he reflected. There was wisdom born from vast experience packed away under that battered sombrero, and the courage of a lion in the heart beneath the greasy buckskin vest he wore. Baldy Bates was one of the last of a fast disappearing clan—the fearless, fighting frontiersman of the old untamed West. Lee felt a wave of affection for the veteran ex-trail driver. Baldy's lightning reaction to the death-threat of those guns undoubtedly had saved Lee's life. Where a less experienced and courageous man would have hesitated, he was instantly in action. An example of coordination of mind and hand typical of the breed.

XII
Juanita

Lee rolled a cigarette and meditatively eyed the red swing-doors. Revelry had resumed its sway in the dance-hall. Music from the Mexican orchestra stole sweetly into the night, the plaintive, appealing strains of La Paloma. Those Mexicans were always good when it came to playing a guitar, Lee mused. There was something seductive and heart-pulling and gay about the tunes they played.

He lit the cigarette and after another cautious glance at the saloon entrance he sauntered slowly up the sidewalk in the direction of Ma Kelly's—became a vague shape in the darkness beyond the glow of the swinging kerosene lamp. He halted, stared back at the saloon. Apparently he was unobserved by spying eyes; he could hear the shuffle of dancing feet, the murmur of men's voices, the shrill laughter of girls, the lively lilt of a gay bolero from guitars and mandolins.

Lee's gaze fronted round to the black mouth of the narrow alley on his right; the cigarette in his fingers fell to the sidewalk, was ground lifeless under boot-heel. He spoke softly—scarcely a whisper.

"That you, Sandy?"

A shadowy form stirred in the blackness. "Shore is, Lee," came the guarded reply.

In a moment Lee was at the cowboy's side. "What's up?"

"Shore was thinking yuh missed the high-sign I sent yuh," muttered the young puncher.

"Saw you duck down this way—follow that girl in the red cloak. Who is she?"

"Search me," grunted Sandy. "Calls herself Juanita. Never saw her before tonight. Met her in Wirt's place. She give me a note for yuh. Come on, Lee, she's waiting in a coulee back of Kelly's Creek." He pulled at Lee's sleeve. "Come on, feller! This gal is a lady—"

"Not so fast," rebelled Lee. "A dump like Wirt Stoner's is a queer place for a lady. And where's the note?"

"She's some sort of dance-hall gal," grudgingly admitted the cowboy. "But I shore know a lady when I see one. This Juanita gal is decent—shore a pippin for looks." He fumbled in a vest pocket and drew out a crumpled piece of paper. "Smells like a lady, too," he said, sniffing. "The shindig drove it clean out of my haid—until she grabbed onto me when I followed you and the sheriff from the bar."

"Let's see it," Lee moved into the deeper blackness of the alley, the note in his hand. Sandy kept pace with him.

"She was beatin' it away from Wirt's when she spotted you go in," the cowboy further explained. "Said she figgered you was Lee Cary and hung round for a chance to git hold of yuh."

Lee halted and by the flare of a match in cupped fingers managed to read the few penciled lines.

"You do not know me, but because of what you did for Ramon Avilla one night in Ensenada I want to warn you of a great danger. The young *vaquero* will bring me your answer. If you would save your grandfather, please Senor Cary do not fail to come to me. I sign myself your unknown friend

                        Juanita"

The match flickered out and like a picture suddenly thrown on the black screen of the night Lee saw again the dingy interior of that Ensenada cantina—the slim, handsome young Mexican hidalgo backed against the adobe wall.

From different angles of the long, grimy room, four scowling-faced men crept toward the defiant-eyed youth. They wore high-peaked sombreros, and cartridge-laden belts crisscrossed their shoulders and girdled waists; long knives glittered in clenched brown fists.

Bandidos! Or so it seemed to the young Americano who suddenly pushed into the room. Behind the bar was a fat man in a greasy apron, watching helplessly with stark horror in his eyes. He shot an appealing look at the newcomer. The latter spoke harshly.

"*Que pasa!* What is this?"

At the sound of his voice the four assassins whirled with startled oaths—to find themselves covered by the Americano's guns. Again the latter spoke and the glittering steel blades clattered on the earthen floor. The young Mexican was on them like a tiger, jerking guns from belts and ordering them with curses to face the wall. He ran to the door, whistled shrilly, three times, after which he stepped back and smiled gaily at the stranger whose guns still covered the quartette huddled close to the rough adobe wall.

"Senor, may I ask the name of the brave *caballero* who this night has saved the life of Ramon Avilla?"

The youth's Spanish was pure, his diction that of a high-caste Mexican.

"Lee Cary." The stranger grinned. "How about tying up these cutthroats, Senor—"

Ramon Avilla gestured. "The affair is done—for

them," he bowed—"for me it is a deed that will live in my heart, Senor Cary—"

"Forget it!"

"My father, Don Sebastian Avilla of Rancho San Juan, and my sister, Senorita Juanita, will greatly desire the honor and privilege of thanking you, Senor." Ramon bowed again. "It is a debt an Avilla will never forget—"

The pounding of hoofs outside interrupted the youth's elaborate thanks and in another minute some half score *vaqueros* were crowding in through the door. A word and a gesture from Ramon, and the four crestfallen ruffians were being dragged out with violent hands—to what fate Lee never knew.

So the writer of the mysterious note was none other than the sister of Ramon Avilla! Conscious of an odd thrill of excitement he followed Sandy Wallace through the dense darkness of the tunnel-like alley.

Five minutes brought them to the deep gully beyond the little stream that flowed from Mrs. Kelly's springs. Sandy came to a standstill.

"There she is, Lee—waitin' like I said—over by that big rock."

Lee went on alone toward the slender figure poised motionless near the large boulder. To his surprise he saw that her scarlet cloak covered the ragged attire of a peon. Her face was turned eagerly to him. He paused, removed his hat.

"I am Lee Cary, Senorita—"

The girl beckoned him to approach. "It is good of you to come," she returned in Spanish. "My note will have told you who I am—"

"Yes, Senorita—that you are the sister of Ramon Avilla—"

"—whose life your courage saved," she broke in.

"It is because of our eternal gratitude—our debt to you—that I am here, so far from my family, with only faithful Fidel with me for protection." She gestured over her shoulder at a man standing by the side of two fast-looking horses. A Yaqui Indian, Lee recognized; a lance-straight grizzled old warrior. He was heavily armed, and the fierce eyes shadowed under high-peaked sombrero roved with unceasing vigilance.

"Yes—Fidel makes a good watch-dog. He would die for me." The girl's tone was affectionate. "He speaks no English, so we could not send him to you. I came because there was no messenger whom we felt you would believe. Our father is too aged for the rigors of such a journey—and Ramon lies on his bed, wounded"—her low voice trembled—"the work of *El Capitan's* cutthroats," she added fiercely.

"Who is *El Capitan*?" Lee watched her closely. "Is he known to you—your brother?"

"No, Senor! We know only that he is a devil. Some say he is one of your own countrymen." She gestured again. "His spies are everywhere, so you must believe the word I bring to you. It has not been an easy thing to do."

The soft starlight was full on her upturned face. She was beautiful, Lee realized, despite the ragged shirt and overalls of a peon. As if conscious of his appraisal she pulled off the tattered sombrero and revealed a wealth of short-cropped black hair.

"It is for disguise I am dressed like this," she confided with a tremor of a smile parting full red lips. "I had to cut my hair." She made another of her expressive gestures. "Tonight—Fidel and I shall be on our way back to Rancho San Juan. We shall ride by night—and hide while it is day—"

"You are very brave, Senorita, to do this thing."

Lee's tone was grave. "Your note implied that my grandfather's life is in danger, but even so he would be greatly upset to know you are taking this risk to warn him. My grandfather would not like it."

"The note did not tell you all, Senor," replied Juanita quietly. "Your own life is in hourly danger, which is the real reason why I came. You must be on your guard!"

Lee was startled. "You should not have incurred such risks," he worried.

"An Avilla could do no less. We owed you my brother's life, Senor." The tremulous smile hovered again on her lips. "Do not be angry—Senor Lee Cary—"

Impulsively he held out his hand. "I can only repeat that you are a brave girl, Senorita," he said, deeply moved. "Now just what is this danger threatening my grandfather and me?"

"It is not easy to explain," Juanita's voice was troubled, "our ranch is large—with many cattle—mostly our Mexican breed, not so fine as your American cows."

Lee's expression was bleak. He felt he knew what was coming.

"Sometimes our Mexican *rancheros* are offered herds of good-blooded cows at prices that make them profitable to buy. We do not ask questions, usually." Juanita gestured. "Questions might cause unpleasant complications, you will understand, Senor—" She gave him an embarrassed smile.

"You mean the *rancheros* suspect the cattle offered them are stolen from ranches on this side of the border," Lee helped her out.

"It has been a custom of many years," Juanita said defensively. "It is practiced by your own countrymen—when stolen Mexican cattle are offered for sale on their side of the border—"

Lee nodded. He was aware that many Mexican cattle

found their way into the herds of American ranchers in a manner not entirely blameless.

"Ramon, who now is in charge of Rancho San Juan, has sometimes purchased good-blooded cattle without being too curious where they came from," the girl went on reluctantly. "Some of them may have been stolen cows, but he didn't much concern himself. He paid our good dollars for them and was satisfied." Juanita shook her head sadly. "Poor Ramon! He was very troubled when he learned that the last herd he bought was stolen from the Smoke Tree Ranch. He complained bitterly to the—the certain person who sold the cattle to him. He was warned to say nothing—if he valued his life."

"It is fine of you to tell me this." Lee's tone was sympathetic. "We need not speak of it again—"

"I would not speak of it," she replied a bit haughtily. She lifted an expressive shoulder. "It is only that I want you to understand why I came to see you. Another herd was recently offered to him—from the same source. Ramon refused to buy and promised he would inform your grandfather. He was attacked and only by a miracle managed to escape with his life." Juanita sighed. "His wounds will keep him in his bed for many days, I fear."

"Who *is* this man you mention?" questioned Lee. "This dealer in stolen Smoke Tree cows?"

"One who is an agent for *El Capitan*, of course," Juanita said.

"*El Capitan?*"

"My brother is positive," asserted the girl. "He was held prisoner for several days in their stronghold—an abandoned mining town close to the border, he told me. On your American side," she added.

Lee nodded thoughtfully. He knew there were

such places in the bleak desert hills, somber ghosts of mad gold-rush days. He could name several abandoned boom camps, and there were others whose hectic existence had been so brief that even their picturesque names were lost from memory. A few dark holes in scabrous hillsides, some dumps of tailings sprawled down the slopes, a few tumbled buildings and corrals—moldering bones in some tiny long-forgot Boothill. Ghost towns, hidden deep in the desolate, remote desert wastes—ideal strongholds for lawless men.

"Your brother did not hear the name of this place?" he questioned.

"He was taken there blindfolded," Juanita told him. "His escape was made in the dark of the night. It is a hard place to find—and to leave," she added. Her voice grew strained. "He managed to see—and overhear strange things. Listen, Senor! He learned of this plot to kill your grandfather—and you. Three men were chosen by lot—they threw dice, Ramon told me—to see who among them would be the assassins."

Lee's eyes narrowed reflectively. "Can you describe the three men—"

"Only from what Ramon told me." Juanita pondered. "One of them is a Mexican—who has lost an eye. Ramon did not get his name. The other two are Americanos. Ramon said that one of these Americanos was an oldish man with whiskers and a little finger missing from his right hand. They called him Panamint. The third man was like any of your gringo *vaqueros*." She gestured. "I can tell you no more about them."

"An old man with whiskers!" Lee grinned. "Doesn't make sense—sending an old man with whiskers on a killing job."

"You are amused?" Juanita shook her head. "Do not

make fun, Senor Cary. It is possible the old man with whiskers was chosen for some special purpose—perhaps to win your confidence because he seems old and not the cold-blooded killer he really is. *Quien sabe!*" She made her little gesture of doubt.

"Something in what you say," muttered Lee thoughtfully.

"Even now they may be in Coldwater—those men," worried the girl.

Lee pricked up his ears.

"*Coldwater!*"

"Ramon heard them talking about Coldwater—something about meeting another man—at the Desert Bar saloon—"

Lee's face was serious. "The Desert Bar," he mused. "Now who would they be meeting at Wirt Stoner's place?"

Juanita shook her head. "Ramon was unable to learn the man's name, save that he would get them jobs with the Smoke Tree—"

"Gil Hawken!" Lee's voice was incredulous. "No," he muttered half to himself, "Gil wouldn't be that sort of scoundrel!"

"I do not trust that h*ombre*," the girl said in a low voice. "He is *muy malo*."

"What do you know about him?" Lee's tone was wondering. His eyes narrowed. "Sandy Wallace tells me he met you in Stoner's dance-hall," he said bluntly. "He thinks you are an entertainer."

Amusement lurked in the girl's dark eyes. "I like your Sandee," she murmured. "Sandee ees a nize boy." She went on in Spanish, "I had not met Gil Hawken until I came to Coldwater about three weeks ago. When I learned he was foreman of the Smoke Tree Ranch I made myself agreeable to him."

"You mean you came to Coldwater on the trail of those three men?"

Juanita smiled faintly. "I pretended I was a famous dancer from Mexico City," she said. "Wirt Stoner believed me—or pretended to believe me when he saw me dance *La Jota*." She gave him a provocative smile. "Some day, I will show you *La Jota*."

"It's a promise," laughed Lee. He shook his head. "It was a mad thing to do—a girl like you—dancing in that place!"

"It was necessary," Juanita said simply. "I wanted to find out more of this plot to—to kill you. There seemed no other way." She lifted a disdainful shoulder. "I came to no harm, Senor. This Hawken—he is a pig. I laugh at him—at his clumsy lovemaking—"

"Those men you followed might have happened to know you," argued Lee. "It was dangerous. You should not have done such a mad thing."

"It was necessary," she repeated. "I was not afraid—until lately—"

"Wirt Stoner?" he guessed.

The girl nodded. "He is different from Hawken—a sly, dangerous man," she said with a shiver.

"He made love to you?"

"In his strange way," Juanita admitted. "He—he made me afraid. I could not read his thoughts. Sometimes I feared it was really that he suspected me. I will be glad to put many miles between me and that cold-eyed snake."

"You shouldn't have done it," grumbled Lee. He was appalled. "It gives me the creeps to think of what might have happened! Why didn't you come direct to the ranch with your story?"

"Ramon and I talked it over. We feared spies—and I thought I would learn more in Coldwater." Juanita's tone was despondent. "It has been for nothing—except that I have been able to warn you. I am afraid to stay longer. Wirt Stoner frightens me. I have told you all that I know," she finished.

"You've told me a lot—and done a lot," thanked Lee gratefully. He grinned. "We'll keep a sharp watch for the one-eyed man, and the whiskered Panamint who has lost a finger." He held out his hand. "*Machos gracias*, Senorita Avilla, for your kindness. The debt is repaid many times and you must go back to your home and tell your brother to worry no more about the affair."

She returned the pressure of his hand. "Ramon will be glad," she said softly. "And I am glad, too, Senor, that I have met the brave man who saved him that night in Ensenada." She smiled. "Some day you will come to Rancho San Juan, no? I will show you *La Jota*."

The flawless beauty of her upturned face quite took Lee's breath. The naive invitation to visit Rancho San Juan had interesting possibilities, he reflected. Another face materialized between him and the luscious Juanita, a lovely piquant face with bright chestnut hair and gallant dark blue eyes that seemed to wistfully beckon him. Lee was suddenly stricken with anxiety. Nan was at that hotel—perhaps in immediate peril. Almost he could hear her voice coming to him through the night—as it had that night of the sandstorm. The memory swept away his momentary hesitation.

"Some day I will come to Rancho San Juan—perhaps," he said a bit hurriedly. He hesitated. "I wish I could ride with you—at least to the border—but an affair of great importance does not permit—"

Disappointment looked briefly from the lovely dark eyes. "It is *adios*, then, Senor," she murmured in a low voice—and turned abruptly to the waiting Fidel.

The Yaqui's fierce eyes were probing the darkness

behind them. With a swift, warning gesture he moved with all the stealth of a stalking jungle cat toward a thicket of low willows. Starlight glittered on the knife in his hand.

"He smells an enemy," Juanita whispered to Lee. "No!" as he reached for his gun—"you might shoot Fidel!"

They stood tense, the girl's hand pressed to her heart, their eyes searching the blackness into which the Yaqui had vanished. Lee's quick glance in the direction of Sandy told him the cowboy was still patiently waiting.

A sound came from the clump of willows, a sudden threshing of branches—a low startled grunt—then silence; and as silently as he had slid away, the Yaqui reappeared.

"*Que pasa!*" Juanita spoke nervously. "What is it, Fidel?" Her eyes dilated at the long blade in the man's hand and she pressed back against Lee. "Ah! Then you have—"

"Si, my Senorita," returned the Indian quietly. "The man is dead—very dead—" He finished wiping the blade and thrust it into his belt.

"Who was it, Fidel?"

"I know not, my Senorita, save that he is a Mexican—and has but one eye that now will spy no more."

Juanita's hand clasped Lee's arm. "The one-eyed Mexican!" she exclaimed in a frightened tone. "It means that my mission here is known—"

"You must ride at once," Lee told her. "You must be a long way from here before the man is missed—his fate suspected by his friends."

"*Si,*" she acquiesced. "I must ride fast and far this night." She swayed toward him and for a moment he felt the press of her palpitant supple body against his.

"Hasta la vista, amigo mio," she whispered. Her lips were perilously close, her eyes challenging. "Hasten the day when I see you again, my friend!"

"Hasta la vista," responded Lee, much moved. "I'll never forget you, Juanita." He pressed both her hands in his. "Now go!" he entreated.

Obediently she turned to her horse and leaped into the saddle. *"Vaya usted con Dios,* Lee," she called softly; "go you with God!" In another moment she had passed beyond the dark wall of the night, the faithful Fidel riding close at the heels of her horse.

Lee hailed the cowboy.

"Dead man lying over there in those willows," he said briefly. "Look him over, Sandy. I want any papers you find."

"For the love of Pete!" Sandy stared at him with bulging eyes. "All right, Boss, I'll search the corpse— but when in hades did this killin' take place?"

"While you were standing there looking at the stars," drawled Lee. He turned away quickly. "You'll find me at the hotel—" His voice faded in the distance.

"Well—hang me for a sheep-herder," muttered the astonished and somewhat crestfallen young cowboy. He went clumping toward the willows.

XIII
The Girl in 213

Baldy Bates was amusing himself with a deck of greasy cards when Lee walked into the dingy lobby of the Coldwater Palace Hotel. The old man was inclined to be grouchy.

"Whar yuh been?" he grumbled. "Thought yuh figgered to see the Page gal."

"Came as soon as I could," Lee told him. He glanced around disappointedly. Save for an enormously fat man dozing behind the desk the place was deserted. "Didn't you give her my message?"

Baldy nodded. "Said she was undressin' for bed an' that yuh could see her in the morning—if you still wanted to talk to her." He uncoiled his long gaunt frame from the rickety chair. "Seems like I ain't so spry as I was fifty years back," he complained. "I'm thinkin' it's 'bout time I hit the hay my own self."

"Got a room?"

"Nope. Hotel's full up, that ol' gander back yonder says." Baldy yawned. "Got my bed-roll in the wagon over at the O.K. feed stables. Can fix me a bed in the hay."

"I'll take you over to Ma Kelly's place," suggested Lee.

"No," refused the old man, after a moment's deliberation. "I'll bed down with the broncs. Be safer." Baldy grinned at the surprise in Lee's face. "Ain't meaning it's me I'm scared about. It's the broncs. Spotted a bunch of Mexicans makin' camp down in that big coulee back of the feed stables," he explained. "Ain't trusting them hombres much when thar's good horses 'round." He moved toward the door. "Waal, *buenas noches*, young feller. Be seein' yuh in the morning."

Lee was disturbed. Growing unease gnawed him. Since his amazing talk with Juanita Avilla he was more than ever reluctant that Nan and her young brother remain alone in the hotel, a place he suspected was secretly owned by Wirt Stoner. The gross, unkempt man dozing behind the desk was nothing more than Stoner's hired man. Meeker was not a bad sort when he was sober, which was seldom, but the hotel, with its drunken Saturday night patrons, was no place for a respectable young girl. And there was the disturbing fact of Stoner's suspicious eagerness to arrange for the rooms, according to Jake Kurtz' story. Lee had never liked or trusted Wirt Stoner. The past hours had not lessened his antipathy toward the man.

The screen door banged open and three cowboys lurched noisily into the lobby. Meeker roused from his nap and morosely handed out the keys to their rooms; after which he lighted a half-smoked cigar and blinked owlishly at Lee.

"No chance for a room in this hotel," he croaked. "Thought you always bunked at Ma Kelly's when you come to town."

The fat man's words gave Lee an idea. If he could persuade Meeker to let him have a room, Nan would not be so entirely alone, without protection. He would be near—if trouble brewed.

"Be a good fellow," he begged as he approached the desk. "You can find me some sort of room, Meeker."

The hotel man shook his head. "Ain't a bed left," he protested. "You're out of luck, Mr. Cary. You can find a room over at Ma Kelly's," he added.

Lee threw a twenty-dollar gold piece on the desk. "I

want a room!" He tempered the curt demand with a sleepy smile. "I'm dead on my feet, Meeker. Want to get to bed."

Suspicion was suddenly rife in Meeker's small eyes as he tried to fathom Lee's unusual desire to patronize the Palace Hotel. Lee invariably made the Adobe Inn his headquarters when in Coldwater. The answer, it dawned on Meeker, was the good-looking girl upstairs. The one who apparently had caught Wirt Stoner's fancy. The thought of becoming involved in matters that concerned Stoner brought a pallor to Meeker's mottled face.

"Your gold ain't good here, tonight," he muttered sullenly. "Sorry, Mr. Cary—" He pushed the gold coin away.

Reluctantly Lee abandoned his plan.

"You've a heart of stone, Meeker," he pretended to grumble as he turned away.

As the door closed behind his would-be patron, Meeker leaned heavily back in his squeaky chair. "Wirt's up to some devilment," he worried. "The young feller kind of suspects something is wrong—else he wouldn't be offering me twenty dollars for a night in this bug-ridden mangy dump."

The hotel man drew a large handkerchief from a hip-pocket and wiped a perspiring face. "Wish I was ten thousand miles away from this hellhole!" He replaced the bandanna and after a furtive glance at the door, produced a flask from a cubby under the desk. He drank deeply. "Got to get away from here," he muttered. "Hell's going to bust loose in this cow-town, one of these days."

He replaced the flask and fumbled under his shiny black coat; a stubby gun slid from a shoulder-holster and lay in his moist palm. Deep lines scored his flabby, pendulous cheeks as he eyed the weapon. That clear-eyed young girl upstairs! She was not like those other creatures who lived in the Palace Hotel! He knew a good girl when he saw one.

The hotel man's bloated, mottled face set in chiseled granite lines and with a muttered oath he returned the stubby gun back to its hidden holster. Wirt Stoner was due for a surprise—if he tried any of his tricks on that girl in room 213, he promised himself . . .

Lee met Sandy Wallace emerging from the blackness of the alley. He had searched the dead Mexican, the cowboy informed him.

"Not a scrap of paper on the corpse," Sandy stated. "Nothin' 'cept the makin's for cigarettes. Feller, I'm shore mystified how that one-eyed greaser got stuck in the gizzard—and me standin' so close I could have heard yuh wink an eye."

"He was trailing the Mexican girl—or us," Lee speculated. "The Yaqui knifed him."

"For the love of Pete," marveled the cowboy. "Shore would hate to have that Injun on my trail. He's sudden death in the dark—that *hombre*."

Lights twinkled at them through the tamarisks and palo verde that shaded Ma Kelly's Adobe Inn. Sandy jingled his gold pieces.

"Mebbe Slim and Willie are sittin' up for me," he hoped as they pushed through the white picket gate. "The poor mavericks are plumb set on trimmin' me—the way I did them last month."

Lee had no answer. He was thinking of what he had learned from Ma Kelly—and from the lovely lips of Juanita Avilla. Most of all he thought of Nan Page. He was wishing he had not allowed her to remain at the hotel. He should have insisted upon seeing her.

He went gloomily to bed.

XIV
Dark Men

It was still dark when the crackle of six-guns jarred Lee from sleep.

He sat up, trying to convince himself that it was only some hilarious cow outfit making a noisy, early-morning start for home. He could hear the muffled thud of horses' hoofs growing faint in the distance. For some reason the explanation failed to satisfy him and after a moment's frowning thought he slid from the bed and lighted the small lamp on the dresser. It was three o'clock, the watch told him—a good two hours before dawn.

Lee hesitated. He was worrying too much about Nan Page, he reflected. His apprehensions were unreasonable. And yet he felt there was something sinister about the burst of gunfire—those rapidly retreating hoofbeats. He would never forgive himself if harm came to Nan Page—

He got into his clothes hurriedly and lamp in hand went quietly down the hall. A door opened; Sandy Wallace's tousled red head peered out at him.

"That you, Lee?" The cowboy opened the door wider, revealed Slim Kendall and Willie Sims eyeing round from a makeshift card-table. Sandy grinned. "Been makin' an all-night game of it," he explained. "Cain't none of us lose enough to want to quit. First I win, then Slim gits it away from me and then Willie takes it from Slim. Which means we start all over ag'in."

"Hear that shooting up the street?" Lee asked.

"Shore did," Sandy said. "We was wonderin' what the ruckus was."

"If you boys were awake, you heard more than I did," Lee suggested. "How did it seem to start, Sandy?"

The cowboy considered. "Seems to me there was a single shot come first, then some yellin'. Right on the tail of the yells them other guns started smokin'. Then we heard you jump out of bed and light yore lamp." Sandy's voice was troubled. "We was wonderin' if you figgered somethin' is wrong."

Slim and Willie crowded to the open door and the former broke into the colloquy. "The first shot sounded like it come from the hotel," he estimated.

"Them other shots was further off," added Willie Sims "I'd say them *hombres* was back of the O.K. feed stables—an' ridin' fast."

"I'm taking a look," was Lee's curt decision. He started down the hall.

"We're takin' a look with yuh," muttered the red-headed Sandy. With one accord the three young punchers reached hastily for discarded gun-belts and trooped at Lee's heels. The latter smiled back at them. "Easy with those boots," he warned. "You'll have the house thinking there's a fire—or a raid."

Silently they made their way into the patio by way of the kitchen, where Lee deposited the lamp.

"Shore plenty dark under these tamarisks," complained Sandy. "Keep off my heels, feller. Can't yuh see me?"

"Ain't got cat-eyes," muttered the offending Willie Sims. "Keep them hoofs of yore's movin' if yuh don't want 'em stepped on."

They reached the starlight beyond the picket gate. "Keep to the street," again cautioned Lee. "Sidewalk's too noisy."

They padded swiftly through the dust under a sky ablaze with stars. The air was chill, the night still. Only the muffled scrape of their own boots, the banshee yip of a distant coyote, disturbed the nocturnal hush.

"Beginnin' to think we dreamed we heard them shots—them horses," muttered Slim Kendall. "Ain't a light showin' in nary window. If we heard guns smokin' and horses on the run," he argued, "why ain't some of these folks stirring, I want to know?"

"You're wrong," rebutted Sandy. "There's a light in the hotel." He hastened his stride to keep up with Lee's increasing pace.

"You'd think the folks in the hotel would have heard a gunshot in the lobby," maintained the argumentative Slim.

"A gunshot don't mean nothin' in Coldwater on a late Saturday night," Sandy sagely pointed out. "Mebbe them *hombres* would just figger old Meeker had committed suicide and let it go at that."

Cautiously the four investigators pushed into the dimly lighted hotel lobby. Lee, in the lead, halted with a smothered exclamation.

Sprawled on the floor between the desk and the stairs was the bulky form of Meeker. A single look was enough to inform their experienced eyes that the man was dead.

There was a gasp from Sandy Wallace.

"You done called the play, Slim! Old Meeker shore has killed hisself—"

"Meeker didn't stick that knife into his back," Lee objected. "It's murder! Meeker has been murdered!"

He stooped; and when he straightened up there was a stubby gun in his hand.

"Meeker's," he said in a hard voice. "One shell empty. It was Meeker who fired that first shot you boys heard." He stared down at the dead man. "Tried to stop them—and got knifed," he muttered.

His face suddenly haggard, Lee went quickly to the desk and scrutinized the open register. "213," the watching punchers heard him say to himself. Jerking at his gun he went leaping up the stairs.

Sandy and the Lazy Y men gaped in bewilderment. They were at a loss to comprehend the very evident and terrible fear in Lee's face. With a stifled exclamation the redheaded cowboy ran to the desk and studied the register.

"Nan Page!" The young cowboy's voice was dismayed. "Hell, fellers! It's the Page gal! She's up there—and her kid brother!" He went clattering up the stairs, gun leaping from holster.

Slim and Willie stared open-mouthed for a brief moment, then jerking at their guns they took the stairs like a pair of crag-leaping mountain goats. Who Nan Page was they neither knew, nor cared. It was enough that she was a girl, and apparently in peril.

Startled faces peered from doorways as the cowboys raced along the hall to room 213. Lee burst from the room and into the one adjoining. He reappeared almost instantly. His face was pale.

"The girl is not in her room, nor the boy!"

The three cowboys exchanged dismayed looks. Lee's distracted gaze fastened on a partially dressed man who lurched from an opposite room.

"You there! Know anything about it?" he demanded.

The man blinked uncomprehendingly. "Whash goin' on?" he wanted to know in an aggrieved tone. "Whash idee—bustin' up a feller's sleep?"

Lee turned away impatiently. No sense wasting time with a drunken man.

"Hey! What's wrong?"

The question came from a girl whose rouged face peered from another door. "What was that shootin' awhile back. Most scared me to death—"

She shook her head to Lee's sharp interrogation. No—she knew nothing of a girl and her kid brother. Her door slammed shut.

Lee's voice sheared like cold steel through the growing uproar as the long double row of rooms spewed out occupants in various stages of undress.

"Meeker is lying dead down in the lobby! Knifed in the back—murdered!" he told them. "Before he was killed he fired his gun. Somebody must have heard the shot—heard *something!*"

There was a stunned silence. Lee's fiercely probing gaze roved from face to face.

"Talk up!" he begged. "A girl and her young brother have disappeared from their rooms. Meeker was killed—trying to protect them—"

An elderly, bow-legged man spoke up. "Heard shootin' a few minutes ago," he admitted. "Wasn't anything to wonder about. Seems like thar's gun-play ev'ry time I come to this cow-town. Always aim to mind my own business," he added dryly.

Several others now volunteered similar information— and like reasons for failing to be curious about the gunshot.

Pressed further, the same quiet-spoken man admitted hearing some noise in the hall, and what he thought some harmless scuffling in the rooms opposite his own.

"I figgered it was some horse-play going on," he sheepishly told Lee. "Didn't think nothing of it."

Others corroborated the man. They had heard what they thought was some harmless scuffling. Nobody had been sufficiently curious to investigate—even speculate. A man with night-shirt tucked into his trousers started to push through the throng of awed-faced roomers. Lee halted him.

"Where are you going, fellow?" he rasped.

"Over to Wirt Stoner's house," answered the man "Gotta tell Wirt about poor old Meeker."

He was one of the bartenders, Lee now recognized. "Go ahead, Joey," he assented. "Wirt will want to know."

He followed the barman down the stairs, Sandy and the Lazy Y men at his heels.

The thunderstruck roomers came to life. Poor old Meeker was dead—*murdered*—and a young girl and her small brother mysteriously snatched from their midst! Like a suddenly unleashed stream the crowd poured down to the scene of death.

"One of you boys stick round and keep an eye on things here," Lee said to his three friends.

His look told Sandy that he was selected.

"I'm trailin' with you," rebelled the cowboy. "You ain't leavin' me behind. I'm ridin' with you after them wolves that's got the Page gal."

"I'll watch things here," volunteered the quiet-spoken elderly cowman. He hurried up, buckling gun-holster round lean hips. "I'm Andy Drew, foreman of the Diamond D," he introduced himself to Lee. "You go ahead, Mr. Cary. No time to lose if you want to pick up the trail while she's hot."

"Thanks, Drew." Lee had heard of the Diamond D foreman—knew him for a decent, trustworthy man. Old Tim Hook, the Diamond D's owner, was long a friend of his grandfather. "Deputize any of the men here you think you can trust," he went on in a low tone. "Get word to Sheriff Day at Palo Verde."

He sped into the street. Sandy and the two Lazy Y men galloped after him.

The Diamond D foreman's calm glance went to a tall cowboy at his elbow. The puncher nodded, jerked tight the buckle of his gun-belt and ran for the door. Five men streamed after him, belting hastily-grabbed holsters as they clattered into the street.

The doors of the O.K. Livery & Feed Stables yawned wide. Lee slid to an abrupt standstill. From the dark interior of the barn came strangled curses. Sandy panted up.

"Pete Smith!" he yelled. "Sounds like the old feller's choking to death!"

He dashed through the doors, gun in hand, Slim and Willie close at his back.

Lee glanced uneasily over his shoulder at the little cluster of men hurrying up. Hands lowered to gun butts. He was not sure of their purpose.

"We boys aim to chip in with you," one of the newcomers told him grimly. He was a tall, brown-faced man in the early thirties. "I saw that young gal and her kid brother when they come to the hotel." He swore softly. "We fellers aim to git up a necktie party if there's harm come to 'em, Mr. Cary. I'm Chuck O'Neil, of the Diamond D," he introduced. "These boys is all Diamond D—"

"Thanks, Chuck." Lee's tone was grateful. He knew the type of men who worked for Tim Hook's Diamond D. Fearless, resourceful, hard-riding fighting men. Those responsible for the murder of old Meeker and the abduction of Nan and Ted would pay terribly for the double crime.

"Come on, fellers! Get yore broncs and fork saddle!" rasped the Diamond D man.

Tight-lipped and fierce-eyed, the cowboys stormed

into the stable, were met with a startled yell from Sandy Wallace. Lee sped through the doors.

"Light that lantern—somebody!" implored Sandy's excited,voice. "Something wrong here!"

A match flared and in a moment the glow from the big stable lantern spread over the scene. Sandy was stooped over the huddled form of Pete Smith. Baling wire tightly bound the livery man's ankles and wrists; a twisted bandanna had been thrust between his jaws.

Sympathetic hands quickly released the old man. He sat up, coughing and spitting and gasping out lurid imprecations against his assailants.

"They was dark-skinned fellers," he told his attentive listeners. "Sneaked in on me and nigh choked me to death before I knew what was goin' on—"

"*El Capitan*," muttered a voice. "*El Capitan's* gang, shore as yuh're bawn."

There was a dead silence. Uneasy looks passed between the men. The night's affair had assumed a new, more sinister aspect. *El Capitan!* The elusive bandit of the border. None knew the identity of this cunning wolf of the cattle ranges, or where he "holed-up." The task confronting them seemed more formidable with each flitting second.

Fear filled Lee's heart as he stared down at the spluttering old livery man. Would he ever see Nan Page again? He fought down his panic, steeled himself to action.

"Get your horses, boys."

He spoke with his usual calmness. Only the lines suddenly scoring his lean brown face betrayed his struggle to retain that calmness.

"Scatter out . . . first man picks up the trail fires three spaced shots as signal."

Soberly, in grim silence the men hastened to their

horses. Lee eyed the livery proprietor. "Tell us all you know," he ordered. "Have you seen anything of Baldy Bates? He said he would bed down here for the night."

"If yuh mean that old longhorn that put up the Page gal's buckboard team, I shore saw him plenty," snorted old Pete Smith. "The horse-faced galoot went chargin' like a buffalo bull after the gang . . . stomped all over me . . . never even took time to untie me." The annoyed livery man spat out a piece of chewed bandanna. "Left me layin' here like a trussed-up hog," he grumbled. "Awful inconsiderate he was—"

"Come on, boys!" Lee was running to the doors. "Baldy's out here—somewhere!"

Closely followed by the Faithful Three he faded into the darkness, leaving the wrathful Pete talking to himself.

"Told yuh that last burst of gunfire come from back of the barn," reminded Willie Sims, pounding along by the side of the long-legged Slim Kendall.

"They've cut across Kelly's Creek and headed for Cat Canyon," panted Slim. "Hi! Lee! What's that—layin' over there?"

It was a dead horse, the tall, hawk-eyed Slim had glimpsed lying in the chaparral.

"Baldy's work," pronounced Lee in a steely voice. "Scatter a bit, boys. I'm afraid the old man's not far away."

They knew what he meant. Baldy Bates would be very dead, when they found him. Grimly they continued the search.

It was Lee who made the next discovery. The others ran up, fear in their eyes.

"That ain't old Baldy!" exclaimed Sandy Wallace. He frowned down at the body sprawled under a big greasewood. "A Mexican—one of the gang," he muttered.

"More of Baldy's work," Lee said in the same steely voice.

"The shootin' old warrior," admired the redheaded Sandy affectionately. He looked at his friends, an odd gleam of hope in his blue eyes. "Fellers! I'm bettin' my stack of chips the old maverick is alive and still full of fight."

"You shore win the pot, young man," drawled a voice out of the darkness.

"Baldy!" Lee's voice was jubilant.

Their startled eyes probed the baffling curtain of the night. From behind a great boulder emerged the lank, stoop-shouldered frame of the ex-trail driver. He approached slowly, and they guessed he was hurt, or weary to the point of collapse. Lee ran to meet him with an exclamation of relief.

"Keep yore paws off me!" Baldy's tone was peevish. "I ain't no case for a doc. Ain't needin' no nurse, mister." He eased down on a convenient boulder and rubbed a shin. "Gimme the makin's, one of you jaspers."

Lee mutely handed him tobacco sack and papers. Baldy grunted his thanks and proceeded to roll a cigarette. Despite his nonchalance they read anguish and despair—gnawing shame—in the deep-set fierce old eyes.

"Match," he muttered, gaze savagely intent on the dead Mexican. Some one—it was Sandy—handed him the requested match.

"I've a mind to take yore skelp," he apostrophized the dead man.

The match spurted to flame against horny thumbnail, the trick Teddy had loved to watch. Smoke curled from hairy nostrils, then with an infuriated, animal-like bellow Baldy was on his feet.

"I'll take the skelps of ev'ry last mangy dog of yuh!"

His long knife flashed and he lurched toward the still form lying under the creosote bush. Lee grabbed his arm.

"Put that knife back!" he rasped. "Take a brace, Baldy. We've got work to do—got to get her back—and the boy! We need your help," he was inspired to add.

Baldy rolled bloodshot eyes at him. "Aye," he mumbled. "We gotta git 'em back—her an' Teddy—" His berserk fury had left him, they saw.

"Git 'em back," he repeated stonily, and peering hard at the young man clutching his arm. "Lee Cary, ain't yuh?" He heaved a deep sigh. "Waal—let's ride. No time to lose."

"Tell us what you know, first," urged Lee. He glanced at the riders spurring up from the livery barn. "We've got a posse ready to ride soon as we know all there is to know."

He was sound asleep in the hayloft when he was awakened by a shot, Baldy related.

"Got tangled up in some baling-wire when I made for the ladder," he detailed. "By the time I got outside a bunch of riders was fannin' it past the barn—" The old cowman's voice choked. "Saw they'd got the girl—an' Teddy. Took after them fast as I could run . . . started my guns smokin'. One of the greasers swung a rope at me an' fust thing I knowed I was being snaked through the chaparral at the tail-end of his riata."

One of the attentively listening cowboys swore softly. "Like to have broke ev'ry bone in yore body— all them rocks and brush," he muttered.

"I'd a couple of shots left," Baldy went on. "Killed

the greaser's bronc. He fell clear an' come for me with his knife, grinnin' like a face from hell." Baldy's own smile at that moment was terrible to see. "My last bullet took him plumb center. He dropped whar he's layin' now, 'longside that greasewood." His eyes flamed. "How come they got the gal and the boy out of the hotel—an' all them rooms full of men?" he wanted to know.

Lee informed him of Meeker's death.

"That was the shot that woke you up," he said. "Nobody in the hotel, upstairs, knew what was going on. Thought some of the drunks were shooting it out."

Baldy glanced at the dead Mexican. "I'd say Meeker earned some mileage back from the hell he was headed for awful fast," he commented briefly. "I'm gittin' me a bronc," he added. "I want a bronc that kin travel clear to hell—if that's whar them fellers hole up." He slouched away toward the livery barn.

"Go with him," Lee directed the Three Musketeers. "Saddle up your own horses and be ready to ride as soon as I get my Buck horse from Ma Kelly's."

The two Lazy Y men and Sandy Wallace hurried to overtake Baldy. Lee turned his attention to the cluster of waiting Diamond D riders.

"Won't be easy to follow the trail while it's dark," he warned Chuck O'Neil. "Take it easy until the rest of us overhaul you. Be dawn inside of an hour."

The hard-eyed Diamond D man nodded. "I savvy," he said curtly. "Come daylight, we'll run like hounds after a wolf, huh?" He swung his horse and melted into the darkness, followed by his equally grim-faced companions.

Lee's heart warmed to them as he watched them go.

Wirt Stoner hailed him as he passed the hotel, now

ablaze with lights. Lee halted, face hard, unfriendly. There were questions he wanted Stoner to answer—later. Standing near the saloon man was the same bearded stranger Lee had observed in Stoner's office the previous evening. Again, as if obeying some covert signal from the saloon man, the stranger drifted from view.

Worry was visible in Stoner's eyes as he confronted Lee.

"This is terrible," he groaned. "Poor Meeker killed— Miss Page—her kid brother gone—"

"I've no time to talk about it, now, Wirt," Lee said in a curt voice. "Not unless you have anything to say that will throw some light on the affair." His chill eyes bored the other man. "I hear it's your doings, Stoner, their going to this lousy hotel of yours."

Stoner swore. "What in the hell do you mean?" he exploded furiously. "Why should I know anything about this business?"

"I'm asking you," Lee said softly. "You mix with a lot of dirty crooks, Wirt. If you have any suspicions—spill them. It's up to you to talk—and talk fast."

"You're loony," declared the saloon man sullenly. "All I know is that a friend of mine has been murdered and the Page children evidently abducted. I was asleep in my house when Joey brought me the news," he added.

The man's horror was genuine enough, Lee felt. His suspicions weakened. Perhaps he had allowed gossip to unfairly prejudice him against Wirt Stoner.

"It's a mess, Wirt," he groaned. "It's as mysterious as it is horrible. Who in the world would want to harm that girl—and her kid brother?"

Stoner shook his head gloomily. "Lee," his voice lowered, "if there was any sort of clue that pointed right, I'd say—*El Capitan* is the answer."

"We found a dead Mexican," interrupted Lee. "Baldy Bates shot him—"

The saloon man gave him a startled look. "A Mexican!" He glanced around uneasily. "Lee—the answer is *El Capitan*."

"Why should *El Capitan* pull off such a stunt—run away with Miss Page and her brother?" puzzled Lee.

Stoner gestured helplessly. "*Quien sabe!*" he said. "The devil probably has seen the girl some place . . . decided he wanted her. Who knows?"

Lee nodded glumly and hurried on to Ma Kelly's. The widow heard his quick step and ran from the kitchen to meet him

"Oh, Lee! I've heard the dreadful news!" she wailed. "The poor lamb—"

She trotted by his side to the stable.

"Your horse is ready for you," she told him. "I knew you'd be ridin' fast, lad. I told Frisco to throw your saddle on."

Briefly he related the few details he knew.

"No telling when I'll be back," he finished. "Explain to Dawson, won't you? Try and keep him here." His face hardened. "If he isn't man enough to understand—then I don't care a hoot if he does run out on me."

"Don't you worry about Mr. Dawson, lad," comforted the widow. "He's a nice feller—not the kind to get cold feet."

The great golden horse melted into the darkness beyond the picket fence; and wiping her eyes, Mrs. Kelly went slowly back to her kitchen.

"God be with him—and them two poor children," she prayed fervently.

Her fingers touched the little faded green wooden cross at her throat.

XV
"Home Is Over There—"

It was all too fantastic to be real, Nan told herself. A ghastly dream! Soon she would wake up—find herself back in that dingy hotel room. As from afar she heard Ted's voice.

"Nan! Do you think they'll kill us? Or maybe sell us into slavery—like those Barbary pirates did Robinson Crusoe?"

There was a quaver in the boy's voice that Nan knew was real enough; and so were those rough adobe walls real, the pile of straw on which she crouched, and the pale dawn filtering through the high narrow window. No—it was not a nightmare! The unbelievable had actually happened! They were prisoners!

Her arm drew Ted closer.

"No," she reassured him, holding her voice steady. "We won't be killed, or sold into slavery."

She was glad it was too dark for Teddy to see the sudden horror she knew was in her eyes. *Sold into slavery!* The thought was congealing. Nan shivered. Such things *did* happen! But she must hold fast to her courage, she reflected. Ted and she would need all the courage in the world—to fight this thing that had happened to them.

"No," she repeated—she was glad she could speak so coolly—"they're only bandits, Ted. I suppose they'll carry us back into their mountains—hold us for ransom."

"Gee!" Ted pondered over this angle. "We'll have

to sell the ranch to raise the money." His tone was disconsolate. "If they make us sell the ranch I won't be a cattle king."

"Oh, we'll find a way out of this."

Nan's positive tone impressed Ted. He brightened.

"Old Baldy'll pick up the trail," he prophesied. "Baldy was an Injun scout. Soon as he knows we've been captured by bandits he'll ride like the wind to rescue us."

The girl made no answer. She was thinking of another man who would "ride like the wind"—if he knew of her peril. Already he had twice magically appeared when death, or worse, reached for her. Perhaps it was Fate that he was destined to make a third timely appearance just when all seemed lost. The thought brought Nan tremendous comfort, buoyed her up.

Sunlight suddenly stole through the narrow opening that pierced the thick wall. Nan knew without looking at her watch that it was nearly six o'clock. The thought of the watch brought a wry smile to her lips. It now rested in the pocket of a dark-skinned bandit. She had heard the man grinningly remark that he would present it to a certain Rosita for whose favors he yearned. They were unaware that she understood Spanish.

That dreadful moment!

She had not been really alarmed by the shooting in the lobby. In fact had scarcely awakened. She was too dead tired. And there had been gun-play earlier in the evening, in the saloon across the street. Shooting affrays could not concern her. Baldy Bates had promised to avoid trouble. She had wished he could have slept in the hotel, but Mr. Stoner had not arranged for Baldy— in fact had not known of Baldy. The old man planned to sleep in the hayloft of the livery barn, Nan recalled.

He would know nothing of the dreadful thing that had overtaken Teddy and her.

Those unbelievable moments! The memory of them sent cold prickles down her back. The door had opened so quietly!

Thinking that possibly the latch was off and a draught from the open window had drawn it open she was getting out of bed to close it. There was no key, Nan recalled. It had not been possible to lock the door. One foot was on the floor when the three men glided into the room. Amazement had paralyzed her tongue. One of them was instantly at her side, a long knife in his hand at her throat.

"No noise—or the knife," he had warned in whispered broken English.

They had forced her to dress. Because she had forgotten her nightgown she luckily had not entirely disrobed. While she dressed under the silent menace of the knife one of the men had hastily crammed her few things into her bag. It was then the watch had been confiscated, along with her treasured ring set with sapphires and a diamond, a gift from her father.

Nan found herself wondering at the smoothness of the affair. It was almost as if it had been carefully planned. She knew that when she left the room there would be no indication that she had ever occupied it. Only Baldy would know she had been there—and Jake Kurtz. It was the work of a cunning mind, she was convinced.

Her thoughts flew to Gil Hawken. Was he responsible for the outrage? Nan's face paled. That terrible man! Or was it the owner of Smoke Tree Range, the grandfather of Lee Cary? The thought stifled her. She went back to those terrifying minutes in the hotel.

She was out in the hall, walking between two of the men. The third man followed closely with her bag. They had gagged her; a knife pressed lightly against her side. They were down the stairs. She would have screamed, save for the gag. The big fat Meeker lay on the floor. He had tried to save her, she dimly realized. He lay there, dead—had given his life for her.

She had felt horribly ill and helpless as the men rushed her into the street. They put her on a horse—bound her to the saddle. One of the riders held Teddy in front of him on his saddle. Teddy was gagged, too. He could only look at her with eyes that silently implored—the frightened eyes of a child who could not understand what was happening.

Nan's own eyes blazed at the memory of that look in Ted's face. Never would she forgive the man responsible. Some day he would *pay*, she promised herself fiercely.

The rest of it was a blur. They had ridden like mad from the town. Several of the horsemen had fallen back—she had heard the crackle of their guns. What they were shooting at she did not know. One man led her horse—another man rode behind, his quirt lashing her animal.

They rode furiously, for hours, it seemed. Once they stopped in a deep gorge and changed horses. A man had the animals in readiness—saddled. Another curious angle of the affair. The more she thought about it the more was Nan convinced that the abduction had been carefully planned. No chance bandit raid had snatched Ted and herself from the Coldwater Palace Hotel. Oh, why had she not listened to Jake Kurtz and gone to Ma Kelly's place!

Where they now were, she had no idea. She only knew that four grimy, cobwebby walls held them captive. A grinning *peon* had brought in a pile of fresh straw and thrown it in a corner for them to lie on. Teddy, exhausted, had gone promptly to sleep. The forgetfulness of sleep was not possible for her. She wished she could have slept. She felt completely done.

Ted's voice again broke into her dismal musings.

"That man took my Winchester twenty-two—and my pistol," he complained aggrievedly. "I told him they were mine and he only laughed and said his little boy could use them."

"The beast!"

Nan felt the fierce killing rage of a tigress wave through her. She could have flung herself tooth and nail on that man had he appeared just then. But would he ever show his face again? Would anyone come— bring them food—water?

She appraisingly eyed the sunlight streaming through the window. Grisly thoughts troubled her. Perhaps nobody would come. Perhaps they had deliberately been left in this wretched adobe hovel to starve to death. Her face blanched.

Teddy saw that she was staring up at the narrow window.

"I could crawl through that hole, if I could reach it," he announced.

His sister's eyes widened at him. "Why—Ted—"

"I could," asserted the boy. "Old Daniel Boone always did things like that when he was trapped by Indians."

Nan looked at him with new eyes. She had the odd feeling that what she saw was not a small, twelve-year-old boy with freckles on his nose, and short, tousled yellow hair. It was a *man* talking to her, a grim-eyed, cool-voiced resourceful grown-up male.

"What sort of things did Daniel Boone do?" she asked meekly.

"Oh, once—when the Indians trapped him in his tobacco-loft—he threw a lot of dried tobacco leaves down into their faces and then jumped over them while their eyes were blinded with the tobacco dust," Teddy informed her. "He was always doing things like that and the Indians never once got his skelp. Daniel Boone lived to be an awful old man."

"Scalp," corrected the girl in a dazed voice. "Not *skelp*, Ted—"

"Baldy always says *skelp*," argued her brother. "Reckon old Baldy knows all about skelps. He's taken lots of skelps."

"Baldy likes to tell tall stories." Nan found herself smiling. "Where did you learn so much about Daniel Boone?" she inquired curiously.

"There was a lot about him on that Winchester rifle calendar Mr. Kurtz gave me," explained Teddy. "Every page for the month had stories about him in small print. It was like a book. I read it all when I went to bed last night—before—before—" He broke off with a gulp and suddenly he was a small boy again. "Wish I was brave as Daniel Boone—or old Baldy," he choked.

Nan held him tight. "I think you are wonderful, Ted," she declared affectionately. "You are as brave as the bravest—and even Daniel Boone couldn't crawl through that tiny window," she added with a thoughtful glance up at the sunlit aperture.

Teddy's interest revived. "Gee, Nan, if I could get up there I'd crawl through in a jiffy. Then I could unbar the door. It's got bars on the outside. I heard the man fasten 'em after he brought us the straw."

"Perhaps you could reach if you stood on my shoulders," suggested the girl. She got to her feet and went to the wall. Teddy joined her and together they studied the proposed adventure.

"I don't think you could quite make it," Nan doubted. "Not even if you stand on my shoulders—and if I could hold you up—"

"You could lean against the wall so you wouldn't teeter," Teddy pointed out practically. "And look, Nan!" His voice was jubilant. "I can get one foot into that hole up there and then make a sort of jump and get right on the window-ledge."

Nan was aware of qualms. She grew panicky as the adventure took on possibilities.

"I don't know, Ted," she objected. "I don't quite like the idea. Even if you crawl through, it's a long way down to the ground outside." She shuddered. "You might break your neck!" she wailed.

"Gotta take chances," declared Teddy stubbornly. "Baldy says *yuh gotta!*"

"Oh, Ted! You sound just *like* old Baldy!" Nan made a gesture of mock despair. "Such language—"

He ignored her. "Give me a boost, Nan," he begged. "Easy as pie—with that old hole there—"

She was appalled, continued to demur. "Those men might be close," she argued. "They'd catch you, Teddy."

"They rode off after they locked us in here," the boy told her. "I heard 'em go. I figger," he said, in the speech of his beloved Baldy Bates, "I figger them *hombres* done made camp down by that thar crik we crost last night."

"You win, feller," announced his sister solemnly. There was vast admiration in her voice. She gave him a kiss and a hug and bent down. "Up with yuh, mister. Reckon I c'n h'ist yuh plenty easy."

With some difficulty Ted managed to climb to her

shoulders. Nan braced herself against the rough wall and gritted her teeth as the little high-heeled boots bit into tender flesh. In a moment one foot had gained the necessary toe-hold in the cranny beneath the window. Ted gave a little upward leap and landed facedown inside the two-foot embrasure.

Nan picked herself up from the earthen floor. That last push of Ted's leg had quite overbalanced her. "Good work, feller!" she applauded. She rubbed her chafed shoulders and stared up with anxious eyes. "How does it look—outside?"

The boy's face peered back at her. A cobweb festooned his nose. "Easy as pie," he announced in a whisper. "There's a pile of straw right underneath. I can drop down easy and make no noise."

She watched, breathless, tense, while he cautiously backed through the narrow window. It was a tight squeeze, even for him. He vanished; she heard a soft thud outside. He was on the straw-pile now, she realized. Her legs oddly trembly, she ran to the heavy door.

The moments dragged; Nan pressed against the door. Why was Ted so long? She could hear nothing! Only the wild hammering of her heart. Something had happened to him! He had hurt himself—was unconscious—or a guard had seized him! She dared not cry out for fear of making matters worse.

Anxiety was at fever heat when at last she heard a faint scuff of feet. Immediately her dread fell away. It was Ted! She began to wonder why he moved so very slowly. Her fears returned. He *had* hurt himself— twisted an ankle.

Gently the bars slid from the grooves—inch by inch. The crudely timbered door began to sag outward. Ted's whisper came to her.

"Move awful quiet, Nan—"

She pushed through the opening; with a warning gesture, the boy noiselessly closed the door and slid the bars back into the grooves. He turned to his sister. "You were so long," she whispered. "I was frightened—"

"Had to make an Injun stalk," Ted explained. "Baldy showed me how to move so quiet you can't hear a leaf rustle. He's saved his life hundreds of times 'cause he knew the Injun stalk."

Nan gave him a misty-eyed smile.

"What shall we do now, Ted?" She might have been a little girl speaking to a big brother.

"I shut the door again so they won't suspect we've escaped," Ted told her. "If they saw the door hanging open they'd know we've escaped and then they'd start cuttin' sign for our trail."

She nodded gravely. "You know so much, Teddy. You're wonderful!"

Teddy refused to be heroized. "Just common sense," he scoffed. "Baldy says yuh gotta use common sense 'bout them sorta things."

She could have hugged him Instead she glanced apprehensively at the sun. What to do now left her in a maze. Teddy's next words pointed the way.

"If we can get their horses before those two men wake up, we can be a long way from here before they know we've escaped," he whispered. "You follow me, Nan. Walk awful silent—like an Injun."

She tiptoed after him, trying her level best to walk "like an Injun." They rounded the corner of their late prison. Nan saw another and larger adobe building. One wall had fallen out, a tumbled heap of crude adobe bricks and mud, evidently the result of an earthquake. The place was an abandoned Mexican ranch, Nan realized. Her heart sank. They were somewhere "below the border."

Ted was speaking in a cautious whisper, and pointing, and Nan now saw the two men sprawled on some straw under the sagging porch.

"They're awful sound asleep," whispered the boy. "Hear 'em snore, Nan."

The stertorous breathings, the straw-covered mescal jugs, told the story. Their guards were in a drunken stupor.

"Where are the horses?" she whispered.

Ted pointed. "Over there, in those trees—"

Stealthily they crept past the snoring guards toward the small grove of ancient, gnarled olive trees, where the horses were tethered with rawhide *reatas*, browsing the plentiful dry Autumn grass. They were fast-looking, sturdy animals, Nan was quick to appreciate. Bandits usually were particular about their horses, she reflected.

One was a buckskin with black mane and tail, the smaller animal, a slender-limbed red-bay, not unlike her own fleet Linda Rosa.

Both horses were saddled, a fact that sent the girl's spirits soaring. Throwing on those heavy Mexican saddles would not have been an easy thing to manage. Apparently their guards had been too lazy to unsaddle, or else wished to be ready for hasty flight in the event of pursuit.

Silently she blessed the potent mescal that had made useless their precautions.

"I'll take the buckskin," she decided. "The red horse is more your size, Ted."

They approached the horses cautiously and reached down bridles from saddlehorns.

"Nan!" Ted's guarded voice was jubilant. "Look!

My Winchester twenty-two—and my pistol and holster—" He pointed at a nearby tree.

"One of those guards must be the man who took them from you," decided his sister. "Quick! Get them, Ted!"

While he gleefully recovered his prized weapons and buckled on the holster, Nan hastily bridled the horses. They climbed into the saddles and rode away at a walk. Nan frantically yearned to be a long way from those tumbled-down adobe walls before the guards roused from their drunken sleep.

Soon they were in a deep gully and out of sight of the adobes. Nan wisely decided to halt long enough to adjust their stirrups. The rawhide thongs were stiff, and tight; she could have wept at the delay. There was no alternative. It was not safe to ride fast with those stirrups dangling out of reach.

She tugged feverishly at the stubborn knots. The remaining members of the bandit gang would not be far away, she worried. Ted's surmise of a camp by the side of some stream was correct, she suspected. The men were not aware that she understood Spanish. She had overheard enough to know there had been talk of making camp in some place they called *Arroyo Orso*—Bear Creek.

Nan pulled savagely at the stiff buckskin tie-strings. Her mind was in a whirl. One thing was sure—they must avoid any sort of a stream—for the time being. Any one of the trails she had observed when riding from the little Mexican ranch might lead them to the bandit camp. She shuddered at the thought.

They climbed back into the saddles.

Which way now?

The girl's gaze traveled blankly over the bleak hills. A rough, unfriendly country. Any moment hostile eyes might see them. She recalled that shortly before their arrival at the lonely prison-ranch they had crossed a wide, sandy dry-wash.

"If only we could see something familiar," she bemoaned. "I'm all twisted around, Teddy."

"We gotta ride North," her brother decided. "That way is East—" He gestured at the early-morning sun. "When you know which way is East it's easy to find North."

"Yes, Mr. Boone," she answered meekly. "We can ride North—and be lost for days and days. I want something more local to point at, mister."

"Let's get out of this gully—up on a hill—so we can see the mountain peaks," suggested Ted practically. "Maybe we can spot old San Jacinto. Then we could head awful close to Los Posos."

"Teddy, positively you are marvelous," she applauded gratefully.

"Baldy says when you get lost you gotta locate a landmark," explained the boy. "Baldy says a *hombre's* gotta use common sense and keep his head when he's lost. He says it's *plumb loco* to go fannin' all over nowhere when a *hombre* gits twisted round. He says yuh gotta locate yore bearin's, feller—That's what Baldy told me, Nan."

His sister leaned toward him from her saddle. "You haven't kissed me, this morning, Teddy," she said very gently. "Kiss me, Big Brother!"

"Gee, Nan!" Teddy flushed. "You're awful brave, Nan—" He gulped and obediently kissed her.

They rode slowly out of the gully, following a cattle trail. It was a steep climb, but worth the effort, the girl thankfully realized as she gazed with starry eyes at the snow-tipped mass of San Jacinto etched grandly against the blue sky.

Below them was the wide dry bed of a river—the dry-wash they had crossed the previous night. The way was before them now. A long trail—and beset with perils.

"Come on, Ted," she said softly.

Nan flung a gesture at the fleecy tip of San Jacinto. "Home—is over there—"

XVI
"Good Old Sanctuary"

The strain of the long fruitless hours was visible in Lee's unshaven, haggard face.

It had been a day of bitter disappointments.

Chuck O'Neil and his Diamond D men had spread out toward the Coyotes, lured by a rumor from the reluctant tongue of a frightened Basque sheepherder. The man had spoken vaguely of horsemen riding past his tent during the night toward Coyote Pass.

Old Baldy Bates and Sandy Wallace, with the two Lazy Y boys, were raking the maze of canyons that scored the rugged flanks of San Jacinto. Lee had arranged to meet them at the Springs near the mouth of Lone Palm Canyon.

He was waiting for them now, after a grueling ride over the hog-back and down the almost impassable windings of Andreas Canyon. It had been rough going for the Palomino. The golden horse was tired. Lee watered him carefully, unsaddled and gave him a refreshing rub-down. He replaced the saddle and himself sprawled wearily on the grass that fringed the spring.

The sun dipped below the ridge; deep shadows crawled the steep canyon slopes; a freshening wind blew in from the southwest, rustled the hoary dry fronds that bearded the giant palm tree towering above the willows. A cloud pushed over the shoulder of Santa Rosa, a smoke-gray cloud that seemed to spread even as he watched. There was rain in that cloud.

His gaze went to the narrow portal of the canyon; the vista of desert beyond the high cliffs was still yellow with sunlight. In the canyon itself the gloom was fast deepening. Where he rested in the willows that bowered the spring it was quite dark.

The view beyond the gap was like a brightly illuminated picture, framed by the sheer, black portal cliffs. He continued to gaze, conscious of a heartache. It was out there he had first met Nan Page. The evening of the sandstorm! He knew now that he had loved her from the first. That unforgettable night under the sheltering old mesquite tree! She had been so plucky.

Lee's long, lean frame tensed. A horseman had suddenly appeared in the gold-tinted background of the picture framed by the towering canyon cliffs. A second rider moved into the scene—a third—a fourth.

Baldy Bates, and the three young cowboys, arriving at last!

Almost instantly Lee knew he was mistaken. It was like looking at a stage-setting from a seat in a darkened theater, with the spotlight full on the players. The four riders stood out clear and sharp—he could see them distinctly—and they wore huge high-peaked sombreros.

He continued to watch while the group of horsemen held their pose in the spotlight thrown by the setting sun. They seemed to be arguing, deliberating; and of a sudden two of them were riding straight for the gap. The other two rode on, were lost from view.

Lee got to his feet, stood motionless by the Palomino. The stallion had pricked up his ears, was staring attentively. Lee's hand closed over the velvety nose. A neigh would draw attention he did not want—yet.

The riders became blurred shapes as they merged with the canyon shadows. Lee knew they could not see him, unless they came fairly close to the willows, which it seemed they were likely to do. He loosened his guns.

Their voices reached him, grumbling undertones—in Spanish.

"We are fools—to look here. I do not like this—"

"He will have our ears if we do not find them—" The second speaker's voice was nervous. "I would not for many gold *pesos* be in the boots of Gaspar Sanchez and Pancho Morena for letting them escape. He will feed their hearts to the dogs."

"We waste our time—looking this way," persisted the first man in a surly tone.

"We saw tracks leading into the canyon," argued the other.

"I will go no further," grumbled his companion. He reined his horse.

"At least we will ride as far as those willows," urged the bolder one.

Lee's hand closed over gun-butt.

"I will go no further," repeated the other man crossly. "I have heard of this place. It is accursed—haunted by evil spirits. The ground rumbles and strange lights are seen floating down the slopes." The speaker's voice was panicky. "It is the abode of Tahquitz, the thunder demon. I have heard strange tales! An old Indian—Andreas, he was called—was snatched away from his wigwam with hands of fire. They say his spirit moans when there is no moon and the night is dark. I tell you I will go no further—"

"We saw tracks," maintained his companion stubbornly. "You are a fool, and a coward, to talk about evil spirits."

"The tracks were burro tracks," said his fellow-rider sullenly.

"But we saw them—the girl and the boy—riding fast from the dunes in this direction!" The man's tone was angry. "Of a sudden they vanished—almost before our eyes. They are hiding here. Come, you fool, we will at least search those willows."

"The Devil has taken them—or Tahquitz," muttered the superstitious one.

The words were scarcely out of his mouth when a hideous scream shattered the canyon's quiet, a prolonged raucous bellowing that rolled from cliff to cliff.

It was too much for the frayed nerves of the Mexicans.

With startled yells of "*El Diablo!* Tahquitz!" they spurred frantically from the canyon.

Lee would have laughed, had he the time or the inclination to find amusement in their terror. He knew the canyon was Paloma's favorite browsing ground. The diminutive burro could be amazingly discordant, especially when her brays were caught up and echoed by the tall cliffs. With fears already worked to high pitch by the superstitious talk, their panic was not unnatural. The voice of Tahquitz had spoken—warned them away from the canyon sacred to the tormented soul of old Andreas.

He was in the saddle, hurling the Palomino down the rough trail. He had heard enough to know that the fleeing Mexicans were members of the gang who had carried off Nan and Ted.

By some miracle the captives had made an escape and been trailed to Lone Palm Canyon.

His face as hard as the rock face of the cliff, Lee sped like an arrow through the narrow portal into the sunset glow of the desert.

The Mexicans were drawing rein and shouting incoherently to their companions who were loping toward them. Four more riders suddenly emerged from behind a dense growth of palo verde bushes. Mexicans, Lee saw by their tall hats. Eight of the men he sought were in front of his guns.

His fury urged him to ride at them full tilt. An act of madness, he realized in time. Their conversation had made it clear that Nan and Ted still lived—were free. The girl he loved was somewhere near—would still be in mortal danger if he allowed rashness to rob her of his protection. Ten yards to the right was a great boulder, as big as a house. He swung behind it and dismounted as the horse slid to a halt.

The men already had seen him. Astonishment held them motionless. Their momentary indecision gave Lee the time he needed. Jerking rifle from scabbard he slipped through the chaparral and crouched behind a creosote bush that spread over a split boulder. He knew the horse would remain behind the protecting boulder, safe from gunfire. He dreaded the thought of a chance bullet finding his beloved Buck.

His location was perfect for a sharpshooter. He sighted at the nearest of the bandits—a man on a flea-bitten gray. The rifle cracked. Lee saw the rider pitch from his saddle.

Instantly his companions were off their horses and seeking cover in the thick brush. Lee fired again, at a tall sombrero that showed above a greasewood. The hat jumped from its owner's head.

Lee grinned, ducked from view as a bullet impinged against the face of the huge rock sheltering the Palomino. They had not yet located his position. He fired again—heard a yell of pain.

Enraged curses came from the attacking bandits. Smoke poured from rifles. Lee could hear the vicious spat of lead flattening against the big boulder.

Silence followed the burst of gunfire. Lee suspected the Mexicans were making a stealthy crawl through the brush, working around to the rear of the big boulder they still believed covered him from their rifles. He began to fear for Buck's safety. He fired again at a tall sombrero that showed for an instant with apparently no effect.

From somewhere to his right sounded the roar of a heavy rifle. Baldy's big Sharps buffalo gun. Lee glanced over his shoulder. Four riders rounded the ridge that shouldered down into the desert.

The fast approaching reinforcement proved too much for the bandits. In a minute they were scrambling for saddles—in frantic flight.

Lee went clumping through the brush to the Palomino. Baldy saw him and swerved from the chase after the fleeing Mexicans. Guns popping, Sandy and his two Lazy Y friends tore away in pursuit.

The old cowman's face was heavily grief-marked. Gaunt shoulders sagged wearily; only his eyes belied the stark exhaustion and despair that racked him. They burned with the light of newborn hope.

"Yuh found her, Cary? The gal's up thar in the canyon, huh? Her an' the boy!"

"Haven't seen them yet, Baldy—" Lee's smile was confident. "My guess is they're round here some place—"

The old man seemed to miss the import of Lee's words. The gleam of hope died in the cavernous eyes.

"Yuh ain't seen 'em?" Baldy's voice crackled, the sweating sorrel under him reared against the savage jerk of spade bit. "I'm followin' them devils to hell—"

A gun roared.

The sorrel plunged, turned end for end, and head down and back humped exploded into a frenzy of bucking. A second shot flared from the brush, was answered by a burst of fire from Lee.

A swarthy-faced man rose from behind a grease wood, took a convulsive step and fell on his face. Lee spurred over to him. The man was dead, he saw. Evidently he had been too badly wounded to flee with his fellows—had thought to take one of the gringos with him over the Great Divide.

Lee eyed him with some regret. He would rather have had him alive. There were questions he wanted to ask. He sheathed his smoking gun and looked to see how Baldy was making out with the frightened sorrel.

The old man rode up and stared with a sour grin at the dead man. There was an ugly red welt on the sorrel's rump—from the bullet intended for Baldy.

"That's one of 'em," muttered the veteran. "Tried to pot me' in the back," he grumbled. He scowled. "He's shore pulled trigger for the last time, that *hombre*."

"Makes two of them," corrected Lee. He gestured at a limp body sprawled near a greasewood. "Got him my first shot."

Guns crackled in the distance. Sandy and the Lazy Y men were making a desperate effort to overhaul the fleeing bandits. The chase would prove futile, Lee saw. The Mexicans had the fresher horses.

"What yuh waitin' for?" Baldy's horse reared under the jerk of rein. "I aim to git me some skelps!" He stared at the younger man. Lee's obvious disinclination to join the chase could mean only one thing "Yuh—yuh know whar the gal is hid out—" Baldy's voice was hoarse.

"I can make a good guess," was Lee's mysterious rejoinder.

They rode in silence. If Baldy was puzzled he gave no sign of his emotions as they rode away from the canyon—instead of toward the canyon—the one logical place to look for Nan and Ted. Where else could they have hidden from their pursuers save in the canyon?

Baldy wisely held his peace and presently saw they were pointing directly for a huge mesquite tree. It was a monster of its kind, the biggest he had ever seen. He darted a sly look at his companion. Lee's face was inscrutable. Baldy's gaze swooped back to the big mesquite and suddenly a wide grin spread under drooping grizzled mustaches.

Lee drew rein. "I'm letting you in on a secret," he said. "I want you to keep it a secret, Baldy."

The old man was scrutinizing the mammoth mesquite tree closely. He drew a gusty breath. "I savvy," he muttered. "I savvy the answer—now—doggone yuh, Lee Cary!"

"You've guessed?"

"I shore have guessed, young feller." Baldy chuckled. "Had me buffaloed for a bit. Never would have figgered they was inside that doggone old mesquite." He began to wonder. "How come yuh figgered they was hidin' in thar?"

"It's a secret hang-out of mine," explained Lee. "I took her there—the night of the storm—"

"I savvy." Baldy's voice was deeply admiring. "She remembered the place . . . took cover when she saw them varmints was on the trail, and closin' in on her. Shore plenty smart—that gal!"

Doubt suddenly assailed him as he swung from saddle.

"Yuh ain't knowin' for sartain they're in thar—inside that doggone mesquite," he worried. "It's only yore guess—" He broke off, went clumping hastily through the chaparral.

"Teddy!" he whooped. "Doggone! It's the kid—"

The boy was crawling through a small opening in the branches of the mesquite. With a shrill cry he scampered to meet the overjoyed cowman.

"Hi! Baldy! We got away from 'em! Nan and I got away from the bandits back in the hills—"

"Gosh, sonny . . . shore glad to see yuh!" gasped Baldy. Tears furrowed his dust-grimed leathery face.

Nan stood framed against the mesquite branches. She held out her hands to Lee.

He clasped them tightly.

Her eyes were bright with tears, he saw, and she was dusty and disheveled and saddle-weary—but smiling the same gallant little smile he remembered so well.

Perhaps she read in his look more than he intended to reveal. The color waved into her pale face; her breath quickened.

"Well," she said, "here I am again, mister, back at old Mesquite House!" The tremor in her low voice belied the casual greeting, and she added softly, *"Good old sanctuary!"*

XVII
Around a Camp-Fire

The rain Lee had suspected was in the clouds pushing over Santa Rosa fell with a pleasant hissing sound that added to the cheeriness of the crackling fire of mesquite wood.

Comfort was entirely relative, Nan drowsily reflected. The past torturing twenty hours had tremendously sharpened her appreciation. No food from the hands of the most renowned chef could possibly have tasted quite so delicious as the fried rabbit and bacon, and the flapjacks, prepared by Lee and old Baldy Bates; and no nectar ever brewed for the gods could have been half so wonderful, so refreshing, as the coffee that came out of Lee's battered, smoke-blackened old pot. Even the pallet of straw, covered with Lee's blankets, seemed soft and restful to her saddle-chafed and aching limbs. All the comforts a tired mortal needed—and an overpowering urge to swoon away in blessed sleep. Only one thing lacking—a bath, with oceans of hot steamy water and lathers of soft fragrant soapsuds. She felt as dusty as any desert rat. The tin basin had been so inefficient. Nan wondered sleepily if she dared go outside to some secluded spot in the cactus and let the dripping sky shower the dust from her—restore her to pristine immaculate whiteness.

The thought amused her. She laughed aloud, at which the others eyed her rather hopefully.

"We'd like a chance to laugh, too," drawled Lee.

"Must be good—if you can sit there and laugh, after what you've been through."

Nan was glad she was sitting somewhat back in the shadows; she knew that she was blushing. It was nothing, she hastily assured them.

"Just foolish thoughts," she said. "Something too silly for words—"

Baldy Bates nodded gravely from the far side of the fire. "Folks git that way sometimes, after a close call," he rumbled reminiscently. "Yuh kind of begin to see the funny things an' want to laugh yore head off. Reminds me of the night I had a run-in with a bunch of Comanches up on the Cimarron—"

"Was that the time you lost your scalp, Baldy?" interrupted Nan. Her eyes twinkled at Lee.

"Was aimin' to tell yuh what happened," he complained. "Waal—as I was sayin'—them Comanches—"

"Now Baldy! You must save it until Teddy wakes up," implored the girl. "He'll be *dreadfully* disappointed, to miss one of your stories."

"He makes a right smart listener," chuckled the veteran scout. "Ted—he don't scoff at a good yarn like you does, Miss Nan." He winked at the grinning younger men and subsided.

"The rain sounds so good," sighed the girl. "Think of it! No dust on the trail—tomorrow!"

"You'll see flowers, soon," promised Lee.

"Flowers!" Nan's low voice was ecstatic. "Rain flowers—out here in this desert! That rabbit," she mused dreamily, "was positively delicious—an epicurean delight! And to think that Teddy got it with the first shot he fired from his new Winchester twenty-two! I'll never forget the look on his face when he brought that rabbit to me." Her eyes caressed the boy, sleeping by her side on the pallet. "The brave

heart. I don't think an earthquake would waken him tonight."

"He's shore earned him a good sleep," muttered old Baldy.

"He was so brave—every moment," Nan told them. "You should have seen him crawl through that little window." There was pride in her voice. "He'd been reading about Daniel Boone from some old rifle calendar Jake Kurtz gave him. He was crammed with Daniel Boone lore."

Baldy yawned. "Was never one to think much of the law myself," he drawled.

"I wasn't talking about the law," laughed Nan. "I was talking about Daniel Boone—the famous Kentucky frontiersman and Indian fighter."

Baldy seemed unimpressed. "Huh, yuh mean that ol' Injun scout feller"—he nodded—"shore, I heard of him. He was pretty fair—not so bad. Been plenty *hombres* as smart an' mebbe some better'n him—not to speak no names out loud." He kicked a fresh mesquite knot into the fire and stared reminiscently at the quick leap of crackling flames. "Now like I was tellin' yuh about them Comanches that time down on the Pecos—"

"Thought yuh said it was down on the Cimarron," put in Sandy Wallace from his corner.

Baldy frowned at him. "Who's tellin' this here yarn?" he began belligerently. Nan interrupted him.

"Speaking of Daniel Boone," she hurried on, "there was another old Indian scout Teddy was always quoting."

"Huh?" Baldy eyed her suspiciously.

Nan's eyes danced in the firelight. "Baldy says *yuh gotta* do this and Baldy says *yuh gotta* do that—and *yuh gotta* locate a landmark when *yuh gits lost*. That was Ted's constant refrain."

Her voice sobered. "So after we escaped from the dungeon we climbed to a high ridge—and *did* locate San Jacinto—just the way Baldy would have done."

There was a low chuckle from across the fire. "The boy's shore l'arnin' fast," pronounced the old Indian scout complacently.

"It's time you got some sleep," Lee reminded the girl.

"I've never been so sleepy in all my life," Nan confessed. Her smile went from face to face of the little group of men sitting around the camp-fire. "It's so wonderful, though—to be here—with my friends . . . feeling so safe—" Her voice died away and they sat in silence, listening to the drip of the gently falling rain— the cheerful crackle of the fire, the subdued stamp of hoofs from the horse shelter.

"I'm worried about Teresa and Diego," the girl went on. "They'll be dreadfully upset—wondering—"

"We'll make an early start, before dawn," Lee promised. "No more saddle work until you've had some sleep. The horses are dead on their feet," he added. "We've got to give them a few hours' rest."

"I suppose you are right," she reluctantly agreed.

The three men rose and Baldy Bates jerked a thumb at Sandy Wallace. "Reckon we don't need to look further for that flew cowhand yuh aimed to put on yore payroll, Miss Nan."

Nan smiled at the redheaded cowboy. He was one of the men who had ridden with Hawken to Los Posos that dreadful afternoon, she recalled. Sandy had resented Hawken's treatment of her—had been pleased when Lee had thrashed the burly foreman.

"I'll be glad if you'll join our outfit," she told him warmly. "Can't pay you much yet, Sandy—but perhaps the Bar-2 will be a big outfit, some day."

Sandy flushed, eyed down at the sombrero in his large freckled hands. "Yuh've hired a cowhand, ma'am," he stammered. "You needn't worry none about the pay. I sort of figger the Bar-2's due to be a real outfit—"

"Then it's settled," she declared.

The cowboy grinned and vanished into the darkness.

"Well, ma'am," Baldy's tone was contented, "yuh've hired a good hand. Sandy—he's one top-hand rider." He followed the Bar-2's newest recruit into the black zone beyond the firelight.

"I like him," Nan announced to Lee, who had lingered. "Sandy—I mean—"

"Sandy's a good cowman—and a fighting man from boot-heels up," Lee declared. His next remark startled the girl. "If you change your mind about running a cattle ranch I'll see that he goes back on the Smoke Tree payroll—as foreman."

"Why!" she gasped, "what are you talking about? Of course I'm going to run a cattle ranch! What has happened has not changed my plans. I'm not to be frightened away from Los Posos—if that is what you are hinting."

"I don't mean anything of the kind."

"You've upset me," Nan complained. "I'll not sleep, unless you explain."

"I mean that Los Posos controls one of the few valuable sources of water we have in this part of the country," Lee said. "Los Posos will be too valuable for cattle grazing."

"Valuable for what?" Nan's tone was skeptical. "I'm afraid you dream—*dreams!*"

"Some day you'll see groves of date trees growing in those flats below your ranch house," he prophesied; "and grapefruit, and other things that will surprise you—and thousands of other skeptics."

She tried to cloak her kindling imagination. "Go on," she laughed, "tell me some more bedtime stories."

"I've been investigating the possibilities for over a year," Lee confessed. "I—I want you to have faith in me—"

"I do!" Nan said quickly, touched by the hurt look in his eyes. "Oh, I do have faith in you, Lee! It's just that I—I don't understand—"

"A man has come all the way from London—a famous expert on irrigation and desert development. He's done big work in Egypt—and other places. I asked him to come and verify my own work here in this desert of the Colorado. He is in Coldwater now—at Ma Kelly's."

"I am glad that you—that you dream—dreams," murmured the girl. "Please tell me some more—"

"My grandfather has been bitterly opposed to my mad schemes, he calls them. He accuses me of having no interest in the ranch." Lee's jaw tightened. "The next few days will surprise him—when he sees what happens to the present Smoke Tree outfit." He went on. "There are others who have been interested enough to set spies on me"—Lee's smile was grim—"spies that to date have been unable to carry any satisfactory information to Wirt Stoner."

Nan sat very erect, eyes dark with excitement. "I'm beginning to understand," she exclaimed. "This old mesquite tree is your secret place of refuge—your—your *sanctuary* from schemers and scoffers—"

"Partly that," smiled Lee. "Principally because it makes a convenient camp. Saves me a lot of trouble. Naturally I've taken precautions to keep the place to myself."

"Blessed old sanctuary," murmured the girl. She looked around meditatively, lifted her face, appeared to listen to the pelting rain, or perhaps she was again hearing the wild ravings of the storm from which she had been sheltered by the same aboreal roof.

Her eyes met his look and suddenly she was on her feet, hands reaching impulsively to him.

"I was thinking that but for your *dreams*— you would not have been here that evening—and I"—Nan closed her eyes—"and I would have been out there, under that old Joshua tree, deep under the crawling sands."

They were standing very close to each other, hands clasped, their eyes locked. A heart-quickening, breathless moment was suddenly hastened on its way by the somewhat peevish voice of old Baldy Bates.

"Lee! What's keepin' yuh!"

Their hands fell apart. Lee stooped quickly to the pile of mesquite wood.

"Coming soon as I fix the fire," he hissed. "Don't make so much noise. You'll waken the boy."

His face was flushed when he straightened up and met Nan's demure smile. The color in her own cheeks was not entirely from the leaping flames of the replenished fire. Lee's eyes twinkled at her.

"Baldy will have my scalp if I don't let you get some sleep—"

They laughed softly, and Lee turned abruptly on his heels, became a vague shadow in the darkness beyond the firelight.

Nan watched, a bit breathless—wondering if he would remember that first night when he left her alone by the camp-fire. His voice came, low and lingering.

"*Buenas noches*—Nan—"

Her answer went softly into the darkness. "Good night, Lee, *buenas noches, amigo mio*—"

XVIII
"I'm Dawson"

Lee found Baldy and Sandy in the horse shelter. The old cowman's mind was not easy. He was untying a slicker from his saddle.

"Should be a guard posted," he worried. "We ain't sartain them *El Capitan* coyotes won't be backtrailin' this way."

Lee agreed with him. "I'll stand first watch," he said. "You can take the next two hours and Sandy can finish it out." He started to take down his own slicker.

Baldy demurred. "Sleep don't worry me," he protested. "You young fellers got to have yore sleep. Me—I'm tough as rawhide." He drifted out, dragging on his slicker.

Lee grinned after him, and Sandy said with a chuckle, "One ol' mossyhorn, that *hombre*."

Lee hugged into his slicker. "I'm riding over to the canyon and see how Slim and Willie are making out," he said. "Get some shuteye," he tersely advised the young cowboy. "We'll be riding before dawn." He swung the silver-mounted saddle to the Palomino's back.

Sandy yawned, frankly sleepy, and stretched himself comfortably on the straw, his saddle for a pillow.

"Slim and Willie 'll get some wet out there—riding herd on the broncs," he observed drowsily.

"Won't be the first time they got soaked riding night herd," grinned Lee. "I showed them a little cave where they can have a fire and warm up their coffee." He buckled on gun holsters and led the horse out.

It was a black night, with not a star visible behind the heavy cloud mass. The rain had increased, if anything, Lee observed. He hoped dawn would bring a clear sky for the ride to Los Posos.

He swung into the saddle and peered round for a glimpse of Baldy. He wanted to tell him of his plan to ride to the canyon. The old man might mistake him for an enemy horseman and start his guns blazing if not warned.

Lack of feed for the unexpected number of horses had forced them to send all the animals save the Palomino over to the canyon where there was plenty of grass. Slim Kendall and Willie Sims, the Lazy Y men, had volunteered for the job of riding herd. Two good men, Lee reflected. He would like to see them on the Smoke Tree payroll. The Smoke Tree outfit needed a proper cleaning out. Gil Hawken would be one of the first to go out on his neck, Lee grimly promised himself. He shrewdly suspected that the "cleaning out" he contemplated would result in a lot of new faces in the Smoke Tree outfit.

Baldy drifted into view from out of the darkness.

"That you, Lee?"

He came closer, peered with surprised eyes.

"What's the idee? Whar yuh goin' with the bronc? Thought I told yuh I was takin' the first hitch."

Lee explained briefly. "Be careful you don't take a potshot at me when I come back," he warned.

"Lucky yuh told me," grunted Baldy. "This is one black night. Cain't hardly tell a greasewood from a human in this dark." He gnawed off a chew of tobacco and filled a leathery cheek. "Start singin' a tune when yuh come back this way," he suggested, "then I'll know for shore it's you—an' not some prowlin' varmint." He laughed silently. "Mebbe better give a owl hoot—"

"Like this?" Lee gave an imitation. "That good enough?"

"Couldn't do a owl hoot better myself," admired Baldy. "You hoot three times an' when you hear me answer yuh'll know I ain't pullin' trigger on yuh." He faded into the darkness, his boots from which he had removed spurs making no noise that the hissing rain did not swallow.

Lee rode away slowly. It was impossible to go faster than a walk through the blackness. Fortunately the Palomino's eyes were keener than his. The golden horse moved like a wraith through the chaparral. Lee let the horse have his head. He knew he could trust Buck to make a beeline for the canyon.

His own eyes and ears were on the alert. What he might fail to see, he might hear. And hear something he did—surprisingly enough the hoot of an owl behind him.

He reined the horse, straining ears for a repetition of the agreed signal. Was it Baldy—or his imagination?

Again the mournful note of an owl. Lee answered, waited for a response. It came quickly. Baldy undoubtedly was signaling for him to return to the camp.

Lee swung his horse round and rode back to the big mesquite. Baldy must have discovered something suspicious.

"Thar's somethin' queer back yonder," greeted the veteran ex-scout. He gestured in the direction of sand dunes. "What yuh make of it, Lee? Cain't be a star— not with these clouds—"

"Not a star," muttered the younger man, staring intently. "It's a light, Baldy. A camp-fire! There's a camp over there!"

"El Capitan's gang!" Baldy's voice was grim. "They figger to find us, come mornin'."

"I'm riding over there," decided Lee.

"No yuh ain't," demurred the old man. "Scoutin' is more my line than yore's."

"We've only one horse," Lee said with a chuckle. "Buck won't let you fork him, old-timer. He's a one-man horse. You'll have to stay with the camp—keep watch—"

"The fool luck," growled Baldy. "Shouldn't have sent *all* the broncs over to the canyon."

Another voice joined the conversation. Sandy Wallace, fully dressed and buckling on gun belt.

"What's all the owl talk for?" he wanted to know.

Lee gestured silently at the tiny flicker of light in the distance.

"El Capitan's gang," muttered the cowboy, unconsciously echoing Baldy's opinion.

"I'm riding over there," reiterated Lee. Horse and rider melted into the black night.

"Looks like I don't get me no sleep after all," Sandy Wallace mourned. "Might as well go unroll that ol' slicker if I'm goin' to stand out here in the rain." He vanished into the mesquite tree.

Baldy's grin followed him. He was quite aware that the redheaded puncher's grumbling was shallow pretense. Sandy was thrilled at the prospect of excitement. No sleep for him when there was trouble in the wind.

The veteran's gaze went enviously to the glimmering little point of light in the far distance. He yearned to be riding in that direction by the side of the Palomino. Instead he followed Sandy to the horse shelter and drew the big Sharps buffalo rifle from saddle sheath.

Lee rode for some fifteen minutes and dismounted in a clump of greasewood. He knew that Buck would not stir until his return. He gave the sleek wet shoulder a gentle slap and stole on through the chaparral, hand inside slicker resting on gun-butt.

The steady hiss of the rain was an aid. He felt he could draw fairly close to the light, which he now saw was a small camp-fire—as he had suspected.

Slowly he crawled forward, eyes straining, ears alert. No bandit encampment, he began to realize. He could make out three horses in the foreground, then suddenly, a man, seated on a boulder and carefully nursing the small camp-fire built under an overhang of rock. Another figure lay on a blanket close to the fire.

Lee halted, puzzled eyes intent on the scene. From somewhere to his left came a low guttural voice:

"Quien es!" Who is it!

Lee flattened, eyes raking the brush for the speaker. Again the harsh challenge sabered the black night.

"Quien es!"

Lee was searching his memory furiously. Where had he heard that voice before? There was something familiar in that fierce, guttural intonation. He had heard it before—and recently.

He continued to hug the wet earth; the slightest stir might draw a bullet. The man must have the ears of a lynx, to have sensed his stealthy approach.

A minute passed, with Lee probing the baffling darkness. Only the beating of his own heart—the rain, hissing into the thirsty ground. He wished the man would make some move. He had the uneasy suspicion that he was being stalked by a past-master. Again he racked his memory for some clue to the unseen one's identity.

His gaze went back to the little camp-fire. The man was on his feet—was peering into the darkness beyond the firelight. There was a gun in his hand. But it was not the man that riveted Lee's amazed eyes. Even at that distance he knew he had never before seen him. It was the slight boyish figure, half lifted from the blankets close to the fire that told him the astonishing truth, solved the mystery of the harsh, challenging voice.

With an effort Lee stifled the impulse to cry out. He would need time to establish his own identity. He knew now to the full his real jeopardy. "Death in the Dark" was what Sandy Wallace had called the savage Yaqui. The man stalking him in the chaparral was Fidel—the knife-wielding bodyguard of Ramon Avilla's beautiful sister.

Lee's nerves were good; he was accustomed to face danger with coolness; but the thought of the Yaqui's great knife turned him cold. He had seen what Fidel could do with that blade. The man was a jungle cat. He could see in the dark.

Something moved under his tense fingers—a smooth stone, he realized. In an instant he was on his feet, the stone hurtling through the air far behind him. He heard the impact of it against a stubborn shrub—the quick rush of the Indian toward his fancied victim. Lee went charging toward the camp-fire.

"Juanita!" He called the girl's name as he ran. "It's Lee Cary! Your friend!"

The tall stranger's gun went up, spouted red fire into the air as the girl struck at his hand. The next moment Lee was inside the zone of firelight.

Still clinging to the man's wrist, Juanita turned a frightened face.

"Senor!" she gasped. "*It is you!*" Her hand dropped from the stranger's arm, went to her heart. "*Madre de Dios!* You were so—so close to death, *amigo!*"

The Yaqui came up with tiger-like leaps, knife glinting in the firelight. Juanita's sharp word brought him to an abrupt standstill.

"It is the Senor Lee Cary! Put your knife away! He is my friend!"

There was a startled ejaculation from the tall man with the gun.

"Did you say *Cary*, Senorita?"

"*Si*, Senor—"

The stranger gave Lee an astonished smile. He was an elderly man, with a rugged, well-tanned face and thick grizzled hair.

"Most extraordinary!"

He held out a welcoming hand.

"I'm Dawson—"

XIX
Two Girls

Nan and Juanita were at late breakfast in the little patio when Lee and his English friend arrived, on their way to the upper reaches of the canyon back of the ranch house, Lee rather vaguely explained. His companion frankly declared that he had persuaded Lee to bring him for the express purpose of inquiring after Senorita Avilla.

The night of exposure to the rainstorm had left Juanita a very sick girl, quite unable to return to her own home in Mexico. Nan had insisted that she stay at Los Posos, where she could have old Teresa's careful attention. The Yaqui had returned to Rancho San Juan with the news of her illness.

"You must take coffee with us," Nan urged. "It's a celebration. This is Juanita's first morning up for breakfast."

"She has been so good to me," smiled the dark-eyed girl. "See—it is one of her best frocks I am wearing!"

The girl was distractingly lovely in the filmy pink dress. Nan herself was in the faded overalls and flannel shirt and boots she had worn the day of her first meeting with Lee. She planned to ride down into the flats, where Baldy Bates and Sandy were stretching the new barbed-wire around the field intended to hold the prospective nucleus of the Bar-2 herd.

She was not to be weaned from her purpose by Lee's talk of flourishing orchards covering Los Posos flats, she told him. She was not interested in growing cotton and her imagination was not vivid enough to picture groves of date and fig trees.

"I'd be a white-haired old lady before I could pick dates and figs from my trees," she declared. "Wouldn't I, Sir Christopher?" she appealed.

The Englishman's eyes twinkled. "It would require patience," he admitted.

Nan liked his rugged, sunburned face, his quiet dignity.

"I'm not a bit patient," she laughed. "I want action for my money!"

"You'll get action enough in the cattle business—and trouble," Lee drawled.

Nan scorned him. She had come West to go into the cattle business, she reminded. She wouldn't for the world disappoint Ted. He had set his heart upon being a cattle king.

"You can be in the cattle business and grow dates, too," argued Lee. "There's plenty of land only good for grazing." His smile was quizzical. "Don't forget that it takes money to start a cattle ranch—buy cows."

"I have enough to pick up a few cows," she informed him. "Sandy knows where I can get a hundred or so young stock—cheap."

The two men rode on their way. Nan declared it was time she attended to "ranch duties."

"I shall soon be leaving you," Juanita regretted. "My brother will be coming for me any day. He will be cured of his wounds by now."

"I'm going to miss you dreadfully," mourned Nan. "I like having you here, Juanita, I never had a sister."

"Nor I," murmured the Mexican girl. "I would have died, I think, if you had not brought me here to the care of your good Teresa." She smiled affectionately at the old nurse who was helping the white-haired Diego remove the breakfast dishes.

"We've both been through enough to last all our lives." Nan pulled the black sombrero over her thick tawny hair.

"Those terrible *bandidos!*" Juanita shuddered.

"Why *El Capitan's* men should run off with Ted and me is more than I can understand," puzzled Nan. "They seemed to know what they wanted—those men. It's all too mysterious! I can't imagine how they knew Ted and I were in the hotel."

"*El Capitan's* spies keep him informed," Juanita suggested. "He thought to hold you for ransom."

"I suppose there's no other answer." Nan reached for her spurs. "Poor pickings for bandits—that's all I can say." She buckled on a spur. "From the look of Lee Cary's eyes I've an idea that Senor *El Capitan* has not heard the last of his little scheme."

"*Un caballero grande, el Senor Cary,*" murmured the Mexican girl.

"I believe you've fallen in love with him!" Nan bent down with the second spur. "Lee *is* nice—and fine, Juanita."

"*Si*—a great gentleman," repeated the dark-haired girl in a low voice. "But it is—*you*—he loves, *amiga mia*—"

"*Juanita!*"

"It is true! His eyes betray him when he looks at you." Juanita nodded. "He loves you greatly."

"I—I think you positively are absurd," declared Nan. "You're making me blush like—like a—"

"—like a girl in love," smiled Juanita. "Kiss me, Nan. I am so happy for you—*both*."

They clung to each other, and Nan, breathless, suddenly shy, ran from the patio. Juanita watched her with a curious wistfulness.

Nan's lightly uttered accusation had been perilously near the mark. Juanita was honest with herself. She knew she easily could have loved Lee Cary. She had been attracted at the time of their first meeting—the night Sandy Wallace had brought him to her.

She had said *adios* and ridden away, not expecting ever to see Lee again—and ridden straight into the hands of *El Capitan's* men.

Don Avilla's daughter was a valuable prize. The bandits knew she would bring large ransom money and three men were detailed to conduct the prisoners to *El Capitan's* stronghold. They would have slain the Yaqui on the spot. Juanita's pleadings, her promise to pay ransom for him, had saved Fidel's life.

Too many pulls at the mescal bottle as they rode made the guards sleepy; *a siesta* was inevitable. Hours slipped away, the bandits snoring—the prisoners helpless. Juanita would never forget the anguish of those hours, lying there under the scorching sun, cruel rawhide thongs biting into tender flesh.

And then the big Englishman . . . the blazing guns—three dead lawless men!

Darkness—and the rain! Her collapse . . . the make-shift camp—and then from out of the black, rain-swept night, the voice of Lee Cary—calling her name.

Juanita's hand went to her heart. The memory of that miraculous moment would never leave her. She would *always* have a prayer for the happiness of Lee Cary.

XX
Jim Cary

Ted rode into the yard while his sister led the red mare from the barn. Nan eyed his horse critically, the trim little bay confiscated when they escaped from the bandits.

"Might be Linda Rosa's twin brother," she observed as she swung into her saddle.

"Sandy says he'll make a dandy cow-horse," enthused the boy. "I like him a lot better than old Pinto. I've named him Rubio."

"Rubio?"

"It's Spanish . . . means red. Lee said so. Like Linda Rosa means *lovely rose*."

"*Si, si*, Senor!" Nan smiled. "Well, mister—let's ride Rubio and Linda Rosa down to the flats and take a look at the new fence."

"I've just come from there," Ted said. "I'm helping string the wire. Baldy sent me for some more staples. He says I swing a hammer 'most good as a man."

"All right, get your staples. I'll wait."

Ted climbed from his saddle and scampered to the tool-shed. Nan's gaze went to the lofty peak of Old Chimney lifting into the cloudless blue sky. Lee and the Englishman had ridden in that direction on some mysterious mission. Lee had been rather vague about it, she reflected. Probably something to do with water.

Her gaze idled on across the rugged flank of Los Posos canyon to the higher ridge beyond. Queer—that dust drifting over Coyote Canyon. Nan straightened up in her saddle. There was no wind—at least not enough to stir up so much dust. It lifted lazily, a long, trailing dun plume.

Teddy hurried back with the staples.

"What do you make of that dust, Ted?"

"It's a tornado," pronounced the boy.

His sister shook her head. "No. Not a tornado—and not a sandstorm. There's no wind blowing."

"Nan!" Ted's voice was apprehensive. "Look! Those men—"

They were riding through the gate Ted had left unclosed, three strangers.

Nan's eyes dilated. She guessed instantly the identity of the tall old man on the Palomino stallion. That haughty Cary face!

He was like an arrogant old eagle—swooping down on her. She heard herself speaking quietly.

"Don't be frightened, Ted. I—I think it is Mr. Cary, Lee's grandfather."

The golden stallion approached with mincing steps and proudly arched satiny neck. Behind the lord of the Smoke Tree rode two alert-eyed cowboys. Both men were heavily armed, Nan noticed.

She grew conscious of a curious deep-toned intermittent roar, like the thunder of distant seas. She was not imagining things. Teddy's startled face told her that he too was hearing what she heard.

"Nan!" The boy's voice was shaky. "That funny noise—"

Jim Cary reined his horse, keen eagle eyes absorbed her from head to foot.

"I suppose you are the Page girl?" His tone was mild.

"I am Nan Page," she admitted quietly.

"I'm Cary—of the Smoke Tree."

"I think I have met your foreman, Gil Hawken,"

Nan retorted. "I told him not to come back." She was resolved not to show fear in front of this arrogant old despot.

His short snowy beard twitched. "Gil Hawken is no longer foreman of the Smoke Tree." He gave Ted a penetrating look. "The boy is your brother?"

Teddy spoke up bravely. "I'm Ted Page. We own Los Posos and are going to raise cattle. Our iron's the Bar-2."

The gleam in the frosty eyes struck Nan as sardonic. Anger welled within her; the color mounted to her cheeks; her eyes sparkled.

"May I inquire the reason for your visit?" she asked in a cold voice.

He stared at her for a moment. "I've been hearing about you from my grandson," he said abruptly.

Nan waited for him to continue. The curious deep-toned muttering was growing more distinct. She turned startled eyes toward the trailing dust banner.

Cattle! That noise was the bellowing of cattle—a trail-herd!

Dumbfounded, and frightened, now, she looked at old Jim Cary.

He was smiling oddly. "I heard how you stood off Gil Hawken," he said. "Lee told me. You are a brave young woman."

Nan found her voice. "Those cattle! What does it mean, Mr. Cary?"

He ignored the question. Instead, he smiled at the wide-eyed Ted. "So the Bar-2's your iron, young man?"

"Yes, sir." Teddy's tone was defiant. "It stands for Nan and me."

"Got any cows, yet?"

"No, sir. Sandy Wallace knows where we can get some young stock cheap."

The old cattleman's shaggy brows beetled. "Been hiring one of my best men away from the Smoke Tree, I see." Again the snowy beard twitched. "I'll have to keep a sharp eye on your Bar-2 outfit."

The two cowboys exchanged grins. Nan crimsoned.

"If you think you can make fun of us—or frighten us—you are mistaken." She kept her voice steady. "We're here to *stay*, Mr. Cary."

He nodded. "Lee told me you weren't easily frightened," he said, half to himself

Nan again gestured at the trailing dust. "I asked you about those cattle. They're being driven onto Los Posos range—" Her breath was coming fast. "Is that your Smoke Tree outfit?"

Again the cowboys exchanged covert grins. Jim Cary looked for a moment at the dust billowing over the ridge.

"My Smoke Tree outfit," he admitted dryly. "Those cattle are going where they belong, young woman. I've run cattle on that range ever since Bill Page disappeared."

"I won't allow it," flared the girl. "You shan't!" She faced him with clenched hands. "I'll—I'll fight you to the last!" she panted. "You'll not run Smoke Tree cattle on our range!"

"Nan!" Teddy's voice was shrill with excitement. "Baldy and Sandy are coming on the jump!" He gave the old cattleman a defiant look. "It's our outfit, Mr. Cary, and coming fast. You'd best turn that herd before there's plenty trouble. The Bar-2 outfit's shore salty."

There was no mistaking the amusement in the old cattle king's eyes; a laugh rose deep in his throat. "That's cowboy talk, mister." He chuckled, rocked in the big saddle. "You're a salty young man yourself, I see."

Baldy Bates and Sandy tore into the yard. The young redheaded cowboy goggled at the Palomino's rider; his jaw sagged. Jim Cary jerked him a nod.

"Hello, Sandy. Hired out with my new neighbors, eh?"

"Yes, sir, Mr. Cary." Sandy's face was red.

Old Baldy leaned forward from the speedy buckskin he rode—the same horse Nan had appropriated from the bandits.

"What's the idee of them cows bein' shoved onto Bar-2 range?" Voice and eyes were belligerent. "I'm foreman of the Bar-2 an' I shore crave to know 'bout them cows!"

Jim Cary was smiling broadly now. It was a kindly, friendly smile, Nan saw with growing bewilderment. Not the smile of a ruthless man come to declare war on her. Baldy glared at him.

"I got hair-trigger fingers," he proclaimed loudly. "Was born that way. I'm awful short on patience."

For some reason Nan made haste to intervene. She was bewildered—completely at sea—but conscious of an odd thrill of hope.

"You are speaking to Mr. Cary of the Smoke Tree," she broke in. "Lee's grandfather, Baldy."

"Huh!" Baldy's tone was perplexed. He glowered at the dust drifting over the ridge. "Waal, what's the answer?" he wanted to know. "Are yuh lettin' them cows go on Bar-2 range, Miss Nan? I'm only yore foreman."

"Those cows are going where they belong," Jim Cary said mildly. "They are Bar-2 cows, you see—or will be when you put your iron on them."

No one spoke for a moment. The bawling herd was pouring round the ridge and spreading over the flats below. Nan's look went to the tall old man on the golden stallion.

"I—I'm afraid I don't *understand*—" She tried to speak calmly. "I don't understand," she repeated more firmly.

The fierce eagle look had left Jim Cary's face. The smile he gave her was curiously gentle—benign.

"Your great-uncle, Bill Page, was my friend—" He spoke slowly. "He was a good man . . . would have made a good neighbor. I was glad to have him on Los Posos. I think," he added, "that I'll get down from my saddle. Hurt my leg some weeks ago. Gets a bit stiff—riding." He swung to the ground. "Get off your mare, girl. We'll sit on this log here while we talk—"

Nan meekly obeyed. She was glad to sit down. There was a trembly feeling in her legs.

"You, too, Ted. Sit here on the other side of me." Lee's grandfather chuckled. "Salty outfit—the Bar-2, eh?" His glance went to the buckskin's wondering rider. "So you're Baldy Bates, eh?"

"Never wore no other name," grinned the Bar-2 foreman.

"Heard of you lots of times," declared Jim Cary amiably. "You used to be with the old Circle C—down in the Panhandle."

"Was trail-boss," admitted Baldy. His grin widened.

"I told you Baldy was famous, Nan!" cried the delighted Ted. "He's awful famous, Mr. Cary. He's taken thousands and thousands of cattle up the old Chisholm Trail and hunted buffaloes and been scalped by Indians. That's why he never takes his hat off."

"Now look here, sonny," Baldy reddened, "thought I put yuh right 'bout that scalpin' bus'ness—"

"I forgot," apologized Ted reluctantly. He hated to surrender the legend of Baldy's scalp. "It was Brazos got scalped."

Jim Cary smiled. "I think Baldy and you and I are going to be good friends," he predicted.

The bawling from the harried trail-herd was subsiding as the cattle spread over the thickly grassed flats and slaked thirsts at the little creek flowing down from the springs. Nan sat in a daze, scarcely taking in the conversation. She was dreaming, she told herself. This kindly old man was not the feared tycoon of the vast Smoke Tree range. Those widening columns of cattle down there were not real.

Suspicion lifted a disturbing head—leered at her. Nan stiffened; Lee Cary had done this thing! Her cheeks grew hot. Lee was responsible! She looked at the old man by her side.

"Is—is this your grandson's—doings?" She flung the question at him hysterically.

Jim Cary shook his head. "Lee knows nothing about those cattle down there," he assured her. "Those cattle belong to the heirs of Bill Page, which means they belong to you and this salty brother of yours." He smiled down at the wide-eyed boy. "Nothing mysterious about the matter, when you know the facts."

"It's the most mysterious thing I ever heard of," Nan asserted. "I—I must be going quite mad!"

Jim Cary's eyes twinkled "Not when you understand. As I said, those cattle belong to the heirs of Bill Page. A few words will make it clear to you. Some days before his disappearance, your great-uncle bought some breeding stock from me. They were never delivered. Bill Page had vanished. Those cattle down in the flats represent the natural increase during a period of some twenty years."

Nan stared down into the flats. The stretch of meadow was teeming with cattle. The thing was preposterous—beyond her powers of imagination.

"There are hundreds—and hundreds of them," she marveled.

"Sixteen hundred and fifty," conceded Jim Cary placidly, "not including young calves. We don't tally calves till next roundup." He smiled at Ted. "Lot of work for your ranch-crew—slapping the Bar-2 iron on those cows."

Teddy was too awed for speech. He continued to gaze rapturously at his new friend. Baldy Bates spoke for him.

"Means more hands on the payroll, Miss Nan," he said contentedly.

"The *natural* increase, understand," emphasized Lee's amazing grandfather. "Of course I had to sell off from year to year as the steers matured to market age. Anything in that herd down there over three years old will be breeding cows." He looked at Baldy Bates. "You'll find around two hundred prime steers—three-year-olds—in that bunch, ready for market any time. I'd hold them for Fall, though. Get a better price."

Nan found her tongue. "How many cows did Uncle William buy from you?" she queried in a weak voice.

"Oh—couple of hundred—"

"Then how can you turn such a big herd over to us?" she puzzled. "You say you had to sell off from year to year."

"Natural increase," Jim Cary reminded. "I sold only beef critters. Never sold good cows. Every season found more cows having calves. Mathematical progression." He chuckled. "Don't worry, girl. I've kept strict tab. Every animal that came from the original herd Bill Page bought from me is ear-notched—a swallow-tail in the left ear. All of 'em wear the Smoke Tree brand, but that special ear-notch marks them for Bill Page cows."

"One white cattleman," muttered Baldy Bates.

"There have been losses, of course," Jim Cary went on briskly. "Droughts—some rustling. Kept strict account. I'm not giving you a cow that doesn't belong to the heirs of Bill Page."

"But the feed—these years," worried the girl.

"Since your uncle's disappearance all this country has been Smoke Tree range. If anything, I owe you money for running my own cattle on Los Posos. We can call it all square between us. I looked after Bill's cows—kept nesters and such out of Los Posos—"

"Of course," Nan flushed, "I didn't mean you could possibly owe us—"

"I've had the use of Los Posos. If anything—I'm ahead—" Jim Cary fumbled in a pocket, drew out a slip of blue paper. "I told you I've sold beef steers as they matured. Less operating costs I've deducted, the sales for the last twenty years total quite a tidy sum for your back account."

Nan stared at the slip of blue paper he put into her hand. It was a check for thirty-three thousand dollars.

Her eyes misted. "It's not true," she said a bit wildly. "I—I can't bear any more, Mr. Cary!" She was suddenly weeping against his rough coat-sleeve. "I've been thinking such mean things about you," she sobbed.

"I'm used to having mean things said about me," Jim Cary told her gruffly. "What I'm not used to, are tears—like your tears." He cleared his throat. "When are you coming over to see me, young fellow? Got a colt you'd like." He gestured at the golden stallion. "Son of El Rey, here."

"Gee, Mr. Cary!" Ted wriggled ecstatically. "A real Palomino colt!"

"Coming on two years old—and the spitting image of old El Rey."

Teddy eyed the stallion critically. "El Rey is the spittin' image of Lee's Buck, Mr. Cary," he declared.

"Buck is a son of El Rey, too," the old cattle king informed him. "All El Rey's colts look like him." Mr. Cary smiled down at the girl drying her eyes on his coat-sleeve. "Smoke Tree Palominos go back to Lee's great-grandfather, Don Felipe Torres. Finest Palominos in the country."

"I'm ashamed of myself," she whispered contritely, "crying like a child—" She straightened up, saw with relief that the two Smoke Tree men and Baldy and Sandy were tactfully gazing down into the valley, apparently enormously interested in the trail-herd. Her smile came. They were gentlemen—these hardy riders of the cattle ranges. Uncouth, illiterate, some of them, but always real men. Teddy was eyeing the golden stallion doubtfully. "I don't know about that Palomino colt, Mr. Cary," he worried. "I've already got old Pinto—and Rubio. Pinto isn't so much—but Rubio is a good horse, Mr. Cary. Sandy says he'll make a top-hand cow horse."

Mr. Cary eyed the trim red bay approvingly. "A right good horse, Teddy. Rubio should make a mighty fine cow horse." He shook his head doubtfully. "A cowman can't get along with only two broncs, Ted. You've got to build up a string. This El Rey colt can be your Sunday-go-to-meeting horse."

Teddy admitted he was impressed by the argument. "I'll build up a dandy string," he declared. "A cattle king's got to ride good horses."

"I see that you and I are going to have some good times," predicted the boss of the Smoke Tree. "We talk the same language." He chuckled. "Maybe I can give you some tips about this cattle king business."

Nan said a bit timidly, "I want to ask you about my uncle—"

Baldy's voice interrupted her.

"I'm askin' yuh about that snake-eyed foreman of yore's—name of Gil Hawken."

Baldy's eyes looked like cold gray slate against the slant of the morning sun.

"I'm riding down thar to the flats. If I meet that coyote—it means gun-play—"

"You won't find Gil Hawken down there with the herd, Baldy. I fired him last week—or I should say Lee fired him." Mr. Cary's smile was a bit grim.

"How about that feller, Slinger Cole?"

"Fired him myself, weeks ago. A lot of new faces in the Smoke Tree outfit," Jim Cary said.

"That's all I want to know." Baldy looked at Nan. "I'm riding down there to take delivery of them cows."

"I'll help you, Baldy!" Ted climbed to his saddle.

"We'll start brandin' quick as I can round up some new hands," Baldy went on. "Sandy's fannin' it to town. He aims to git Willie Sims and Slim Kendall on the Bar-2 payroll."

"In the meantime my boys will give you a lift," Jim Cary promised. "Andy Drew is foreman now. Lee hired him away from the Diamond D to replace Hawken. Didn't *really* hire Drew. Got the loan of him from Tim Hook—till Lee found a good man." Mr. Cary waved Baldy away. "You tell Andy I said for him and the boys to stay on the job long as you want 'em."

"I'll say it's shore white of you, Mr. Cary." The Bar-2 foreman grinned cheerfully at Nan and rode away with Ted and Sandy. The two Smoke Tree men made no move to follow.

Lee's grandfather noticed Nan's surprised glance at them. His beard twitched with his silent laughter.

"More of Lee's work," he chuckled.

"Lee seems to have been very busy these past few day." There was a wondering note in the girl's voice.

"He's the real boss of the Smoke Tree these times," Mr. Cary beetled shaggy brows at the lounging cowboys. "Lee's orders. He won't let me leave the house without a couple of his picked men tagging at my heels."

He gave Nan a brief account of the plot revealed by Juanita Avilla.

"Lee went through the outfit with a fine comb . . . threw Hawken out on his neck—and a half score of his gunmen with him." The cattle baron chuckled. "Lee is on the prod—these days. I've been misjudging him, and what I thought were his fool notions. That Englishman he brought to the house has given me something to think about."

"Oh, I'm so glad, Mr. Cary!"

He eyed her shrewdly. "He has talked to you about his plans—his schemes to make the desert bloom?"

"Enough to give me a faint idea," Nan confided. She hesitated. "I—I want to know about my Uncle William—his disappearance—"

Mr. Cary extracted a long, thin cigar from a leather case. "Mysterious angles to that affair," he said. "Lee is convinced that your—your adventure with *El Capitan's* outlaws the other night is an outgrowth of a crime committed many years ago."

"You mean my Uncle William's disappearance?"

"I mean his murder." The fierce eagle look was back in Jim Cary's eyes. "Bill Page was murdered. I've suspected a certain man for years. No real proof . . . not enough to count in a law court."

Nan's face was pale. She had never personally known her grandfather's adventurous younger brother, but the thought of his death at the hands of an assassin appalled her.

"I let the fellow know my suspicions," Jim Cary continued. "I warned him that if he attempted to possess Los Posos he would dance on air with a Smoke Tree rope squeezing his neck." The old lord of Smoke Tree Range nodded grimly. "He knew I'd keep that promise—which leads up to the rather singular events of the past two weeks."

"I'm all confused," Nan confessed. "The affair seems to involve all of us—"

"Hawken was too anxious to run you off the place," Mr. Cary went on. "If he had told me the names of the squatters on Los Posos I'd have known who you were. It was from Hawken that Wirt Stoner must have learned about you." Jim Cary's tone was grim "And Wirt Stoner is the man I suspect guilty of the murder of Bill Page."

The revelation drew a startled exclamation from the girl.

"Mr. Cary! It's as clear as daylight! Wirt Stoner is responsible for what happened to Ted and me—that night! I've always thought it so strange those men knew we were in the hotel. Nobody else in the place was harmed." She sat up, eyes dark with excitement. "It was Mr. Stoner who insisted we stay there. He even arranged for our rooms."

"Lee and I think the same way." Jim Cary's eyes were bleak. "When Stoner learned about you from Hawken he planned to get rid of you, which leads to another phase of the mystery. Stoner knew that as long as I lived he would not dare possess Los Posos, which he covets because of the valuable springs. So he arranged with *El Capitan* to have Lee and myself murdered."

"It's ghastly!" Nan shuddered. "He's like a dreadful spider—spinning a web of death—"

"Juanita Avilla warned Lee at the risk of her life," continued the old cattleman. "It seems that Lee saved her brother some time or other. She told him that *El Capitan* had sent three men to do the job. One of the chosen killers we know to be dead—knifed by the Mexican girl's Yaqui servant. The others are still loose, which explains my bodyguard." Mr. Cary heaved a sigh. "As if I'm not able to take care of myself," he grumbled.

"This *El Capitan*," mused the girl. "Wirt Stoner must be very close to him—"

"The man is a mystery we've got to solve," growled Jim Cary. "I've lost over three hundred head of beef steers to him the last year or two. The Lazy Y and Tim Hook's Diamond D are in the same boat."

"Wirt Stoner could tell you all about *El Capitan*—if you make him," suggested Nan thoughtfully. "Don't you agree, Mr. Cary?" Her eyes were oddly bright. "Wirt Stoner must be *forced* to tell all he knows," she declared.

"Lee is working now on that angle of the confounded thing," Jim Cary told her with a grim smile. He got up from the log. "What do you say to riding down to the flats for a look at your Bar-2 cows—"

Side by side they rode down the trail; and despite the mystery of intrigue and death, Nan found her spirits soaring. She had a new friend in the grandfather of the man she loved. The ogre of Smoke Tree Range had proved a myth. Life was opening, more beautiful than her dreams.

Clattering hoofs behind, chilled her glow of content. Those two wary-eyed cowboys following so closely were grim warning that death still stalked the road to happiness.

XXI
Terror

"I'm the hardest-worked law-officer in ten counties," bemoaned Sheriff Day, over his glass of sarsaparilla. "Too much ground to cover. Wore out six broncs in three days."

"Need somethin' stronger than sarsaparilla." The drink dispenser winked at Wirt Stoner leaning against the bar. "Ain't that right, boss?"

"No, Joey!" The wiry little sheriff was firm. "I gotta keep off the hard stuff—the way I'm on the move these days—and nights." He chuckled. "Not that I'm disparaging the quality of your whisky, Joey. Wirt wouldn't sell bad whisky to his sheriff—would you Wirt?"

"It's always the best in the house for you, Sheriff." The saloon man smiled sleepily. He disliked being up so early in the morning. It was usually long after midnight before he got to bed. "You should get one of these newfangled horseless buggies," he advised.

"Not for me," scoffed the sheriff. "Get out in the middle of the desert in one of them things—and break down. Seen too many of these automobiles being dragged home at' the tail-end of a wagon." He drained his glass. "When I get too old to fork a bronc it's time I quit the sheriff business."

"All wore out chasin' this *El Capitan* jasper!" The barman grinned, mopped the wet rim left by his customer's glass. "Wore down to a shadder—that's what you are. Even the buzzards won't take a look at you—soon."

The sheriff grinned. "You're a liar," he said pleasantly, and turned to Stoner. "Heard any more rumors, Wirt? That last lead you gave me didn't pan out," he added sourly.

The saloon man shrugged well-groomed shoulders. "I'm beginning to think there's no such animal as the *Senor El Capitan*," he drawled.

"You're wrong!" Sheriff Day scowled. "That raid on the hotel the other night was no happen-so. I've talked with the Page girl. She told me she heard the bandits mention *El Capitan* several times. She savvys Spanish. Didn't overhear enough to give me any real information, worse luck."

"Mebbe *El Capitan* ain't his real name," offered Joey, trying to be helpful. He slapped at a buzzing fly with his damp cloth. "Those fellers shore fixed poor old Meeker, that night." The barman chuckled. "You'd laugh to hear old Pete Smith rave about the way them *hombres* hog-tied him in his own stable. He's still spittin' straw."

"It's a well-organized gang," Sheriff Day asserted. "Whoever *El Capitan* is—he's got the brains of a fox!" He frowned thoughtfully. "Young Slim Kendall said something to me awhile back—the night you had the gun-play here, Wirt. He said sometimes you go looking for a stray all over the range and then find the critter feeding in the home pasture." Sheriff Day nodded. "Kind of stuck in my craw."

Joey sneered audibly. "That kid! Trying to tell you how to catch *El Capitan*! That shore calls for a drink on the house." He slid the sarsaparilla bottle forward and poured himself a drink of whisky.

Wirt Stoner was more impressed.

"I'd say there was something in the kid's idea," he argued. "Perhaps you *are* hunting too far afield, Sheriff."

"Wirt!" The harassed little sheriff gulped his sarsaparilla and banged his glass down. "If you got any notion—spit her out. I ain't despisin' no crumbs that fall from the table—"

"You'd rise up on your hind legs if I told you what was in my mind." Stoner seemed reluctant to continue the topic.

"Spit her out!" insisted the law officer. "It's an order, Wirt. It's every citizen's sworn duty to aid an officer—no matter where the chips fall."

"It's a crazy idea," demurred the gambler uneasily. He shook his head. "Drop it, Day. Sorry I spoke."

"Like thunder I'll drop it!" rasped the sheriff. He was like a hound, suddenly scenting the blood-trail. "Talk up, Wirt—if you don't want to see the inside of a jail for refusing to give information to the law."

Stoner made a gesture of surrender.

"I got to thinking about young Cary—the way he disappears for days at a time. Didn't it ever strike you as queer, the way he goes off—nobody knows where?"

Sheriff Day's terrier jaw sagged.

"Lee Cary!"

His eyes narrowed. "Listen, Wirt! Don't you say things to me about Lee Cary you can't back up with plenty proof!"

"I've said all I intend to say," Stoner's voice was angry. "You can take the idea for what it's worth." The saloon man swore. "Knew you'd say I'm crazy!"

"I'll say you're crazy!" exploded the sheriff. He jerked a nod at the goggling Joey and stalked into the street.

Stoner's gaze roved speculatively over the array of bottles.

"I'm breaking my rule," he grumbled to the barman. "Mix me a double shot, Joey." His smile was not pleasant to see. "Give that fool sheriff a warm tip—and what happens?"

Joey wisely held his tongue. The boss was always irritable when he got out of bed too early.

Stoner lifted the glass. "You saw how he took it, Joey. Went hog-wild—told me I'm loony." He sneered. "The Cary's can do no wrong!"

Stoner swallowed his drink and slid the glass into Joey's practiced fingers.

"To hell with the Carys!" he snarled. "The Cary throne is tottering!"

The barman rinsed and polished the glass. There was a frightened look in his bulging pale eyes. He had never seen his boss so angry.

Sheriff Day's boots rapped sharply down the board sidewalk; dust and splinters flew from scuffed high heels. The sheriff was more disturbed than he had cared to admit to Wirt Stoner. He fervently hoped that Pete Smith would have a decent horse ready for a fast ride.

The aged proprietor was sun-dozing in a rickety chair tilted against the opened barn door. He eyed up resentfully at the skinny little man who was so rudely shaking him awake.

"Take your paws off me," he shrilled. "Give me a bad dream, yuh did. Dreamed a smelly buzzard was clawin' my bones!"

The sheriff wrinkled his nose.

"Don't you ever do some cleanin' round this barn of yours? Smells like a nest of skunks!"

The insult brought Pete Smith wide awake; chair legs thudded to straw-littered ground, he bounced up—shook a gnarled fist at his accuser.

"Yuh dang-gasted ol' liar!" he yelled. "Ain't no cleaner feed barn in ten thousand miles than the O.K.—"

The law officer grinned; he had learned how to make the old livery proprietor sit up and take notice. Pete was inordinately vain of his O.K. Livery & Feed Stables.

"I want a good horse, Pete," he hastened to explain. "Sheriff business," he added laconically.

The livery man was still inclined to be belligerent. "Come clawin' me out of my chair and talkin' about my barn stinkin'," he gloomed. "That's all the thanks I git for keepin' the sweetest smellin' stable in the state—"

Pete ended his monologue with an annoyed grunt. He wrinkled his nose—sniffed suspiciously. "That onery skunk!" he exploded. His face reddened. "I shore will nail the critter's hide to the barn door! Prowlin' round and ruinin' the good name of the O.K." He vanished into a stall; and in a few minutes the sheriff was riding away on a tall, raw-boned sorrel.

Jake Kurtz had not opened for business, he observed, as he jogged past the general merchandise store.

"That's queer," he reflected. "Jake must be sick—or something."

Mrs. Kelly hailed him from her gate. The law officer drew rein.

"What's on your mind, Kitty?" His tone was resigned. More trouble!

"You got a worried look on that sweet face of yours." The sheriff had known her since the demise of Terence Kelly had left her a youthful widow.

"Mr. Day! God bless you! It's that glad I am to see you! There's good reason for me to look worried. It's in mortal fear I am, Sheriff." She opened the gate. "But get off the horse and sit with me under the tamarisk while I tell you—"

The old sheriff sighed, climbed down and followed the widow into the garden. To his surprise Jake Kurtz was sitting in one of the rustic chairs. The chubby storekeeper's usual beaming smile was missing. He greeted the sheriff with funereal solemnity.

"Ach! It is goot you are here, Sheriff Day! Such writings we get!" Jake wiped his perspiring face with a large red silk handkerchief

The sheriff sank into a chair and looked inquiringly at the widow. "You do the talking, Kitty. Ain't got much time to spare you."

"Jake and me have been threatened with death if we don't get out of Coldwater in forty-eight hours," Mrs. Kelly told the officer.

"A joke," grunted the sheriff. "Somebody is having a bit of fun with you."

"No joke, Mr. Day." Ma held out a crumpled sheet of paper. "Jake got one of 'em, too. They're from *El Capitan*."

Sheriff Day read the brief scrawl carefully.

"Sounds like he means business all right," he finally muttered. "Let's see the one you got, Jake—"

"They're both the same," Mrs. Kelly said.

"Yeah, word for word," agreed the sheriff. He folded the pieces of paper and tucked them into a pocket of his unbuttoned vest. "Showed 'em to anybody?" he inquired.

"Not to a living soul," answered Mrs. Kelly. "Jake was going to show his to Wirt Stoner but I told him he mustn't."

"Why not?" The sheriff had a faraway look in his light blue eyes. "Maybe Wirt would buy your place— and Jake's store—if he knew you were leaving the town."

"I wouldn't give him that much satisfaction!" The widow's eyes snapped. "Stoner has tried enough times to make me sell the Adobe Inn to him!"

"Tried to buy you out eh?" Sheriff Day's tone was

thoughtful. "Maybe it would suit him if you got scared out of Coldwater. You'd sell to him cheap."

Mrs. Kelly eyed him shrewdly. The law officer shook his head.

"No—not that, Kitty—"

"It might be," she argued. "I wouldn't put it past Wirt Stoner to try and scare me out of Coldwater—the sly, schemin' fox!"

"What do you think, Jake?" queried the sheriff.

"Himmel!" Jake mopped his brow. "I cannot think! It is too terrible! Ach! Mein store that I build up from a peddler wagon! I will to the ground burn my store if I am made to go away."

"You're not running away—any more than I am," declared Mrs. Kelly firmly. "Don't you talk foolish, Jake."

"Forty-eight hours, those letters say," babbled the storekeeper. "In forty-eight hours—or less—we are dead, maybe—"

"Jake Kurtz! I'm ashamed of you!" Mrs. Kelly's eyes sparkled indignation. "Are you going to be coward enough to run away and leave me to be murdered all by myself?"

"Don't worry about Jake," chuckled the sheriff. "It's thinking about his store upsets him. I know Jake Kurtz. Had him in my posse more'n once. Jake'll fight his weight in wildcats. And that's some weight," he added dryly.

"What shall we do?" worried the widow.

"I was headin' for the Smoke Tree to see the Carys when you stopped me," Sheriff Day continued. He looked at Mrs. Kelly under lazy-lidded eyes. "Never suspicioned that Lee was maybe *El Capitan*, did you Kitty?"

"Good gracious!" The comely widow gasped. "What

a question! Who in the world ever put such a crazy notion in your head?"

"Lee is away a heap of times," the sheriff pointed out. "Goes off for days at a time. Nobody knows where he goes."

"I do—for one," she snapped. "He's got some sort of irrigation scheme. He's been prowlin' all over the desert and the hills, studying things. He didn't want folks to be laughing at him for a fool, I suppose. Been keeping his mouth shut 'til he was sure."

"Yeah?" Sheriff Day was suddenly attentive. "That's Wirt Stoner's pet bug, ain't it. For a man that sells whisky Wirt shore thinks a heap of water."

"I guess that's why he wants me to sell out to him," asserted the widow. "Wirt is wild to get hold of my springs." She went on. "Lee told me only a few days ago not to sell. He told me the place would make me rich. There's an Englishman come to see him—a big expert who's worked in Egypt. He stopped with me 'til he went to the Smoke Tree. A real nice man. He told me our desert country reminds him of places in North Africa. The elevation and fine dry air makes it good for winter resorts and for folks with asthma—and things." Mrs. Kelly's eyes kindled. "Why—he says we'll see big groves of date trees growing all round Coldwater—"

"Yeah!" Sheriff Day tilted his dusty Stetson and rubbed his sparse grizzled hair reflectively. "Maybe there's plenty water under that no-count desert homestead I got south of here. Guess I'll sink me some wells and get rich too."

"He got me all excited," confessed the widow. "He talked a lot about it—even said Coldwater would be known all over the world and that thousands of people would come to spend their winters here. Said if I was smart the Adobe Inn would be famous."

"Yeah!" The sheriff rubbed his head again. "I think," he mused, "I think I'll pick me up a few town lots. There's a piece of ground down by the O.K. stables that old Pete Smith wants to sell." He eyed the widow shrewdly. "Maybe this *El Capitan* feller has got some sort of notion of the prosperity reachin' out to Coldwater—figgers to hog it all for himself." The sheriff wagged his head. "I shore would like to know that *hombre's* real name. We got to smoke him out of his hole. This country is going to be too good for wolves like him."

He drew his lean frame from the home-made garden chair. "I'm riding to the Smoke Tree for a talk with the Carys. It's time old Jim took a hand in this here wolf hunt."

"It's maybe the last time you see us, Sheriff," Jake Kurtz said gloomily. "Forty-eight hours—the letter give us—"

The sheriff's meditative gaze went through the trees to a cluster of cowboys riding up the street. His eyes brightened.

"Tim Hook, and his Diamond D outfit!"

The sheriff grinned—moved quickly toward the gate.

The bearded elderly owner of the Diamond D answered his hail with a delighted whoop. They were old friends.

"Hello, old-timer!" greeted the cattleman. "What's on yore mind 'cept that old hat you wear?" He chuckled, winked round at his grinning riders. "Some day when I feel real wealthy I'm shore goin' to get you a new Stetson. It ain't decent for our sheriff to wear a hat so ventilated with bullet holes! You'll be catchin' cold—you old penny-pincher!"

"Where you headin' for?" demanded Sheriff Day, ignoring the insults to his headpiece.

"Waal—if you must know—we're headin' for the Lazy Y to pick up a bunch of cow critters I bought for feeders," Tim Hook told him. He eyed the law officer suspiciously. "Don't you go and tell me you're deputizing me and the outfit so soon again, mister."

"I'm doing just that same thing," Sheriff Day retorted dryly. He gave a brief account of the peril confronting Mrs. Kelly and Jake Kurtz. The Diamond D men listened attentively.

"I'm riding to the Smoke Tree now for a talk with the Carys," the sheriff wound up. "In the meantime you and the boys stay on guard here at the Inn. Ain't right to leave 'em without protection."

"You bet we'll stay," assented Tim Hook promptly. His face was grim. "If that bunch of killers come round they'll get a dose of lead poisoning they won't forget this side of hell. Huh, fellers?" He glared at the circle of grim-eyed faces.

"You've said it, boss," muttered one of the riders. He was recalling the time Ma Kelly had nursed him through a siege of pneumonia.

Sheriff Day called the widow and Jake over to the gate and explained the arrangements.

"Don't neither of you leave the Inn till I say so," he warned them.

"But mein store!" agonized Jake Kurtz.

"This is one day the Coldwater General Merchandise Emporium don't open for business," Sheriff Day said firmly. He climbed stiffly into his saddle. "So long, folks. Keep a stiff upper lip, Kitty. Tim Hook and the boys will take good care of things here."

"You bet we will!" chorused the Diamond D outfit.

The little sheriff chuckled contentedly and soon the tall sorrel was moving gallantly up the trail to Smoke Tree ranch. Far ahead of him four horsemen showed for a moment against the skyline as they dropped over the ridge.

Sheriff Day's eyes narrowed thoughtfully. There was something familiar about one of those briefly glimpsed riders.

"Looked like Gil Hawken," he muttered. He shook his head. "Guess my eyes fooled me. Hawken wouldn't be ridin' to Smoke Tree. Jim Cary fired him."

He pressed the sorrel to a faster pace.

XXII
"It's Reckoning Day for You—"

The baffling problem of *El Capitan* increasingly worried Lee. He had reason to believe that two of the bandit chieftain's hired killers still prowled Smoke Tree country, seeking an opportunity to remove the Carys from life. He knew too, that one of the lurking assassins was an elderly bearded man whose little finger was missing from his right hand.

Lee was not overmuch concerned for himself. His anxiety was for his grandfather—and for the safety of Nan Page and her young brother. He had forced old Jim Cary grudgingly to accept an armed escort and extracted a similar promise from Nan. As an added precaution for the protection of Nan and Teddy he had posted alert Smoke Tree men at vantage points guarding all trails leading to Los Posos. There could be no let-down of vigilance until *El Capitan's* identity was revealed and the man exterminated.

He said as much to Sir Christopher as they rested their horses in the shadow of Chimney Peak and gazed down the tortuous descent of Los Posos Canyon. It was their second trip to inspect the upper reaches of the big gorge.

"We'll have to postpone things," he reluctantly told the Englishman. "The most important business now is *El Capitan*. He's got to be wiped out."

"I don't blame you," Dawson agreed. "Frightfully unpleasant situation."

"The man has to be *wiped out*," reiterated Lee. "I can

think of nothing else until this country is rid of him and his cutthroats." He frowned. "Can't expect you to waste your time here while I go bandit hunting. Sorry! There's a lot you'll want to see before you will care to express a final opinion, I'm afraid."

"I've seen enough to convince me that your ideas are sound, my dear fellow. No trick at all to throw a dam across the elbow of that gorge. The place is a natural reservoir for enough storage water to irrigate several square miles below the mouth of the canyon."

"How about the flowing wells in the flats?" Lee's tone was anxious. "Will Nan's wells be injured in any way?"

"Not in the least," assured the expert. "The flow from those wells comes from a great depth. The water you will store behind the dam will be surface drainage—won't hurt the springs in the slightest." He gestured at the gray-brown expanse of chaparral reaching toward the horizon. "Water lying under the desert floor," he declared. "You know how the streams sink below the surface a few miles after leaving the canyons. Undoubtedly they flow into vast subterranean cisterns. Tap the ground at the right spots—and you'll have an unfailing supply of artesian water. Of course, in many places the formation won't allow a natural flow. You'll have to use pumps—windmills."

Lee was silent for a minute. A picture spread before his eyes—green fields and low-roofed houses embowered by groves of tall graceful date-laden palm trees.

"Then I haven't been dreaming wild dreams," he finally said in a low voice.

Sir Christopher laughed. "Such dreams are worthwhile," he stoutly maintained.

"Means lots of work," mused the younger man. He

straightened in his saddle, eyes suddenly bleak. "It will have to wait. I've another job to do—first —"

They talked for a few minutes; and Sir Christopher pointed out certain necessary work preliminary to the construction of the proposed dam.

"I'm riding on down to Los Posos," he finally said. "Promised Juanita I'd drop in and say adios. She expects her brother to come for her today—or tomorrow." The baronet's eyes twinkled. "Charming young lady, the senorita . . . Sometimes makes me regret I'm not a few years younger." Chuckling at his little joke the big Englishman swung his horse into the down trail.

Lee's grin followed him. The jovial baronet was good company. He would be sorry to see Dawson go. His grandfather liked him, too. Dawson had quite won Jim Cary over to Lee's long secretly nursed scheme to develop the plentiful water supply now going to waste. The prejudiced, intolerant old cattleman had amazingly altered his opinions in the past few days. Jim Cary had noticeably changed in other ways, Lee reflected as he rode along the narrow trail that twisted over the ridge. Nan Page had worked a miracle with the dour old lord of the Smoke Tree. Jim Cary had strangely mellowed. His enjoyment of young Teddy Page's company was undisguised. Lee shrewdly suspected the boy was in a way taking the place of the great-grandson for whom old Jim Cary secretly yearned. The thought brought an enigmatic smile to the sternly chiseled lips of the last of the Carys.

The trail took a sharp hairpin turn; the Palomino snorted, went up the steep ascent with a plunge; shod hoofs clawed for foothold in the slippery, sliding shale. Too late Lee realized the target horse and man made—skylined on the ridge. From somewhere in the deeps of the opposing ravine came the vicious scream of a bullet—the echoing roar of a rifle.

Head low on Buck's neck, Lee sent the horse leaping down the trail to a clump of concealing manzanita trees.

Safe for the moment from the quick-eyed marksman, he dismounted and jerked carbine from saddle-boot. One—or both of the bandit killers lurked in ambush somewhere below him. Or perhaps the unseen rifleman was Gil Hawken, seeking revenge for his discharge from the Smoke Tree payroll. Hawken and Slinger Cole—both dangerous men—friends of Wirt Stoner. Their close association with the suave-tongued saloon man was one reason why Lee had insisted Jim Cary fire them off the place. Lee's distrust of Wirt Stoner was fast becoming concrete suspicion. It was at the latter's Desert Bar Saloon that *El Capitan's* men were to contact a certain person who was to get them jobs with the Smoke Tree outfit. That person was either Gil Hawken—or Wirt Stoner, Lee now was firmly convinced. Which indicated that both probably were in close touch with the mysterious bandit of the border. The abduction of Nan and Ted from Meeker's hotel was highly suspicious in view of the fact that it was Stoner who had urged the girl to spend the night there—had even engaged the rooms. Also Jim Cary suspected Wirt Stoner guilty of the murder of William Page. The man had motives in plenty to plot against the lives of the Carys and the Page children.

He took stock of his surroundings. The manzanita bushes grew along the edge of a bluff, he observed. Dragging his rifle he crawled forward to the brink, careful to keep the screening branches between him and the sharp eyes he knew were watching the hillside for any movement that would betray his presence.

Slowly he parted the branches, inch by inch, until the opening was wide enough to give him a view. It was almost a sheer drop to the floor of the ravine. He could see the trail looping below to the creek fringed with willows and alders, where it disappeared, to emerge lower down the canyon and climb the opposite slope.

Patiently he studied bush and boulder for some sign that would locate the hidden enemy. Nothing stirred; the canyon seemed devoid of life. Only a lone buzzard soaring against the blue sky as if watchfully waiting for a feast soon to be spread somewhere in that boulder-strewn ravine.

Patience won the trick. Stealthily a hat pushed up from behind a big boulder that had most intrigued Lee's attention. A head came into view.

Even at that distance—at least three hundred yards, Lee recognized the swarthy vicious face of Slinger Cole.

His rifle spoke—the gunman fell forward against the boulder—slid from sight.

Close on the reverberating crash of Lee's carbine roared a second shot—a bullet spatted into the manzanita bush. And like an echo of the second shot came the crack of a third gun from high up the opposite slope. The hidden marksman in the ravine rose from behind a boulder, staggered a few feet and sank on his side, rifle falling from nerveless hands. A bearded man, Lee's brief glance informed him.

His astonished gaze raked up the hillside for a glimpse of his unexpected ally. Astonishment grew to amazement as he recognized the wiry little sheriff riding down the trail on a tall sorrel horse. He rode at a slow walk, rifle ready in his hands, gaze sweeping the canyon floor.

There was something grim and implacable about the

diminutive law officer's unhurried approach. Curses floated up to Lee, drew his attention in time to see Gil Hawken and a man he knew as Paso Wells, rise from behind boulders and dash toward a thicket of willows, obviously bent on getting to their concealed horses.

Again the sheriff's rifle roared. Paso Wells staggered—sprawled his length.

Hawken's voice raged; he whirled—rifle leaped to shoulder. Lee's trigger finger tightened and as the crash of the carbine echoed from cliff to cliff the tall ex-foreman of the Smoke Tree spun round—sank slowly to his knees and fell forward on his face.

Lee went back to his horse, mounted and rode leisurely down the trail. Sheriff Day threw him a casual nod of greeting.

"Good shootin', young feller," he said dryly. "My gun stuck on me. Hawken would have got him a sheriff if you hadn't pulled trigger when you did."

He was eyeing down at the wounded bearded man. "Stranger to me—this here whiskered hombre," he muttered. "Ever seen him before, Lee?"

Lee shook his head. "Heard of him, though." His voice was steely. "See if he's got a little finger missing from his right hand, Sheriff."

The sheriff obliged. "He's shore short a finger," he declared. "What's your name, mister?" he asked the dying outlaw. "Where're you from?"

"I know where he's from," Lee said grimly. "*El Capitan* sent him to do a job of murdering. Isn't that right?" he asked.

"That's right," muttered the bearded man weakly.

"There were three of you," Lee went on. "The one-eyed Mexican is dead. Who is the third man?"

"Slinger Cole," the outlaw groaned. His head sagged. "You got him first shot."

Lee was conscious of a cold chill. Slinger Cole had been on the Smoke Tree payroll three days before Jim Cary had discharged him the afternoon of Lee's brief visit. His grandfather had been perilously close to death. But for Lee's fortunate visit the killer would have remained on the payroll—found his chance to successfully put an end to Jim Cary's life.

Sheriff Day was explaining his timely arrival.

"Saw it was Gil Hawken with 'em," he drawled. "Figgered he wasn't up to any good—"

Lee was eyeing the bearded man more closely. "I'll take back what I said about not having seen this fellow before," he broke in. "I saw him once in Wirt Stoner's saloon office—and again the morning of the raid, talking to Stoner in front of the hotel." His eyes scorched the outlaw. "What's your connection with Wirt Stoner? Who is the man known as *El Capitan*?"

An ugly grin distorted the whiskered face, glazing eyes rolled. "Seein' as I'm due to cash in, might as well talk," gasped the outlaw. "Reckon I—I'm goin' right soon—"

"All right—talk fast," urged Lee.

"Wirt Stoner—Wirt Stoner—he—he is—*El Capitan*—"

Blood frothed from the bearded man's lips. He went limp.

Lee regarded the dead outlaw intently for a moment—turned wordlessly to the Palomino

Sheriff Day found his tongue. "Hey—where you goin'?"

There was a chill light in Lee's eyes, suppressed fury in his level voice.

"I've business in Coldwater," he said.

The salty little sheriff came to life.

"Hey, young idiot! Wait for me! Wirt Stoner's my meat!"

He ran to his tall sorrel.

The sorrel was a sturdy horse, but no match in speed for the fleet Palomino. Steadily the distance widened between them—dust lifted, drifted in Lee's wake—to hover maddeningly over the more slowly moving and gunslinging law officer.

A Diamond D cowboy, hanging over Ma Kelly's neat picket gate, cigarette drooping from lip, was the first to catch the staccato thud of the Palomino's pistoning hoofs. The cowboy's eyes bulged. He let out a shrill yell.

The widow's trim feet led the stampede to the gate.

"Land sakes!" she panted. "What's wrong now, Pascoe?"

Pascoe—he was the youthful cowboy whom Ma Kelly's nursing had saved from an early grave— mutely pointed down the street.

"Land sakes!" repeated Mrs. Kelly, "it's Lee Cary— and riding like the wind. Somebody's chasing him, too," she added nervously.

Big Tim Hook hurried up, trailed by noisy-booted Diamond D men, jerking guns from holsters.

"By thunder!" The bearded owner of the Diamond D's voice rose to a bellow. "Lee Cary—and shore comin' like a bat out of hell!" He peered intently. "Who's the feller chasin' him, Pascoe? Cain't make out for dust—"

"Looks like the sheriff," muttered the young cowboy, staring through funneled hands

"By thunder!" The old cowman's voice was startled. "It *is* the sheriff!" He darted a puzzled glance at the widow. "Now what in hades is he fannin' after young Cary for?" he muttered uneasily.

There was a set look about Mrs. Kelly's attractive mouth; her chin went up.

"Don't you go gettin' crazy notions in your head, Tim Hook!" she snapped.

Despite her fiery retort, the widow was miserably conscious of a quaking sensation in her bosom. She could not help recalling Sheriff Day's odd question about Lee. The law officer had wanted to know if she had ever suspected Lee might be the mysterious bandit of the border. Loyally she throttled the ghastly, chilling thought.

"He's riding *with* Lee—not chasin' him," she staunchly declared.

"Fork saddles, boys!" Tim Hook's tone was brittle. "Whatever he's doing—there's trouble in the wind!" He jerked open the gate and ran for his horse; the outfit clattered at his heels.

Jake Kurtz panted up to Mrs. Kelly's side.

"What is it?" he wanted to know breathlessly. "Mein gootness!" he ejaculated. "What now is it gone wrong?"

His own eyes gave him the answer. "Lee Cary—" His eyes bulged. "Undt the sheriff trying to catch him." The chubby storekeeper's eyes were wide with astonishment.

"Don't be a fool!" hissed the widow crossly. "He's not chasing Lee—you—you fat dumbbell!" Mrs. Kelly was quite sure now that she would never, never marry Jake Kurtz.

She had no time for further reflections about the storekeeper. The great golden stallion was rocketing up. Mrs. Kelly caught a glimpse of Lee's face. His expression was taut, his eyes like hot coals. He stormed past without even glancing at the wondering widow, or at the Diamond D men tumbling into saddles.

Ma darted a look at the trailing sheriff, and then

stared back up the street with fascinated eyes. Lee was off his horse—was moving with quick jerky strides to the swing-doors of the Desert Bar Saloon. She could see the dust spurt from his boot-heels. In a moment he was lost from view, behind the doors.

Mrs. Kelly's gaze shifted to the sheriff. He was coming fast.

The Diamond D men were splitting, several of them with Tim Hook grouping to await the nearing sheriff. Four others went galloping toward the saloon.

Mrs. Kelly's heart was hammering; she clung to the gate-post in an agony of suspense.

From the moment of the bearded outlaw's shocking revelations one thought had dominated Lee Cary. He was resolved to destroy a wolf—not a human being, but a cunning and cowardly snarling-fanged ruthless killer.

The instant Wirt Stoner saw him, he read his doom in the chill, implacable eyes that seemed to lift him literally from the table where he was dealing faro.

The gambler's face went a chalk white, his eyes were dead, lusterless glass. Lee moved closer to him, spoke.

"Stoner—*El Capitan*—" His low voice cut like a sword point through the sudden hush. "It's reckoning day for you! Hawken—and the others—have paid their account!"

Startled, incredulous looks fastened on the quaking saloon man.

"Gawd!" muttered an awe-stricken voice. "*El Capitan!* He's callin' Wirt—*El Capitan!*"

Lee ignored the interruption.

"It's reckoning day for *you*," he repeated in the same deadly tone. "Do you hear me, *El Capitan*—you foul monster of deceit—murderer of William Page!"

His calmness was terrible to witness. Those nearest him blanched. Sweat suddenly beaded their faces.

Noises floated in from the street—the drumming beats of hoofs drawing close. Lee spoke again.

"You heard me, Stoner," he said more loudly. "Go for that gun you carry in that hidden shoulder holster—or must I shoot you down like a mad cur?"

Stoner had remained wordless, nor did he speak now. For a moment his dull eyes flickered over the hostile faces intently watching him. No mercy there for the inhuman being known as *El Capitan*. Sweat suddenly broke from the pores of his livid face.

"Go for your gun!" repeated the implacable voice of the man from Smoke Tree.

Stoner's white, well-tended fingers stole inside his coat, fumbled over the slight bulge that to knowing eyes betrayed the secretly carried weapon.

Lee's tenseness was suddenly gone—tall, muscular frame relaxed—he leaned forward just a trifle, hand hovered over the butt of holstered gun.

Horses were sliding to a halt in the street beyond the swing-doors, the clatter of hurrying boots, the rasp of dragging spurs, came to unheeding ears inside the long barroom. The swing-door slammed violently open—framed the wiry little sheriff. Crowding behind him showed the excited faces of Big Tim Hook and his Diamond D riders.

Stoner made no attempt to look at the newcomers. He spoke for the first time, lips twisted in a dreadful grimace.

"I'm fooling you, Cary." His voice came in a husky whisper. "You'll never say your bullet killed *El Capitan*—" The hand thrust inside his coat knotted—there was a sharp explosion—smoke poured from under the coat; and with a ghastly grin the man who was *El Capitan* crumpled to the floor.

Sheriff Day pushed through the crowd and stared down disappointedly at the dead bandit leader. His look went to Lee. The latter had not shifted out of his half crouch; gun hand still hovered over the black walnut butt of undrawn six-shooter.

"Killed himself!" The salty little sheriff's tone was withering. "Killed himself—rather than shoot it out with you, Lee!" He snorted contemptuously. "The crawlin' snake!" Sheriff Day's gaze roved around the long barroom, riveted the vista of staring eyes on himself.

"That's the last of *El Capitan!* Bit himself and died of his own poison."

The dour little sheriff's smile was suddenly extraordinarily cheerful. It had occurred to him that at last he was done with long futile rides in chase of the man who for so many months had eluded him.

XXIII
Spring

Linda Rosa minced along haughtily. If the golden horse at times came too close, laid-back ears and the disdainful toss of her head, quickly warned him to keep his distance. Not that it was Buck's fault if he pressed alongside. It was his rider's odd tendency to lean toward the chestnut-haired girl in Linda Rosa's saddle. Buck's occasional dancing step indicated an inclination to resent such a display of slack horsemanship.

A spray of scarlet ocotillo nodded in the red mare's bridle, above her ear; and a chaplet of delicate desert verbena adorned Nan's black sombrero. Spring reined in the desert—and in the hearts of Nan and Lee.

They rode past the giant old mesquite tree. Memories rushed back to them. . . .

They rode on, presently, through the narrow portal of the canyon, past the stately bearded palm reaching its crown of living green to a flawless blue sky.

Contentedly they followed the winding trail, higher and higher, until at last they rested on the lofty ridge overlooking Los Posos Canyon.

Below them lay a miniature mountain lake, formed by a dam thrown across a narrow bend of the gorge.

"It's marvelous what you have done—since last Autumn," Nan said softly.

"I wasn't sure it could be done, until Dawson showed me," Lee confided.

"You dreamed a dream—and the dream has come

true!" There was pride in the girl's voice—and a great gladness. "Green fields," she said, "that's the picture-to-be, you told me, and low-roofed homes embowered in stately palm trees laden with great clusters of luscious dates. Happy homes . . . happy families . . . in a land your dreams have brought to life."

They rode down the hill and up the opposite slope to the ridge beyond. Below them in the distance were the ancient walls of the house reared by Don Felipe Torres, great-grandfather of the last of the Smoke Tree Carys.

Silently they gazed down at the rust-red roof showing through the green trees. Three horsemen rode out of the canyon directly below them. Nan laughed softly

"Your grandfather!" she exclaimed, "and old Baldy Bates—with Teddy riding between them. Teddy adores those two old dears." She watched for a minute, lips curved in a tender smile. "Baldy and your grandfather are almost jealous of each other at times, I think."

"Ted is riding the Palomino colt," Lee said.

"He's named him Oro," laughed Nan. "He told me you said Oro was Spanish for gold."

Far in the distance lifted a banner of dust. Lee gestured.

"Ramon—and Juanita coming—for the wedding," he said contentedly.

Nan's breath quickened. *Her* wedding day—tomorrow!

"Ma Kelly has made the most marvelous cake," she told Lee.

Her gaze went back to the ancient gray walls and red roof showing through the green trees. Her home to-be!

The red mare and the golden horse were closely shoulder to shoulder. Lee's arm went gently around the girl's waist. Her eyes were like stars.

Linda Rosa and Buck stood very still, patiently resigned to the inevitable.

☐ YES!

Sign me up for the Leisure Western Book Club and send my FREE BOOKS! If I choose to stay in the club, I will pay only $14.00* each month, a savings of $9.96!

NAME: _____

ADDRESS: _____

TELEPHONE: _____

EMAIL: _____

☐ I want to pay by credit card.

☐  VISA   ☐ MasterCard.   ☐ DISCOVER

ACCOUNT #: _____

EXPIRATION DATE: _____

SIGNATURE: _____

Mail this page along with $2.00 shipping and handling to:
Leisure Western Book Club
PO Box 6640
Wayne, PA 19087
Or fax (must include credit card information) to:
610-995-9274
You can also sign up online at **www.dorchesterpub.com**.
*Plus $2.00 for shipping. Offer open to residents of the U.S. and Canada only.
Canadian residents please call 1-800-481-9191 for pricing information.
If under 18, a parent or guardian must sign. Terms, prices and conditions subject to
change. Subscription subject to acceptance. Dorchester Publishing reserves the right
to reject any order or cancel any subscription.